THEY HAD LAUGHED AT HIM
AND CALLED HIM A FOOL . . .

But it was they who were the fools.

He was going to offer the Lord something that the crass mercantile Church could never understand. Something that the Prophets in the Old Testament would have loved. Something directly from the spirit.

He was going to offer God a sacrifice. A real wondrous event, like the miracles of old. A human sacrifice. And if he was lucky . . . very lucky . . . more than one.

S. J. CASSIDY

THE ALTAR BOY

BERKLEY BOOKS, NEW YORK

THE ALTAR BOY

A Berkley Book / published by arrangement with
the author

PRINTING HISTORY
Berkley edition / September 1982

ISBN: 0-425-05533-7

PRINTED IN THE UNITED STATES OF AMERICA

THE
ALTAR
BOY

HE WALKED into the bedroom and shut the door behind him. His hands had gone a little cold and he could feel the baby's hand squeezing his stomach again. There was a sharp pain in his side and he experienced a breathless sensation. It was almost as if he had already done the deed itself. He could feel the surge of emotion welling up inside of him.

He slid the chair away from the desk and picked up the leather book his father had given him long ago. Quickly he looked through the pages—pages written in anger and grief and helplessness. He had thought for a long time that everyone had deserted him: his friends, his family, the Church. But that was before he understood what had to be done could only be done by himself. And once it was done they would all see that there was no way he was going to go on being a weakling, a loser. They had passed him over—he who had done more for them than anyone else—but now, now he was going to show them. He was going to show everyone.

He picked up the fountain pen. He stared out-

side at the cool, dark night and saw a woman
walk by with her son. She was a large red-haired
woman, and her son held onto her hand tightly,
as though he were afraid of being left behind. He
smiled to himself and began to write over the
white, creamy pages.

The words came from memory, like a frag-
ment of a puzzle he had lost long ago. Chapter
30 of the *Rule of St. Benedict:*

How Boys Are To Be Corrected

Every age and degree of understanding
should have its appropriate measure of discipline. Therefore, as often as faults are committed by boys, or by youths, or by those
who do not understand the greatness of the
penalty of excommunication, let such
offenders be punished with severe fasts or
chastised with sharp stripes. . . .

He stared down at the words and felt tears
come up in his eyes. For a second he wasn't sure
he was crying, but then he felt a great relief in
his back and he began to relax. He was crying,
he knew, because he was happy. Not happy like
he had once been, happy with illusions. No, now
he was happy in a new way, one in which he
would show them all how strong he really was.
There was going to be discipline for them all
right, but it was going to be a lot worse than
mere fasts, or sharp stripes. He was going to rise
up, like a shadow, and cover all of them with
himself. They were going to hear him at last, and
then the children and their parents would wish to
hell they had never been born.

Sunday, 7 a.m.

KATE RIORDAN woke before the clock radio went off. When it clicked on, she switched it from the droning voice of a bible-study preacher to WROR-FM. Ah, Air Supply. That's better, at least a melody you can listen to. Getting up on a Sunday morning was her least favorite thing to do in the world. Why Monsignor Merja insisted on this ceremony before the Palm Sunday Mass for the new senior altar boys was beyond her.

As she went into the hall towards the bathroom, she knocked gently on the door across from it.

"Danny," she said softly. "Time to get up, kiddo."

She heard a groan and then a crash. She was going to open the door, but then she remembered an argument they had had last week: I'm ten now. Don't come in my room unless you're invited. She had protested, but in the end decided that he was right, he deserved a little privacy. So be it. But what if he had broken his neck in there?

"Hey, astronaut, are you all right?"

3

"Very funny, Mom. I tripped."

"Do you want me to come in?"

"M-m-m-m-o-m-m-m!!!"

"Okay, okay, but don't say I never offered to help you."

She had everything on but her makeup as she headed toward the kitchen. A neat print dress, sensible shoes (as her mother would have called them), and her long blonde hair up in a bun. I look too prim, she thought, too prim for thirty-one. And then she laughed to herself. But I am going to see a Monsignor this morning. You can never look too prim for a Monsignor.

She opened the door to the kitchen, which led to the small back yard. It was only April, too early to put the screens in the storm door. The catch that would allow her to prop the storm door open was broken, so she used a waste-basket instead. Looks real classy, she thought to herself. But the kitchen was stuffy and she needed some air. The radio had said it was going to be a very warm day for April.

Pouring herself a glass of orange juice, she pondered what to fix Danny for breakfast until she remembered that that too had been a source of contention lately.

Rubbing his leg, Danny appeared. She looked up at him and felt her heart melt a little. With his reddish-brown hair hanging in bangs over his freckled face, and in his blue and red striped t-shirt, his oldest Levi's (she had tried to buy him a pair of new jeans, but when he saw they were designer jeans he had made her take them back), and tennis shoes, he looked like the All-American Boy. Huck Finn himself, though she didn't make the mistake of calling him that any more. He hated that term, felt that it made him into some kind of hayseed, and he didn't want that at all. He was growing up fast, Kate thought, too fast maybe. Even in bucolic and old-fashioned William's Crossing, kids seemed to find everything out too early. He stood there still rubbing his leg and squinting at the sun-filled room.

"Damn," he said. "That hurt."

She put down her coffee cup a little too loudly on the table.

"Danny, I told you about your language. And you cannot go to church dressed like that. Not in those old jeans."

Danny rolled his eyes and yawned a little.

"Aw, come on, Mom. I'm not going to be wearing these in church anyway. I'll have my cassock and surplice on. Besides, Billy the Horse and Skeeter wear them underneath every week."

Invoking the other boys. She supposed it was in some ways a healthy sign. Just last year he wasn't getting along with them well enough to mention what they were allowed to do. That meant they had accepted him a little more. It wasn't easy being the smartest kid in the class. She remembered the jealous girls in her own past calling her "Brainiac" and "Four Eyes." Mediocrity made its own inviolable laws.

"Listen," she said. "We don't really care so much about what Billy and Skeeter wear. It's out of respect for the Church that we dress up. It's important that we pay attention to those old rituals, Danny. They mean quite a lot. Especially Palm Sunday. The most beautiful liturgy of the year, I think."

"Well, okay. But I don't see what's so important about it. Monsignor Merja doesn't really care about Palm Sunday or anything else. He just likes to act like a big shot. He's always yelling at us."

Suddenly he arched his back and looked sternly at her. In the most pompous voice imaginable he said:

"When I was a young man there was . . . ahem ahem . . . respect for the Church. I mean . . . real RESPECT . . . ahem. . . ."

Kate felt herself start to smile. God, he was a wonderful mimic. Just like Paddy used to be.

"That's entirely disrespectful," she said. "Now go in there and put on some decent clothes. Then you've got to have some breakfast. Okay?"

"Okay, Ma. For you I'll do it."

He smiled and shook his head like the stern Monsignor, then turned and went back into his bedroom. From her seat at the kitchen table, Kate could see his toys scattered haphazardly all over the place. There was his Dracula doll, and his Star Wars rocket ship, and his old Creature from the Black Lagoon model, and what looked like all the comic books in the world. She worried about letting him read such stuff. The world was a violent enough place without the synthetic horrors of the comic book world thrown in on top of it. Still, Kate had to confess, he seemed to love the comics, and she hated to play the conservative, censoring mother. There seemed to be, she thought, a little dazed, no right path sometimes. If she let him read them, he might end up with nightmares, and if she took them away from him, then she made him resentful. So what she had tried to do was read some of the comics with him, offering her own warmth and jokes as a silent rebuttal to all the violence. Motherhood, she thought, was sometimes impossible.

And yet, when he came back out, dressed in his good clothes, grinning at her with that innocent smile, she knew that nothing she had ever done in her life would equal the warmth and joy she felt.

"I'm hungry," he said.

"Coming right up," Kate said, smiling. "How about pancakes?"

"Great. Hey, Mom, I'll tell you what. While you cook breakfast, what if I sort of clean up my room a little?"

"What?" Kate said, flabbergasted.

"I knew that would blow your mind, Mom," Danny said. He chuckled to himself and then went back into the room.

"It's so messy in here sometimes," Danny called, "that even I can't stand it. Hiya guys."

She looked in and saw him pick up the Creature from the Black Lagoon. She smiled to herself, and got the pancake mix and Log Cabin syrup out. He seemed genuinely happy now. Thank God. Things were going to be all right at last.

It hadn't always been that way, not since Paddy had gotten sick. His illness seemed impossible then, and even now she couldn't really accept it. Paddy Riordan had been the archetypal young energetic husband. That is, until the day he complained of the pains in his chest. The doctors had done a biopsy and, suddenly, with little warning at all, they had found themselves listening to an oncology specialist at Mass General tell them that he had advanced Hodgkin's disease. Six months to go. Paddy had been brave, incredibly brave, and, during the first few months, it seemed possible to believe that the doctors had made a mistake. There had been no change in his condition at all, but when the real symptoms emerged, the disease stopped him in his tracks. All at once Paddy was helpless, could barely lift himself out of bed. And then, unbelievably, he was gone. The blow had staggered Kate. There were times when she felt that she couldn't stand it. But it had affected Danny even worse. He loved, indeed, worshipped, his father. And too often after his father's death he came home from school with his shirt ripped off and his eyes blackened.

Kate had scarcely known where to turn. Finally, after talking with the school counselor, she had discovered the root of the problem. Danny had been furious at his father for dying and leaving him behind. And he felt so guilty for the anger that he had to punish himself by getting into daily fights at school. Kate had spent a precarious three years building up Danny's sense of self-worth, trying to be father and mother to her lively, intelligent, and sensitive son. None of it had been easy.

At the time they had been living in South Boston, a place she detested. Southie was the antithesis of all she had hoped for. It was parochial, stifling. The physical surroundings of the neighborhood were drab and unyielding, its people forlorn and without hope. But Paddy loved

Southie, loved drinking in the bars, playing in the sandlot leagues, marching in the St. Patrick's Day parade, being an acolyte in the endless religious processions.

Paddy's family and Kate's family had both moved from Southie to William's Crossing, a suburban Catholic ghetto, after the Second World War. But Paddy was a man unswayed by mountain greenery. He had been a street kid, and soon after he and Kate were married, he got a good job in a printing concern in Southie. Though Kate had dreaded it, they had emigrated back to the old neighborhood. Life there had been loud, hot, and noisy. Kate was constantly fearful. For the first few years of their marriage, race relations had been strained to the breaking point, and Kate would wake at night convinced that Danny had been stomped to death in a riot, or hit in the head with a brick, or run over by a police car. She would hold on to Paddy, who laughed at her and assured her that as long as he was alive, he would take care of their son. But suddenly Paddy was gone. And with him was Kate's shield from the rough-and-tumble world of Southie.

So she had moved back to William's Crossing. It had been, in many ways, a tougher move than the one to Southie. She had to give up her friends and start again. With one exception. This time she started as a widow with a seven-year-old "troubled" son. Everything had been hard. Finally, after being nearly broke, Kate had landed a job as legal secretary to Jeremiah Manning, the town's leading wills and estate lawyer. She liked her job and was good at it. And now, she thought, as she put the pancakes on her son's plate, now at last, Danny, too, seemed to have found his place in her old hometown. He was starting to make friends. He was doing much better in school, and he had achieved senior altar boy status.

"Breakfast is ready," Kate shouted happily.

"Okay, Mom," Danny said. "I'll be right there."

She looked in and saw him pick up Dracula.

"See you later, Drac," he said. "I gotta go to church."

Kate sat in an aisle pew and awaited the start of the Mass. During the ceremony preceding the Mass, she had been pleased that Danny seemed to take what Monsignor Merja had to say with such seriousness. Billy Conley and Skeeter Bannon, the other senior altar boys, had exchanged looks during the priest's admonishing talks, but Danny had listened intently. She had felt great pride in her son, and now she looked forward to the Mass itself.

Suddenly an older woman appeared in the aisle. She wore a dark gray suit a couple of inches too long and a couple of years too late. Her gray hair was frizzed around the edges, and she appeared to have put twice as much rouge on her left cheek as on her right. It was Paddy's mother, Maura Riordan, a woman who had become like a mother to Kate, since her own mother had passed away three years ago.

"I made it," Maura said enthusiastically. "I wouldn't miss this for anything in the world. I just saw him in the back. He looks adorable."

"Yes he does," Kate said. "But, for Lord's sake, don't say that to him. He hates to be called adorable."

"I know," Maura said. "He's at the age where he's trying to be cool."

"Chill," Kate said.

"What?" Maura said, knocking her hat off as she sat down and then bumping her head as she tried to pick it up.

"Chill," Kate said. "They don't use 'cool' any more. That's out of fashion, only said by the old generation, meaning me."

"What's that make me then?" Maura said. "The fossilized set?"

She laughed a little too loudly at her own joke and a couple of people in the pews up front turned around and shushed her.

"Look," Kate said, straining to see the back of the church. "There he is."

She saw that the procession had formed and was nearly ready to begin. First came Danny, serving as thurifer, carrying the lighted censer full of fragrant and steaming incense. Behind him were Billy and Skeeter, carrying armfuls of palm branches.

Behind the altar boys was Brother Michael, carrying the paschal cross which he himself had constructed and colorfully decorated. And, finally, in his bright red vestments, the celebrant of the Mass, Monsignor Merja, the pastor.

From the lectern in the front of the church, the deacon intoned, "Please rise; the processional hymn for this Sunday, Palm Sunday, the last Sunday in Lent, is 'Hosannah in the Highest,' to be found on page twelve of your missalettes."

As the procession moved down the center aisle, Kate found it hard to concentrate on the words of the song, for her eyes had moved to her son who walked so solemnly and who looked so positively beatific.

Even Skeeter Bannon and Billy Conley looked wonderful, Kate thought, though perhaps not quite as terrific as Danny. Kate looked around the packed church for the other boys' parents. She found George and Arlene Conley two rows in front of her. George was a sales rep for McGraw-Hill and his territory was the Northeast. He wasn't home a lot and this led to his wife, Arlene, a school teacher, taking a very strong interest in community affairs. George was known for his now all but faded high school athletic exploits; Arlene, for her authoritative presence on the town's finance committee. No one in William's Crossing wanted to end up on the wrong side of Arlene Conley.

George seemed quieter now that Paddy was gone. He had often told Kate he missed his boisterous running buddy. "It took a little out of me," he said, "when he went. But you have the boy. Don't ever forget you have the boy, in Paddy's image." Not quite, thought Kate, but close enough. Kate also wondered whether the peculiar quietness that gripped George came from his wife's emergence. She never felt comfortable enough with the question to ask either of them. Tall and laconic George would shed no light on the matter. And Arlene, pretty and dark, who had once been described as a young Ava Gardner, would have a glib response all ready. She was not about to let anyone get close.

Several rows in front of the Conleys were the Bannons. John Bannon was the manager of the local Finast store. He had worked for the food chain since he had graduated from high school more than fifteen years ago. He had started as a stock boy and worked his way up through the ranks from produce manager to head cashier, then to assistant manager and finally to the top post. The William's Crossing store was a small one, but John had kept it profitable through tough economic times. He was much admired in the firm's Somerville headquarters and he had refused transfers to bigger stores and even to the home office itself. He was a William's Crossing boy and this was where he intended to stay. From where she stood, Kate could see the sunlight reflecting off John's bald head. He was by no means a good-looking man, but he had an appealing quality to him. Kate liked him enormously. She always had.

On the other hand, Kate felt sorry for Nancy Bannon. She was a short, stout woman who for all the world was like the Kerry housewives who had been her ancestors. She had bleached-blonde hair, much too short to be fashionable, and she always wore clothing designed to enhance her earth mother image. Nancy was a very good mother, kind and gentle and patient. But she had few friends. Her life, it seemed, was her husband and her three children.

As the procession neared the altar rail, it paused for a moment. Monsignor Merja removed his crimson biretta and handed it to Brother Michael. He took two of the palm branches that Skeeter had been carrying and gave one apiece to parishioners on each side of the aisle as the solemn and formal procession celebrated Christ's entry into Jerusalem, the paschal mystery. Kate noticed Monsignor Merja was wearing a cope today instead of his usual chasuble and, before he turned to address the congregation, Billy and Danny helped him remove it.

Monsignor Merja mounted the pulpit and looked sternly at the parishioners.

"Brothers and sisters in Christ, for the five weeks of Lent, our charity and self-sacrifice have been preparing us to help participate in our Lord's paschal mystery. Churches throughout the world join with us in this celebration. Christ enters Jerusalem in triumph to complete this work so that we may have life: He will suffer for us, die, and rise again. Together as one with Him in His suffering in the garden, on the way to Calvary, and on the cross, may we participate in His resurrection and new life."

As he finished, Skeeter stood in front of him with more palm branches. Merja blessed the branches with holy water in silence. Then he said, "Lord God, we pray you bless these branches and make them holy."

"That is the end of the procession of palms," said Monsignor Merja. "We will now begin the Mass proper."

Maura pressed Kate's hand and sighed deeply.

"He *does* look adorable," she whispered.

Kate was sure that all eyes in the church were focusing on Danny. With a great deal of self-assurance, he put Billy and Skeeter through their paces, making sure they properly flanked the altar. He made sure each of the deacons had

palms and when Monsignor Merja seemed to
hesitate crossing to his seat, Danny firmly took
his arm and led him. This was Danny's show. He
had practiced for weeks and no one was going to
foul it up on him.

Kate half-listened to the long reading of
Christ's passion, remembering how as a child she
had fidgeted since it was much longer than the
usual gospel selection. But Danny seemed trans-
fixed. He was listening to every word. She felt
chastised and tried to concentrate. It was no use.
She thought about what she had done as a child
at Mass to arrest her wandering concentration.
Three Hail Mary's. Three Our Father's. Three
Glory Be's. Should she do that now? No, she
was an adult.

Monsignor Merja had begun his homily and
again Kate tried to listen. The Conleys were listening. The Bannons appeared to be listening.
The boys were listening. How long Monsignor
Merja had been talking, she was not sure. She
came in only at the end as he finished up.

"Christ is entering Jerusalem as the King of
Peace. Remember, brothers and sisters, He has
none of the trappings of a warrior. His only mis-
sion in the city is to reunite God and man. From
outside the walls of the city, the peace of our
Lord will flow to all nations. In a very few days,
during this holy week, our Lord will ascend His
throne to dispense God's peace. From this
throne, Christ will speak the eternal language of
peace. Remember Christ's words to them:
'Father forgive them, for they know not what
they do' and 'This day you will be with me in
paradise.'"

He looked up and concluded.

"Blessed is he who comes in the name of the Lord."

Almost involuntarily, Kate felt the responsorial escape her lips.

"Hosanna in the highest."

The remainder of the Mass moved swiftly. Merja received the gifts for the offertory. She watched during the communion rite as he broke the Host over the paten, placed a small piece in the chalice while the congregation sang the Agnus Dei. As the communicants queued up, she made sure she got on the line which would bring her to Merja and Danny. When her turn came, she heard Merja mechanically intone, "Body of Christ." Looking at Danny, who held the gold paten under her chin, she replied, "Amen."

Kate had always regarded the post-communion time as the most precious in the Mass. She felt exhilarated. Everything was going to be all right. As the communion vessels were cleansed on the altar, Kate found herself murmuring a prayer of thanksgiving.

Then, finally, the last antiphon of the Mass was recited. Merja, almost triumphantly, announced, "The Mass is ended. Go in peace." This time the procession did not exit the center aisle of the church, but rather quietly genuflected in front of the altar, and then entered the sacristy door to the left of the altar.

Kate and Maura greeted the Bannons and the Conleys as they walked across the lawn outside the church.

"Didn't they look beautiful?" Arlene said. "You'd never know Billy was the terror of the playground."

"They did look wonderful," Nancy Bannon said.

"That they did," Maura concurred. "And here they come now."

She looked up as Billy Conley and Skeeter Bannon walked from the church toward their parents.

"I suppose Danny is horsing around inside," Kate said, smiling.

"I think he went to the bathroom," Skeeter said.

Billy Conley turned and cuffed his friend on the head.

"Watch your mouth, jerkoid," Billy said.

Skeeter punched him on the arm and ran away.

"Now, now," George Conley called. "Let's calm down."

"Oh well," Arlene said. "At least they looked angelic for a few minutes."

Kate smiled and pressed Arlene's hand.

"I better go get Danny. He's got a Little League game later today. See you at the carnival meeting."

"Right," Arlene said.

"I'll be right back," Kate said to Maura. "You wait here, and we'll ride you home."

She walked across the lawn and into the side entrance. In the sacristy where the boys changed their clothes, Danny was nowhere to be seen. She walked over to the lavatory and knocked on the door. No answer.

"Danny," she called lightly, hoping no one else was inside.

There was no answer. Kate could feel herself tensing up. She hoped he wasn't playing a joke on her. She wasn't in the mood for childish games just now, not after seeing him look so grownup as an altar boy.

"Danny, please come out," she said. "Grandma's waiting here with me. Besides, you've got a game this afternoon. We really have to get going."

She waited, knowing that sometimes he found it hard to stop playing once he had begun. But after a full thirty seconds, there was still no reply.

Slowly she opened the door of the lavatory and looked around. There was no one inside.

She felt a sharp needle in the back of her skull, then told herself she was silly to be worried. He could be back inside the church. He could have gone out another door. She went back outside toward Maura, who waited patiently by the car.

"Have you seen Danny?" she asked.

"No," Maura said. "Is he missing?"

Kate smiled, turned and walked around to the other side of the building passing the azaleas. Most of the parishioners were gone now, all but a few cars had left the lot.

She called out his name again, a little desperately this time. She told herself not to be an alarmist, that nothing could have happened to him right there in church.

But he wasn't on the other side of the church. Kate turned and, feeling a panic sweep her,

she went back inside the church. Nothing. Light
shone through the stained-glass windows onto an
empty altar, an empty aisle, and empty pews. He
was gone. She hurried back outside and caught
up with George just as he was about to join
Arlene and Billy in their car.

"I can't find Danny." There was no mistaking
the rising hysteria in her voice.

George Conley took her arm. "Nothing to
worry about. I'm sure he'll be back momen-
tarily." He thought for a second. "Let's get
Jimmy Lawlor, the sexton. He knows all the
places kids like to play. I'm sure he can turn him
up if he is here."

They found him and he went off to search the
bowels of the church where the parishioners
rarely went. Kate asked Maura to check the
sodality room.

George tried to comfort Kate. "Jimmy's a
good man. He'll find Danny."

In spite of the panic she felt, Kate laughed.
"George Conley, you've never said a bad word
about anything or anybody in your life. Jimmy
Lawlor's a drunk and couldn't find his way to the
men's room without help."

George looked at her sheepishly. "Hey, we
don't need him as tour guide—we just want
Danny back, right?"

Maura came back from checking the room
where the sodality usually met at the rear of the
church. "He wasn't there, dear. Though only old
people go in that room. I'll bet he's never even
been to a sodality meeting."

Oh, spare me, Kate thought to herself.
Danny, I'm going to brain you for pulling this.
Just wait until I get my hands on you.

George offered to check the area behind the baptismal font. There were lockers behind it where the vestments were kept. Lockers big enough for a child to crawl into and pretend to disappear.

Kate listened to George's steps echoing through the empty church. In a matter of minutes Jimmy Lawlor, Maura and George had completed their appointed rounds. Still nothing.

"I'm sure he'll turn up," George offered. "You know how kids are. We were all the same way."

"It just doesn't make any sense. Why would he just up and disappear?"

Jimmy Lawlor piped up, "Don't worry, Mrs. Riordan, sometimes the kids like to play hide and seek in the church. It's a big old place and it fascinates them."

"I know all that," Kate said impatiently. "But why now? He's got a game this afternoon. He's got to go home and get changed. All his equipment is there. Look, George, I don't want to hold you up any longer. Arlene and Billy are waiting for you. Besides, there's nothing more you can do. You go on your way and I'll just stay here and wait for him to turn up. Maura, I'll see you at noon as we planned."

The others went out the side door. Kate remained in the sacristy. With the lights turned out and the place empty, she felt all too alone. She shivered. This is silly, she thought, I'm going to go through the church again, open every door, and find him.

She opened the basement door, flipped the light switch, and started down the steep stairs.

The stairs were covered with dust. No one's been down here in a hundred years, she thought disgustedly. If Jimmy Lawlor did look around, he certainly didn't look here. The air in the passage was cool and damp. Large old oak doors led to all the rooms. She tried them in sequence—all bolted shut, not much of a chance Danny could have opened any of them to hide behind them. At the end of the long corridor was a set of big double doors. Kate recalled that the life-size ceramics which formed the parish manger scene were kept in that room. How the men would groan at Christmastime when Monsignor Merja would ask for volunteers to lug the heavy pieces from the cellar and up the narrow stairs. "Danny," she called out tentatively, though she knew there was almost no hope of finding him in the dim cellar.

She climbed the stairs quickly and slammed the basement door behind her. She shuddered involuntarily. God, that's not a place you want to be unless you have to. She decided that one more circuit of the church proper was in order and if that failed to produce Danny, she would go home, home to wait for him.

Kate took the long way home through downtown William's Crossing. As she edged the yellow Fairmont out of the church parking lot, she tried to remember Danny's favorite haunts. In sequence she thought of the library and the video game arcade, both of which were closed, and then a number of ice cream parlors. Which did he like best? Brigham's, yes that was it. He thought their coffee milkshakes were the best.

At Friendly's they were sloppy and always leaked through their paper containers.

It was a bright spring morning and there were plenty of people out. Kate knew most of them and waved as she slowly cruised Main Street, looking for her truant son. I've got no time to be more sociable, she thought. I've got lunch to fix for Maura at twelve and then I've got to tote him off to his game. I'll kill him for doing this to me, she thought.

The Brigham's parking lot was full, so she left the Ford in the street, double parked with the hazard lights on. Inside, she recognized the shift manager as one of her boss's law clients. His name was Ed Fredericks and Jerry had gotten him a divorce from the red-haired Sullivan girl a year ago. He came right over when he saw Kate waving at him. "Need something to go, Mrs. Riordan?"

"No, no. Listen, Ed, you haven't seen my son Danny, have you?"

"Gee, not this morning. He usually comes in after school but not on Sunday mornings."

"Okay, if he comes in, I want you to call me."

"Mrs. Riordan, is he in some kind of trouble?"

"He will be if he misses this afternoon's game."

"I'll tell him if he comes in—"

"Ed, remember to call."

It was now quarter of twelve, Maura would soon be coming and she would worry if Kate wasn't home. It was frustrating trying to balance the needs of both of them and then finding herself squeezed in the process. Kate was suddenly angry at both of them.

Sunday, 12 noon

MAURA HAD already let herself in when Kate pulled the yellow car into the driveway. Kate fumbled with her keys and found that she didn't need them. Absent-minded Maura had left the door unlocked.

"Any luck, dear?" Maura wanted to know.

Kate put on a bright face. "No, but I'm sure he'll be along. Just a little rebellion I'm sure. It's his age."

"Yes. His father was like that too."

Kate turned away and went into the kitchen. She hated being rude but she couldn't stand hearing one more time about Paddy as a child. Maura had committed his every waking moment to memory.

"Dear, dear, are you there?"

"In the kitchen," Kate said musically. "Fixing our lunch." She put out three table settings and then put one away so as not to upset Maura by emphasizing who wasn't there.

Sunday dinner was being saved for after the game. Lunch was just sandwiches. Maura ate heartily. She and Kate said little. Kate finished quickly and excused herself.

She went into her bedroom, got out her address book and called several other parents to see if they had seen Danny. She had no luck. Her original sense of uneasiness returned. It was now close to one o'clock. His baseball gear was still laid out in his room. He never missed a game. Where could he be?

She went back into the kitchen where Maura sat and attempted to keep her mind off Danny's absence. The attempt was unsuccessful. Maura asked her, "Who will pitch the game if Danny doesn't show up?"

Kate laughed. "I'm sure they'll find someone," she said.

Maura sighed and took the dirty plates to the sink. "Kate," she said quietly, "if Danny were somehow injured—what I mean is, shouldn't we get more people to be looking for him?"

Kate was thoughtful for a moment. "It's important not to panic. Little boys sometimes get strange notions in their heads. They're not entirely rational sometimes."

"But Kate, what reason would he have to disappear? Honestly, honey, I'm very worried. I think we ought to call the police."

"Not yet. I'm going to check out the game and see if he shows up there."

"I'd like to come with you."

"No, I think this is something I should do myself. If he is there, I'm going to have it out with him."

"But dear—all his equipment is here. You don't think you'll really find him there, do you?"

"I just don't know what to think. But what choice do I have?"

As she backed the yellow car down the slight incline into the street, she continued to watch for her son, but the short ride into town proved unavailing. As she approached Strobe field she noticed all the fathers and sons beginning to arrive. She sought out Coach Williams and asked if he'd seen Danny. He said he hadn't. Now her alarm grew. She waited until the game began and when Danny had not shown but Billy and Skeeter were arrayed at third and second respectively, she decided she had no choice. She would go to the police. Maura was right. What if Danny were hurt and needed help? Waiting any longer might place him in further jeopardy.

Kate held the dime in her hand. This was a call she felt strange about making. The chief of police in Mt. Olive was Brian Dolan, a man her own age. Indeed, a man she had almost married.

She placed the coin in the slot, dialed, and asked to be put through to Brian.

"Brian," she faltered, "this is Kate Riordan. My son is missing." She began to cry.

"Kate," he said quietly, "where are you?"

"I'm at Strobe Field."

"Where did you last see him?"

"In church this morning. In the sacristy."

"Okay, listen. I'll meet you at the church in five minutes."

"Okay." Professional and bloodless, she thought, that was Brian. She had never learned how to read him, maybe that had been the problem fifteen years ago.

Brian Dolan hoped his voice hadn't shown the surprise he felt at hearing from Kate Riordan. It

had been a long time since he'd even passed her
on the street. Poor woman. Bad enough to lose a
husband. Now to have a child missing.

As he edged his car into the church parking
lot, he felt uneasy. He considered himself a man
of faith still, but he never went to church any
more. Just driving into the lot made him feel
repentant, like missing Mass when he was a
child.

He let himself in the sacristy door and then he
saw her. It was amazing how little she had
changed. He crossed immediately to her. "Hello,
Kate," he said softly.

"I don't know where he might have gone," she
said. "It's not like him. He's never done anything like this before. Oh God, I know something has happened to him."

Brian used the most reassuring voice he could
muster.

"Listen, Kate," he said. "Try to remain calm.
There's every reason to believe he's all right. It's
almost impossible to believe someone could take
a ten-year-old boy right out of a church. Just tell
me what happened. Okay?"

"I'm trying to," Kate said. "He left the altar
with the other boys. He was undressing with
them. They said he had his things on, and then
he simply didn't come out. I looked everywhere.
I've called all his friends."

"Did you have a fight with him recently?"
Brian prodded. "Something that could have
specifically precipitated his running away?"

"No, nothing like that. In fact, recently we've
been getting along well."

"Okay, how about something less obvious.

Something that you might not have picked up on until now. Not an argument per se, but something subtle. I mean, sometimes a mother will ask a boy to make his bed with a little sharp tone in her voice, something she's done a hundred times before, but this time, this day, the boy is worried about how girls see him, or he's upset about something in school. I mean, say he's flunked a test, and he's worried about showing a paper to his mother. Well, on this day he gets angry, panics, and decides to play hooky from home for a while. Then, when he gets home, his mother will be so glad to see him that she forgives him the bad marks."

"I see what you're driving at," Kate said. "And I've been going over in my mind just this type of thing. Did I jump on him about anything? Did I have an argument with him? But I can't come up with anything. You see, Brian, Danny and I have been going through a really good period. When Paddy died, there was a period when Danny was difficult. He's a very, very bright and sensitive boy. He missed Paddy terribly—as I did—and there was a time when we, well, got on each other's nerves somewhat. I felt, I don't know, I felt lost for a time, Brian. But you probably know all this."

She looked down at the floor and a tear came down her face. Brian found himself quickly reaching for his handkerchief.

"But that was a while back. During the past couple years Danny and I have become close. I mean really great friends. He worries about me, how hard I work. He tries to help."

The tears came down her cheeks and would

not stop. Brian realized that further talk was useless now. He would have his forensic man come
up and sweep the church for evidence. "We'll
find him," he said, but his voice lacked the con-
viction he wanted it to have.

Sunday, 4 p.m.

BRIAN DOLAN cursed quietly as the yellow light flashed on his dashboard. CHECK THE ENGINE it read, but Brian knew there was little point to that. He already knew what he'd find: a rusted-out carburetor, and an electrical system which looked like an old man's veins. Damn, he needed a new car. He'd been telling O'Toole, his lieutenant, just the other day. If there was an emergency, he was through. And now it appeared there was a crisis in William's Crossing, where nothing ever happened. It was strange, Brian thought, as he drove toward the Conley residence. The town seemed the same. Nice, neat clapboard and shingled houses, close-cut lawns, beautiful oak trees. The scene was so tranquil, so typically small-town America that it could have come off a Norman Rockwell calendar. The early spring sun was on his face as he drove.

He found 21 Pine Lane, a white clapboard house with an adjoining garage, with a basket-ball hoop nailed up over it. Looked like such a friendly place. But he thought of what he'd learned already about Billy Conley, and his argument with Danny. He sucked in his breath. He'd never really "questioned" a kid before.

He knocked lightly, almost apologetically on the door, shifted his weight, and tried to get a relaxed, casual look on his face. He might have to scare the kid, but he didn't want to start off that way. There was no point in that.

He wished that George Conley was going to be there, but he knew that George had formed a group of fathers and they were out scouring the town looking for Danny. From George he knew he could expect cooperation.

Arlene Conley and her ten-year-old son looked angry. Arlene sat stiffly across from him, her arms folded, her dark brows knitted. And stocky little Billy sat next to her in the same position. He looked, Brian thought, like a midget sumo wrestler—short arms, legs folded as though he were about to begin a match.

"I won't beat around the bush," Brian said. "You both know that Danny Riordan has disappeared. It's really important, Billy, that you try to help us with this. If you have any idea of where he might be, well then, please say so."

"Gee," Billy said, "I don't know. I mean, he said something about going to the game this afternoon and then to the movies. They've got these scary pictures there. *The Fog* and *Halloween*. They're really scary."

"Right," Brian said. "Were you going to go with him?"

"I played in the game, but I already seen the movies the first time they came around."

Arlene Conley touched her brow and ran her

hand down her cheeks. She looked as though she were trying to keep herself reined in.

"Now, Billy, you're sure that he didn't say anything else?"

"No." Billy Conley gave a slight smile, almost a smirk, Brian thought.

"I guess Danny is a pretty good baseball player. Isn't that right?"

"Not as good as me," Billy blurted out. "He can't hit nearly as good as me. He thinks he's so smart."

"Is he?"

"I guess he's a brain," Billy said, staring down at the floor. "He always gets like 95 and stuff on his tests. But I can hit a baseball a lot farther than him, so who wants to be a brain anyway."

"And did you and Danny have arguments because he was a brain, Billy?"

"Chief Dolan," Arlene Conley said, "I didn't invite you in here so you could accuse my son . . ."

"Hold on," Brian said. "I'm not accusing him of anything. But this could be important. Please, Mrs. Conley, let me ask the questions."

Arlene Conley stared through Brian Dolan, but kept her peace.

"Now, isn't it true, Billy, that you and your friend Skeeter had some arguments with Danny about a week ago? What were they about?"

"Gee, I don't remember," Billy Conley said. "Oh, yeah. He was saying he could hit as good as me, and Skeeter and I said he was full of crap."

"Billy," Arlene Conley said, "I didn't teach you to talk like that."

"I'm sorry, Mom, but he got me really mad. He thinks he's so smart and stuff. He uses big words. Sometimes he makes me so mad I just want to . . ."

Billy Conley looked up at the Police Chief with a guilty blush on his face.

"You want to do what?" Dolan said.

"Nothing," Billy said. "It's nothing."

"Yes," Arlene Conley said. "It is nothing. Kids go through these kinds of things all the time. Besides, I can account for what happened to Billy today. He came right out after church, and we went down to McDonald's for lunch. Though it's ridiculous to have to say so, my son has a perfect alibi. And I've been with him all afternoon."

"Yes," Brian said, "I'm aware of that. But we don't know exactly what went on in the church, do we? Did you and Danny have an argument today?"

"I don't remember," Billy said. "I don't remember anything else."

He pouted out his lower lip and stared into the Chief's eyes defiantly. He looked just like a little bulldog, Brian thought.

"It would be real good if you could remember," Brian said. "Like Skeeter did. He remembered that you and Danny and he were arguing about who was the biggest chicken."

"Chief Dolan," Arlene Conley said, "you are baiting my son."

"No, I didn't hit him very hard," Billy Conley said, starting to cry. He reached over and held his mother's hand.

"Billy," his mother said, "you hit Danny?"

"Well, sorta. He said I never saw *Halloween,* that I was afraid to sit through it the last time it was in town. But I had to leave that Saturday because you said I had to get home. I wasn't afraid of it. I ain't afraid of nothin'. But he kept saying I was, and so I hit him, kinda, on the arm, and he fell down. But he got right up, honest."

"And then what happened?" Chief Dolan asked.

"He just got up and went into the bathroom," Billy Conley said. "I don't know what he was doing in there."

"I see," Brian Dolan said. "And you didn't see him come out."

"No. Me and Skeeter left then and went outside to go home. That's the truth. I didn't really hurt him or nothin'. I just didn't want him calling me names like that."

"All right," Brian said. "Thank you, Billy. You can go now."

Mrs. Conley nodded her head and Billy left the room.

"I'm sorry," Brian said. "But I had to talk with him and get his feelings out in the open."

"And now that you have," Arlene Conley said, "do you think that maybe he knocked Danny unconscious and then flushed his body down the toilet, or what?"

"No," Brian said. "I think there was some animosity between your son, Skeeter Bannon and Danny. Maybe he was upset by getting hit and just took off. Kids have been known to do that. Especially boys who are maybe worried about being sissies. Especially if they get hit by bigger boys."

"You mean bullies," Arlene Conley said. "But my son is not a bully."

She stood up and put her hands on her hips and glowered at Brian Dolan. She looked exactly like a bully, he thought.

"Thank you for your time," he said. "I'm sorry if I shook him up. But this is serious."

"I know it is," she said. "That's why I allowed you to talk with him. But you must see that there's no relationship between their childish scrapes and Danny's disappearance. Everyone picks on Billy because he's more developed physically. Why not pick on Skeeter?"

Brian was noncommittal. He merely smiled and thanked Arlene Conley again and left.

Outside, while trying to get the Dodge started again, he thought about Billy Conley. He wasn't a likable kid. He led the malleable Skeeter around by the nose. But he was still a kid, and it just didn't seem possible that he could have taken part in any crime against Danny Riordan. Still, Danny could have been afraid of him. Maybe the thought of having to face up to Billy and Skeeter was too much for him and he ran away. Brian felt a surge of empathy for the boy. He might be out on the highway, pulling the old run-away-from-home scene. It was a dangerous and lonely place to be for a kid of ten. But still, Brian thought, it was the best hope they had. If he was out there, chances were some driver would pick him up and return him home. If he wasn't, then something else had happened. Something too frightening to contemplate.

It was nearly six by the time Brian pulled up in front of the small white house where Kate Riordan lived. Brian parked the car in the driveway and thought of Kate Riordan. He thought of the way she had looked when they used to go to the movies together when they dated in high school. She had a red and white dress, Brian remembered, a dress that clung to her, and she had brown skin and the softest hair. But she also had a great scent; he could remember smelling her skin as they necked in their car. But then Paddy Riordan had moved in. Of all the people he had to lose her to, Paddy Riordan was the worst. He and Paddy had had a very bad fight in high school. He had never liked Paddy or any of his buddies. They were loud and crazy, though he had to admit he was just a little bit jealous of them, too. Paddy was the best athlete in school. He had even been recruited by colleges for his play on the high-school football team. But he had always been just a working guy at heart. He took Kate, Brian's Kate, as easily as he would have taken a cherry from a tree. Or so it seemed to Brian. The next thing Brian knew, they were having Danny and moving to Southie, and the very next thing that happened was Paddy's death. Since Kate had moved back, Brian had called her a couple of times, just in a friendly way, but she had seemed distant, cold. Paddy's death had taken something out of her, Brian thought, and now this. If anything happens to Danny, she won't be able to go on. That's the truth. Brian climbed out of the car.

Maura Riordan answered his knock on the door.

"Brian Dolan," Mrs. Riordan said. "Thank God you're here. Have you found our baby yet?"

"No," Brian said. "I'm sorry, Mrs. Riordan, I can't say we have. But I am working on it. May I see Kate, please?"

"Yes, you can," Maura whispered. "But please be gentle with her, Brian. She's terribly upset."

"I can imagine," Brian said, walking into the room. He was immediately struck by the homeyness of the place. The blue and gray tweed sofa, the green curtains, the cheerful white brick fireplace, and the magazines, *Good Housekeeping* and *Ladies' Home Journal,* sitting neatly on the coffee table. Then he saw something that made him shiver. It was Danny Riordan's baseball hat, and pants, all laid out on the sofa. Beneath them, on the floor, were his shoes and glove. Brian walked through the living room to the kitchen, following Maura, who walked slowly, as though she were afraid to make a sound.

"Kate," Maura said, "Kate, honey, Brian is here." She stepped aside to let Brian pass and went back into the living room.

Kate Riordan waited at the kitchen table. She had changed into a plaid shirt and a pair of jeans. Her blonde hair was pulled back in a ponytail, which to Brian gave her the look of a teenager. He walked over to her and offered Kate his hand. She squeezed it and looked into his eyes.

"Kate, I've got to ask you a few more questions. Sometimes when a mother and son are alone they do get a special bond," Brian said gently. "I mean, sometimes the little boy begins to unconsciously think of himself as the man of the house. Then, if the mother starts to date another man, well, there can be a problem."

Kate Riordan looked up and smiled.

"I've had a few dates, but *very* few in the last year. I just haven't met anybody, and haven't had time to even look. I work for Jerry Manning of Manning and O'Rourke, the law firm. I frequently work late. I don't have much time for dates."

Brian Dolan could feel his face turn hot, and offered up a silent prayer that he wasn't blushing. "But there could still be a problem in this area," he said.

"Yes, if my son wasn't Danny," Kate said. "You don't understand. Please don't think I'm just a boastful parent. Look up his school records if you want. He's a very good student. He's open and sensitive, and I've always encouraged him to talk about his problems. He's encouraged me to see other men since Paddy died. He says he doesn't want me to be lonely. He's very, very sweet. But there isn't anybody now."

Kate Riordan began to cry. Her hands shook, as she rubbed her eyes.

"It's getting dark out," she said. "God, what if something . . . if someone has taken him. Tell me that hasn't happened, Brian."

"We don't know yet," Brian said, handing her a tissue from the box on the kitchen table. "There are some other possibilities. You and I both know that peer pressure can be a very big factor for a boy Danny's age. I mean, sometimes a boy who gets straight A's has problems with his classmates. Other boys are jealous and afraid of the superior intellect. You remember, we used to call them brains. My best guess is he had a fight with Billy Conley, lost and ran away to lick his wounded pride."

"Oh Brian," she said, "I can't believe that. He's been doing so well lately. He's grown up a lot lately. He's learned to stand up for his rights."

"Then let me ask you another question. Is there anyone who would be mad at you? Who would take Danny off to get even with you? Maybe like a man you wouldn't date. Or some ex-boyfriend, or even a relative. I mean, there are cases in which irate grandparents have taken a child because they didn't feel he was getting the proper upbringing. Perhaps for religious reasons."

Kate shook her head slowly.

"Danny gets along well with my father. My mother has been dead for three years, and my father is retired and has moved to Florida. Maura is his only grandparent, and she is one of my dearest friends as well. As far as people outside the family, I don't know. It just seems impossible."

Brian blew out his breath and sipped his coffee.

"There's no family tension that you can think of then?" he said softly.

"No," Kate said sharply, then immediately apologized. "I am sorry, Brian. I'm just so damned jumpy. Look, I've been thinking about possibilities all day, but I can't imagine what has happened. I mean, if somebody takes a child, doesn't he usually do it for money? Well, I don't have any money. You know that, Brian."

"Okay," Brian said. "But we haven't gotten to that yet. I have to ask some more about men you might know."

"Why?"

"Because you're a bright and intelligent lady.
You were like Danny in school. The bright girl.
Some men, as I'm sure you know, don't like
bright women. They like to take them down a
peg or two. Well, let's say you saw somebody
. . . I mean, just on a friendly basis, and then
you decided to stop seeing them. What if they
wanted to get even, to bring you down a peg or
two?"

Kate managed a small smile for Brian.

"There hasn't been anybody like that, Brian. I
saw one man for a while. His name was Mike
Baines, but it just didn't work out."

Brian felt a tug of the old jealousy.

"And what happened to Baines?" Brian asked
in a voice which sounded too detached to be
real.

"We broke up," Kate said. "Okay, it wasn't
really great breaking up. It was my idea. . . . Oh
damn."

"What is it?" Brian said.

"It was the way we broke up. He didn't really
like my spending so much time with Danny. He
was jealous. But it was a harmless thing. I mean,
he just needed a lot of attention. He wasn't
ready to deal with a woman with a child. That's
all."

"Maybe that's all," Brian said. "I'll have to
check it out. Do you have his address?"

"He's over on Northwest Ridge," Kate said.
"A ski instructor. He lives in a condo. I'll get
you the address before you go."

"Is there anyone else?" Brian asked.

"No," Kate said. "I saw him for quite a while.

He would go away for a while, then come back. It was good to be close to him, but it was good to be by myself, too. I couldn't stand being that close to someone again, Brian. I was afraid they were going to die on me."

Brian nodded, silent.

"What was Danny wearing today?"

"He wore dress Levi's and a white shirt to the church. And a pair of Thom McAn loafers."

Then Kate remembered the Polaroid shot.

"Oh, I've got a picture of him I took outside this morning, Brian. It's in his room."

Kate got up and headed into the room. Brian Dolan watched her walk away. She was back in control of herself. She hadn't broken down when describing her son. That was good. She might have to be a lot tougher before it was over.

Kate came back with the photograph. Brian looked at it. The likeness to Paddy was uncanny. And to Kate herself.

"He is a handsome boy, Kate," Brian said.

"I know," Kate said. "Oh God, Danny . . ."

Suddenly she began to cry again. Brian reached for her, but Kate put her head down on the kitchen table, and sobbed deeply.

"We have got to find him," she said. "God, if anyone has taken him, I'll kill them. I swear it. I can't stand this. What are you going to do?"

"Well, if he isn't home by tomorrow morning, I'll call the FBI. Meanwhile, you stay here and wait. If anyone does contact you, then you call me at my home. Here's my number."

He wrote it out for her and felt her fingers. Ice cold.

"But what about tonight?" she said.

"Tonight I'll have every man in the force combing the area. But try not to worry too much, Kate. Though you can't think of anything, there's still a good chance he is just out being a boy. I ran away from home myself once when I was a kid. For two days."

Brian smiled and took her hand in his. He patted it reassuringly.

"Try and get some sleep, Kate," he said. "Maybe your mother-in-law will stay with you tonight."

"Yes," Kate said. "Maura will be here. But I doubt if I'll get any sleep. Brian, I'm afraid. I don't want to be. But I'm terrified."

"Listen, Kate," Brian said, "I promise you we're going to find him. Nobody is going to steal your kid while I'm around."

Kate stepped back quickly as though Brian had hit her.

"What's wrong?" he said.

"Paddy said the same thing," Kate said. "Two days before we found out about his illness. I'm sorry, Brian. I'm just exhausted. And scared. It's getting cool out there and he doesn't even have a jacket."

Maura came in from the living room.

"It's all right, Kate," she said, handing her a brown sweater. "It's all right, dear."

It was dark by the time Brian tried to start the Dodge again. The CHECK ENGINE sign came back on and he stared down at it, and then back at the yellow lights inside the cozy house. He shut off the ignition and leaned back against the seat. This night he was flooded with memory and dread. Of the church. Of Paddy and Kate in high school. Of his own failed longings. And how bizarre this little boy should have disappeared from the church.

Religion, he thought to himself, is something that never leaves you. They give a healthy dose to you when you're young and you can never shake it. But it was the damn ambiguity that always got him. Kind of like being a policeman.

They brought you up on a Latin Mass and then they switched it all around on you. Now it's got all these songs in English that were written in the sixties. Where's the mystery? Where's the exclusivity? And it used to be such a private thing. A reverie, something you did by yourself. You prayed quietly and alone. Now it's like a goddamn Rotary Club meeting, people turning around and saying things like, "Peace be with you." And shaking your hand. You can bet Thomas Aquinas didn't shake anybody's hand at Mass.

None of this was comforting to Brian Dolan. It all served to increase his sense of dislocation. And he knew there were other men out there, like himself, even more confused—men who were unable to tell right from wrong. Irrational men. The kind who simply killed a child, dumped him in a river or a shallow grave, and then disappeared. Who moved on to the next town.

There would be little or no hope of catching such a man. And with all the confusion inside him, Brian Dolan still could pray. A small voice inside asked God not to let it be that kind of man.

HE WAS out of breath, panting, and he could feel his heart beating wildly. There was no stepping back now. He had done it, at last it wasn't just a dream. He had taken the Riordan boy right out from under their noses. God, they would be howling tonight. He walked over to the corner and turned on his Panasonic radio. And waited.

The news came on, a bright-sounding woman. She talked about today's top story, a laundromat robbery in the south end of William's Crossing. A robbery? What was that? No, they didn't have it on yet. Not yet. He had to be patient. But how to stop the excitement inside of him. He hadn't felt this way since . . . no, that was wrong. He had never, ever felt this way. It was like seeing snow for the first time. It was like going for his first swim. It was better than those things. It was going to be infinitely more satisfying. But he had to remain calm. He had to try to keep himself together.

Time to read. And think of the surprised look on the boy's face. The total surprise. Ah, it was wonderful.

He picked up his book. Tonight again he read from the *Rule of St. Benedict.*

In these days of Lent, let each one, over and above the measure prescribed for him, offer God something of his own free will in the joy of the Holy Spirit. That is to say, let him stint himself of food, drink, sleep, talk and jesting, and look forward with the joy of spiritual longing to the holy feast of Easter.

Yes, he would look forward to it. In the proper style. Though they had laughed at him and called him a fool. He was going to look forward to offering the Lord something far and away beyond his meager station. He was going to offer him something that the crass mercantile Church could never understand. Something that the Prophets in the Old Testament would have loved. Something directly from the spirit, from the deepest regions of the heart. He was going to offer God a sacrifice. A real wondrous event. Like the miracles of old. A human sacrifice. And if he was lucky, very lucky, more than one.

Sunday, 9 p.m.

As BRIAN made his way to St. Dominic's rectory, a neat two-story frame building located in back of the church off Mayhew Street, he was struck by how quiet the town was. No one would ever suspect that a child was missing.

Brian had put off going to the rectory until last. As he reconstructed the day's events in his head, he realized that this was a subconscious maneuver on his part. The priest as an authority figure was something he had had a hard time dealing with as an adolescent. Even now, it was not something he was totally comfortable with. Who were these men, educated to have such great power over the lives of their parishioners? Brian had been brought up to believe that priests were above suspicion. Maybe that was why he was so mistrustful of them. If they were not accountable here on earth, who knows what trouble they could get themselves into?

Mrs. Mullen, the gray-haired housekeeper, answered the door and let him. He decided to talk to her before interviewing the priests. She led him into the kitchen. "Would you like a cup of tea, Chief?" she asked.

"Yes, ma'am, that would be nice."

"It's an awful thing, a child disappearing. I was a child when they took the Lindbergh baby and I remember being terrified that someone would come and steal me. I had nightmares for years."

Brian didn't know too much about Lorna Mullen. She had only recently come to work at the rectory—after old Mrs. Foster had died. But she had come with the best of references. She had once been on the household staff of Cardinal Medeiros and had been chief housekeeper to the auxiliary bishop of Worcester. As she had gotten on in years, she had been looking for a less demanding situation, and when she had heard about the St. Dominic's job, she had eagerly lobbied for it, getting both the Cardinal and the Bishop to write her personal letters of recommendation. She was hired right away.

By all accounts she was an excellent housekeeper and a prodigious cook. Not that she cooked particularly well, though her culinary skills were adequate, but there was lots of everything—roasts, hams, turkey, mounds of potatoes and vegetables, infinite varieties of pies and cakes. Monsignor Merja had had to remind her that she was no longer feeding diocesan armies, only three priests and two brothers.

Brian knew little of her personal background, though he had read the file supplied by Merja earlier in the day. Mrs. Mullen was in her late sixties, a widow, no living children. A daughter had died in a tragic boating accident a number of years ago. From her employment history it was clear that most of her life had been devoted to the priests.

"Mrs. Mullen, do you know Danny Riordan?"

"Yes I do, and a lovely boy he is. So well-mannered. On the Friday mornings when he serves the six o'clock Mass during Lent, he comes over to take a tray of hot cross buns to the good sisters. He's a quiet and respectful young man. Why would he run away? Who would want to take him?"

"That's what we're trying to find out. Do you know if he had any conflicts with people in the town here?"

"Well . . ."

"Please, no confidences. His life may be at stake."

"I do remember a couple of weeks ago that that fine man Coach Mick had to break up a fight on the basketball court on the side of the school between Danny and Billy Conley. They used to fight all the time, I heard, but recently I was told that they were getting along pretty good. The strange thing is they were both playing on the same team."

"Do you have any idea what caused the fight?"

"Billy claimed Danny had tripped him and that he had warned Danny not to do it again."

"But they were teammates."

"Doesn't matter. Billy Conley thinks he is the toughest boy in the school and that other boys must do what he says. It's a trait that Coach Mick is trying to breed out of him."

"Do you know anyone else who might have a grudge against Danny or want to harm him?"

"No, I can't say that I do."

"How is his relationship with the priests here?"

"How could it be better? Monsignor made him a senior altar boy. He's a star player for Coach Mick and Father Joe's been giving him personal guitar lessons."

"Since when?"

"Oh, a number of weeks. Danny comes to the rectory one day a week after school. Personally, I prefer to see young children beginning on the piano. But it's a new age, Chief."

"Well, you've been very helpful. Now I've got to talk to the other priests and brothers."

"You'll probably be wanting to sit in the front parlor."

"No, right here is fine. If it doesn't interfere with your work, Mrs. Mullen."

"Thankfully my work is done for today. I like to be in bed by nine. I'm up at five with the baking, you know."

Mrs. Mullen went out and brought back Brother Charles. He and Brother Michael were diocesan brothers who did all the handiwork around St. Dominic's. They were excellent carpenters and both were possessed of green thumbs. Additionally, Brother Charles was a licensed electrician. He was a tall, angular man in his late fifties. He was a kind man, but a bit aloof. Most people found him to be a bit shy. Brian had often seen him around town, but had never had an occasion to speak to him. Tonight he seemed strangely ill at ease.

"Brother Charles," said Brian. "Have you had any recent contact with Danny?"

"I hardly know the boy," he said quietly, "though I've seen him around some."

"Is he troublesome?"

"I really don't know."

"Do you know any reason he'd run away or anyone who'd want to hurt him?"

"No. No. Neither."

Did he know more than he was telling? He was singularly uncommunicative, but somehow there seemed more to be gleaned here.

"Did Danny have any problems with the other priests?"

"I really wouldn't know. I only see the priests at meals or prayer. Rarely am I around when they are with parishioners."

There was nothing in the man's past that should make Brian suspect him. He had an exemplary record working at various rectories over the past twenty-five years. He was known as quiet, industrious, and earnest. Why was Brian getting a second sense this man was holding back?

Brian decided not to press. "Well, that's all for now, Brother. I'd appreciate it if you would send in Brother Michael."

Brother Michael was a small man in his mid-thirties. Like Brother Charles, he was quiet and had little contact with the parishioners. No one knew too much about Brother Michael. He had recently come to the parish.

Michael was a little over five feet tall and of nondescript appearance. No matter how many times you saw him, you never remembered exactly what he looked like. His features were average: his eyes the right distance apart, his nose like anyone else's and his chin distinctly plain. He seemed to have been ordered out of a mail-order catalog. His only distinguishing fea-

ture was his beard, which obviously had been
carefully cultivated. Another of God's wall-
flowers, thought Brian.

"Brother, can you shed any light on Danny's
disappearance?"

"I'm sorry, Chief Dolan. I've never met the
boy."

"Are you active in *any* parish affairs?"

"No, my duties are confined to maintenance."

Brian surveyed the man's hands. This was a
man who was used to outdoor labor.

"Well, Brother, if you see or think of anything, be sure to let us know."

"It would be my pleasure."

Curious duck, thought Brian. Quiet, but quite
self-possessed.

"Ask Monsignor to join me, please."

"Certainly," Brother Michael said evenly.

Monsignor Merja was about five foot nine,
and quite trim. His eyebrows were thick and
knitted together in what looked like a permanent
frown. An ascetic and remote man by nature, he
tried hard to relate to his parishioners but it was
not his forte. In fact, it was not even his interest.
Brian knew that at one time he had been in line
for better things. But during the time of the Second Vatican Council he had been slow to grasp
where the Church had been going, and he had
been superseded in ecclesiastical politics by
younger, more liberal priests. Now there were
men much younger than he who were bishops.
These men, he knew, were less scholarly, less
pious even, dared he think it, less holy. But they
were now in charge. And Merja, a man of the
old guard, a World War II refugee, representing

the conservative thinking not in favor during the sixties, was resigned to the oblivion of St. Dominic's. Five years ago, at fifty-five, he had been made a Monsignor. But this rank served only to further underscore his disappointment. It highlighted what might have been in his life.

Still, Brian was aware Merja was nothing if not an organization man. And so he gave his best and was clever with money. In a time when most parishes were going broke, St. Dominic's showed a healthy profit. A testament to Merja's managerial skills. And why not, this was a man who had been subadministrator at the chancery in diocesan finances. He had collected there in a day what St. Dominic's took in in a year. Life was full of crosses to bear, and St. Dominic's was his. He would do his best.

A Polish pastor in an Irish parish seemed unthinkable, about as plausible as a Polish Pope. But here he was, and here, he supposed, he would remain.

Brian noticed that Merja was carrying his breviary.

"I hope I didn't disturb you, Monsignor."

"No, no, I can finish later. I am sure that God will wait." Merja tried to manage a smile.

"Monsignor, I understand that you and Danny had a run-in a couple of years ago."

The priest looked embarrassed. "Yes, this is true. Danny went through a period where he had trouble controlling himself in class. He was very fidgety. On this particular day, he would not keep quiet. He was warned a couple of times and then I slapped him."

Brian just stared at the priest.

"I lost my temper," said Merja. "I really shouldn't have hit him. But you know, God acts in mysterious ways. From that day on he has never given us any trouble. Maybe it was discipline that he so badly needed. Children these days get very little discipline, and Danny has no father."

"Do you feel the boy's mother is too lenient with him?"

"The boy's mother tries very hard. She loves her son."

"That wasn't my question."

"All children need discipline."

Brian decided not to pursue the matter further.

"Do you have any ideas on the boy's disappearance?"

"I have searched my brain. I do not."

"Well, I guess that's all for now, Monsignor. Would you please ask Father Joe to come in?"

"He is on vacation."

"He is? Since when?"

"Actually, he was due back today, but he called and said he had some family business and he might need a day or two to complete it."

"What kind of business?"

"He didn't say. A priest is entitled to his privacy."

"I see. Well, please have him get in touch with me when he returns. One last thing. I hope to involve the parish in finding Danny."

Monsignor Merja shifted in his seat and seemed to stare through Brian.

"Let me say this. I just learned from Frank Fahey of your idea to involve the Knights of

Columbus. I do not endorse this, but I will not oppose it."

"Hell, Monsignor, a child is missing."

Monsignor Merja smiled ironically.

"It is the task of the police to recover missing children, is it not?"

Brian felt like a schoolboy again.

"Monsignor Merja, we're talking about a young boy's life."

Merja gave a peremptory wave of his hand. "I have scheduled a novena to St. Anthony. That is all we can do."

Cold son of a bitch, thought Brian. Wonder what his problem is.

Sunday, 10:30 p.m.

KATE SAT at the kitchen table, her mind racing a hundred miles an hour. Maura sat across from her, stirring her tea.

"I can't help thinking," Kate said, "that Danny has to be near or in the church. I think I'll go back and search the parish hall and maybe take another look in the cellar. I just know he's got to be there somewhere."

"Nonsense, dear, it's after ten o'clock. I'm sure the church is all locked up now anyway."

"I could find Jimmy Lawlor and make him go with me. Make him really search the place this time."

"Kate, I don't think that would do any good."

"It's just I can't stand this waiting any more. You'd think Brian Dolan would have turned up something by now."

"Now we can't take the law into our own hands and besides the police are only human. These things take time."

"That's the point, Maura, we don't have time. Danny may be hurt. Maybe he did have a fight with Billy as Brian thinks, got a black eye or

worse and was too embarrassed to come home.
He might need medical attention right now."

"Let's at least wait until we hear from Chief
Dolan."

"Okay, I'll stay here for now but I better call
Jerry and tell him I'm not going to be in in the
morning if Danny doesn't show up."

"That's a good idea, dear. Maybe Jerry will
have some advice."

More advice, Kate thought, as she moved to
her bedroom to make the call in privacy, was
what she didn't need. Jerry's wife Karen answered and volunteered to get Jerry from his
garage where he and his son were building a
small rowboat. Jerry and Mike were avid sailors
and loved to explore the Merrimack when the
spring thaws came, which would not be too long
now.

Jerry was the most respected lawyer in the
town of William's Crossing. His father had been
a district court judge in the town for more than
thirty years and his uncle had been attorney general of the Commonwealth. In fact, as a girl Kate
remembered going to church when a red Mass or
votive Mass was celebrated for the Manning family. These were very infrequent and only to help
members of the legal profession exercise their
equitable capacities. Kate never knew quite why
these Masses had to be held, but she did know
that the Manning family had a lot of clout in William's Crossing.

Jerry sounded glad to hear from her on this
Sunday evening. "Hi, Katey. What's up?"

His ebullience set her back. "Jerry, Danny's
missing. He disappeared after Mass this morning."

"Wow, hold on a second. Tell me what happened."

She ran quickly through the events of the day. He was silent but then asked, "Kate do you think he disappeared on his own or that someone took him?"

"I just don't know, Jerry."

"What does Dolan think?"

"If anything he leans to the idea Danny did it himself."

"Listen, I've got an idea—I'll put up a reward. Maybe we can get some information that way."

Kate was touched. "Jerry, I'm very grateful but I think that would be premature. Anyway, this phone call is by way of telling you I may not be in tomorrow."

Manning drew a long breath. "Kate, I'm surprised at you. That goes without saying. Call me as soon as you have any news. And remember, the reward is there if you need it."

"Thanks for all your support, Jerry." She put down the phone, knowing he was one person she could count on.

Monday, 12:30 a.m.

THE LAST person Brian wanted to talk to was Mick Shea. Mick was about forty and in his day had been an All East fullback at Boston College. Everyone said he could have played pro, but he had turned to coaching instead. First junior high and then high school. But somewhere along the line it had come apart for Mick Shea. Brian wasn't sure what the exact circumstances had been. Some people said the bottle. Others said Mick's hot temper. Now that Mick's dreams of coaching glory seemed largely behind him, he contented himself with the parish CYO teams. And there was no question that all his teams were winners. Athletics were a very serious matter to Mick Shea.

Brian decided to stop at the Wishing Well Tavern on Fulton Street to see if he could locate Mick, who was a prominent customer there. The bar was a big barnlike place with a juke box filled with old fifties' standards. Every time he went into the Wishing Well, Brian imagined to himself just how at home Perry Como and Patti Page would be in a place like this.

It was after midnight and the tavern was largely empty. At the long slate-topped bar, though, was Everett Moody. Moody was a tag-along sort, about Mick's age, who never did much, Brian knew. But he idolized Mick. If anyone knew where the Mick was, it would be Moody. Brian walked over and took a seat next to him.

"Hey, Moo, seen the Mick around?"

"Don't believe I have, Chief. Haven't seen him in a couple of days." Moody continued: "He's in and out. Might have gone to the Celtics game tonight."

Brian ordered a Miller Lite and said, "Say listen, Moo. What do you know about Danny Riordan and the Mick? They get along?"

Moody laughed. "No more than most. You know the Mick. He gets carried away sometimes, you got to put a clamp on that boy. He don't mean bad. Just wants to win. Never saw anyone who wants to win as bad as he does, even going back to our B.C. days."

"Any specific problems between them?" Brian turned around and looked Moody full in the face.

"Naw, the Mick don't favor one boy, more or less. He treats them all the same—like dogs. He likes to say that's how Vince Lombardi became a winner."

Brian had another sip of his beer. "That sounds real enlightened."

"Aw, Chief. The Mick's just had lots of disappointments. Many's the time he's sat here and told me about them. You know he should be coaching pro now. Hell, at least college. That's what the Mick says. Instead, what's he doing?

Stuck with a bunch of little kids. That can get a man awful pissed off. Know what I mean?"

"But you don't remember anything between the Mick and Danny?"

"You asked that, Chief. Boy, you must be losing your mind. You need more sleep. Look like hell, too. Got to take better care of yourself. Don't let them get you down!"

Brian shook his head in assent, fished out two quarters and left them as a tip.

"Thanks for the advice, Moo," he said. Vic Damone's version of "On the Street Where You Live" wafted through the Wishing Well.

Monday, 1:30 a.m.

KATE LAY in her bed but sleep would not come. She felt powerless and even as she said the third decade of her rosary, she found no solace. She put the beads on the night table, flipped on the light and sat up. It was no use. She knew she had to search the church again. Quietly, she got dressed again and let herself out the back door, tiptoeing with each step so as not to wake Maura, who slumbered peacefully on the couch in the living room.

She got into the Fairmont, released the parking brake and shifted the car into neutral. When it had rolled gently down the slight incline into the middle of the street, she turned the ignition on. Driving through the darkened town was eerie. She saw no one on the darkened streets. But as she drove purposefully towards St. Dominic's, she felt a sense of peace descending over her. For she knew that Brian Dolan was out looking for Danny and that gave her comfort. Moreover, she knew that if Paddy had still been alive he would have scoured every inch of the town. She could do no less.

Leaving the car in the church parking lot, she walked around to the front of the building. The church had been locked at 8 p.m. recently after a couple of incidents of minor vandalism. Kate gave a tug at one of the doors and to her surprise it opened. Jimmy Lawlor in the excitement must have forgotten to lock it. More likely he had had a nip or two and simply was unable to perform his duties. Kate knew it wouldn't have been the first time.

Kate blessed herself with holy water from the scalloped dish in the vestibule. She made her way into the main hall of the dark church, all the way to the front. She could see nothing except shadows caused by a few votive lights. She knelt in the first bench and began to pray. But the words would not come. Her heart would not lift. The church which meant so very much to her had abandoned her, left her by herself to face this terrible crisis. Was this why she was now so fearful?

She made her way in front of the altar rail to the right side of the church where the door to the sacristy was. In the glassed-in room used for crying babies she thought she saw a glimmer of movement. But that was ridiculous, she told herself; who would be sitting in a dark church? Suddenly she was filled with dread. Was it her imagination or simply a reflection of the flickering votive candles?

Nobody used the crying room any more, did they? It had been built back in the fifties when there were many more babies in the parish than there were today.

But Kate looked again and could see a solitary

figure in the room, kneeling in the near darkness. She crossed to the door of the room, scared, but determined to find out who this apparition was.

She recognized the woman kneeling on the prie-dieux, her gaze fixed on Kate's face. It was Mrs. Mullen, Monsignor Merja's housekeeper. She appeared to be in some kind of trance. Kate put her hand on the woman's shoulder and she recoiled, as if she had been bitten by a rattlesnake. Then she spoke, quietly, barely above a whisper. "You scared me, Mrs. Riordan. Oh, Mrs. Riordan."

"Mrs. Mullen, what are you doing in here with all the lights out?"

The strange look did not go away. "I came to pray for your son and my daughter."

Kate Riordan shuddered involuntarily. She no longer wanted to search the rest of the church, all she wanted was to be free of the place.

DANNY RIORDAN could feel the panic running through him like silverfish swimming through his blood. He tried not to move too quickly because the pain was so bad in his head. Oh, it felt soft back there, very soft and squishy, and he thought of a Spiderman comic, when Spidey was bashed in the head, and it looked like a crushed fruit there. There was hair, but beneath it was this soft spongy-looking stuff, and lots of red blood. He had to not think of that. He had to figure out stuff, like his dad had told him to. Think with your head. Don't just scream and cry. He had only done that when he was a little kid. But then nothing like this had happened to him. God, if he could just not be real scared. Because maybe ten minutes ago he had gotten so scared, so scared that he had tried to jerk his hands free, and rip the tape off his mouth, but the knots had only gotten tighter, cut into his wrists, and he hadn't been able to breathe at all for a time. What had happened then? Had he passed out? He wasn't sure. It was so dark in here, dark and so cold. And he was on a hard floor. It felt like concrete, with no rug, and it was cold. Maybe he was in Dracula's castle. Maybe a vampire . . . But no, no it wasn't a vampire, because they didn't really exist. It was a man, a kidnapper. Maybe a kidnapper was scarier than Dracula. You could trick Dracula, 'cause he had to go back to his coffin. But if he was real, a real guy, he could come kill you. But sometimes they didn't. Sometimes, Mom said once when they were watching TV, sometimes a kidnapper is just a sick person. He wants money and then he lets a kid go home. But sometimes too, he gets the money and . . .

Danny started to cry a little, but then got mad with himself. He wasn't a baby any more. He was ten years old. You weren't really a little kid any more when you had two numbers to your age. And he was an altar boy. He had led the whole church procession. Monsignor Merja had told him that when you were an altar boy, you were really becoming a man in God's eyes. He tried to think of God watching him when he was going through the procession. God would be pleased with him, but now, now, maybe God was testing him. To see if he would really get scared, and he didn't want to disappoint God. That would be horrible. He tried to move his feet but they were tied together at the ankles. He scraped his legs back and forth on the cold concrete, and then he felt a shock. He had on his dress jeans, and if he did that, he would wear a hole in them and then Mom would be furious with him when he got home. Home. Oh he wanted to be back in his room, under his secret quilt, which was really an ultra shield, and when

he was under there, none of the bad guys from
Sonic Space I could get him. He wished he was
under the quilt right now, because if he was, the
ropes would come free and he would figure out
where he was.

But he wasn't with his quilt.

He wasn't in his room.

He was somewhere bad. Somewhere dark and
awful.

Now Danny shut his eyes tight and tried to
make them dark, darker than the room. And
when he opened them the room would be a little
lighter. There had to be some light somewhere.
He opened them and looked around. But there
was only darkness, a darkness he had never
imagined before, even when he had deliberately
tried to scare himself by turning all the lights out
and going down into the basement of his house.
This was darker than that.

And so he tried to think of something else. He
would listen. He would listen, and he would hear
something. He sat and strained.

But there was nothing. No sound at all.

No, wait. One sound. His own heart beating,
the sound of his legs scraping nervously (and he
had to stop that, Mommy would be mad if he
messed them all up).

He edged up against the wall and then he realized something. The wall was hard too, hard and
cold, and he knew that it would only be cold if
he were underground somewhere. But the real-
ization scared him even worse. For if he was underground, then maybe he was dead. Maybe this
was what it was like when you were dead and
buried somewhere. He wanted to cry out for
help, but the tape was on his lips tight.

Then he thought of something. Tape was made with glue. Glue like on a Band-Aid. If you cut your knee, and you put on a Band-Aid, and then you went out and ran around for a while, you would get all sweaty, and the glue would come loose on the Band-Aid, and it would slide off. Danny felt a little better. If he could lick up over his mouth, get his tongue up on the glue, maybe it would wear it out and he could get it loose. He tried it, but there was a problem. He didn't have any spit in his mouth. His tongue was dry, completely dry.

He tried it again, and that time he could taste some of the glue. It was horrible. He looked around and then he saw something. It was over in the corner.

Danny froze with horror. It was big and it looked like a box.

He was so afraid that he wasn't able to lick the glue any more. He wasn't able to move at all.

He sat still and then, suddenly, he heard a rumbling sound. It was loud, so loud, and it seemed to be coming from somewhere outside of the room. What was it? Like an engine. Maybe he was in some kind of secret airplane place, or a rocket factory. But it didn't sound exactly like an airplane. It was like something else.

What was it?

Danny put his head up against the cool wall and listened to the rumbling again. Then it stopped, as quickly as it had begun, and he was alone.

But somehow he felt better. There was something to figure out. If he stayed very still and worked on the tape, and maybe shuffled his legs a little—even if he did dirty up his new pants—to loosen the ropes on his ankles, which suddenly didn't seem as tight as the ones on his arms, if he could try to think about the loud noise and what it might be—then maybe he wouldn't cry and act like a baby, and make everyone ashamed of him.

Like Billy Conley. If *he* was kidnapped by someone, he'd fight back.

Danny rubbed his legs around, and slid forward until he found a little rough spot on the floor. He could maybe use it like a knife.

And wet the glue. Oh, it tasted awful, and think about the noise.

And don't look over in the corner. Don't look there at the dark shape.

There, he was doing better. He was going to help himself. It was going to be all right.

As long as the man didn't come back.

Monday, 7:30 a.m.

KATE SAT up in bed, the covers twisted around her like a tourniquet. She felt the cold sweat run down her back, and tried to stop herself from shivering. The night had been the worst of her life. Worse even than when Paddy died. She had barely been able to sleep at all, and when she had finally fallen into unconsciousness, she had a dream in which her child was swimming out into the ocean. She was on the beach watching the tide take him out. Behind her was a lifeguard. Kate ran towards him, screaming, but the words made no sound. Breathless, she had run up to the lifeguard stand and grabbed the lifeguard's toe to get his attention. His foot was made of papier-mâché and came off in her hand. Kate then ran to the ocean and watched Danny disappear into the mouth of what looked like a huge whale. She had wakened from that dream screaming so loud that Maura had to come into the room.

Now she stared at the sun, and the phone next to her. The telephone had taken on a horrible new significance for her. She could barely stand to hear it ring, and it seemed to have been ringing all night. By now Danny's disappearance was all over town. She pulled herself out of bed, walked over to the maroon drapes, and pulled them back. The sun came flowing into the room, but she felt not one bit happier for it. In the kitchen downstairs she could hear Maura banging pots and pans. Suddenly the doorbell rang. The sound of it was like an electric needle through her heart.

Kate began to rush forward and cracked her elbow on the bedroom door. The pain went like a shock wave up her arm, but she barely noticed it. Perhaps it was Danny. . . .

By the time she had gone down the three steps to the living room, however, she realized that it was not Danny at all, but a police officer with red hair, a red nose, and a large stomach. He smiled sympathetically at both Maura, who had answered the door, and Kate herself.

"Lieutenant O'Toole, ma'am," the large man said, smiling and walking into her living room. "Brian sent me up here to help you. The morning papers have a rather large story on your son, and I have come over for a while to man the phones. A couple of the other boys from the station would like your permission to go through your son's room. We'll be as neat as pins, Mrs. Riordan. I know how terribly upsetting this all is. But we need to look at anything that might give us a hint as to where the lad might be."

Kate felt her heart sink into a dejection so low that she could barely speak.

"Then there's no news," she said flatly.

"Not yet, ma'am," O'Toole said. "But with

the boy's picture in the paper and on TV, well,
we hope that someone will see him today."

O'Toole handed the paper to Kate. Maura
walked to her side and the two women stared in
disbelief at Kate's son. The picture was the
snapshot she had given Brian last night.

"God help him," Kate said. "I can't believe
this. Just yesterday I took this picture."

Maura put her hand on Kate's arm and
squeezed tightly.

"The other boys are out in the car," O'Toole
said gently. "If you wouldn't mind terribly, I
think that it would be a good thing if they go
over things a bit. Meanwhile I'll take care of the
phones."

"Who will call up?" Maura said.

O'Toole shook his head as he gestured to the
men outside.

"The question is who won't call up," O'Toole
said. "You see, Mrs. Riordan, in a case like this
a lot of people call up. Some are trying to be
helpful, some are just crazy, the kind that read
the paper for plane crashes, or think they're psy-
chics, or—well, you get the idea. But we have to
take the calls. All of them. Many a case has been
solved by one chance phone call."

"So it's a case then," Maura said under her
breath, causing Kate to jerk away from her.

"I'm sorry," Maura said. "It's just dawning on
me that . . . I'm so sorry, Kate dear."

Suddenly Maura began to cry. The tears came
all at once with a suddenness that surprised Kate
and O'Toole.

Two uniformed police came into the house.
They had a large case with them, and a camera.

"Officers Mears and Cole," O'Toole said, pointing to the blond man and his shorter, chunky partner. "They're good boys. Now, if you could just show them Danny's room."

"He actually has two rooms he uses," Kate said. "There's his bedroom, and there's a kind of TV play room, next to the kitchen. But what are you looking for?"

"Clues," said Mears. "For example, you mentioned toys. A lot of times a kid has a favorite store he goes to. You could maybe show us some toys, tell us where he got them. A lot of missing kids are found in toy stores."

"Toy stores?" Kate said incredulously. The idea seemed so incredibly dumb that she could barely talk to the two men. Didn't they realize who her son was? He was the smartest ten-year-old around. He wasn't likely to run off and show up in a toy store.

"Look," Kate said. "This is ridiculous. I mean, my son is a responsible . . ."

But she stopped then. They had no way of knowing Danny. And they had no idea of where he might be. They had to try everything, look at every possibility. The phone rang and Kate, standing next to it, automatically picked it up.

"Hello," she said.

"Hello," a man's voice said. It was deep and sounded desperate. "Mrs. Riordan?"

"Yes," Kate said, suddenly feeling terrified. "Who is this?"

"No need to get excited, Mrs. Riordan. I'm a friend. A good friend. I read about your child. I don't blame you, Mrs. Riordan. I can't stand children either."

"What are you saying to me?" Kate said tensely.

"That I don't blame you for killing your son and burying him in St. Dominic's cemetery. That was a pretty smart thing to do. I did it to my kid too. They're in there together, Mrs. Riordan, and to hell with the thankless little bastards."

"My God," Kate said. She felt overwhelmed. She was falling backwards, falling quickly.

Suddenly O'Toole was behind her. Holding on to her. He gently took the phone out of her hands and sat her down on the big sofa.

"Mears," he said, "get Mrs. Riordan a glass of water. Right away."

Kate reached up and held onto O'Toole's hands. She felt cold again, clammy, and the room was swimming in front of her.

"Oh God," she said. "He said he was glad I'd killed Danny, because he had murdered his child. He said he buried him in St. Dominic's cemetery. God. Is it possible that he was giving us a clue?"

"I doubt it, Mrs. Riordan," O'Toole said. "That's why we'll be manning your phones. You're going to get all sorts of calls now. You don't want to be bothered by them. If they're important and the person wants to talk to you, then we'll get you. If not, you won't have to deal with it."

"But what if one of them is turned away who actually could tell me something about Danny?" Kate said, taking the glass from Mears.

"We have to judge that," O'Toole said. "And we have had more experience in this type of thing than you have. I worked on the Boston police force for quite a while in my younger days, and I've seen all sorts of things. Now just drink and relax."

Kate looked up at the kind Irish face, and beyond it to Maura. She suddenly felt a fury, a cold, wild fury. What kind of person could have killed his own child, or even made a joke about it? The kind of people who read the *National Enquirer* week after week in order to get a cheap thrill out of some famous movie star's cancer, or some fat woman's horror story, or some neighbor's ghastly murder. The kind of people who laugh at accidents on the highway, or hang around plane crashes or trials of famous assassins. This was the world she was entering now. And the thought terrified her. But not nearly so much as the fact that Danny might already be in that world. Not on the outskirts like herself. Instead, he might become a headline in the *Enquirer*.

"I want you to know, officer," she said suddenly in a voice that she didn't recognize as her own, "that if one of those people has taken my child, I will kill him. I mean it."

O'Toole looked down at her and nodded. He had seen this before. The rage of the helpless, a rage that would burn itself out after a while. Either that or it could turn in on itself. When a child was lost, there was anger, then a guilt which sent some mothers over the edge into madness. Mrs. Riordan looked like a strong woman, he thought as he held her hand. But there was nothing so bad as losing a child. It was a blow that could finish off the mother's life as well as the child's. Now all he could do was smile and offer her comfort. And silently be thankful that his children were grown and married. And that his own grandchildren were present and accounted for.

Kate went to her room and sat with the Raccolta, a kind of all-purpose prayer book. Maura had given it to her when she and Paddy had gotten married. She had thought it old-fashioned at the time but now she had taken it down from the shelf and begun to thumb through. When she was younger she had often turned to the prayer for solace. But when Paddy had died, all that praying had seemed in vain. Now again, in her hour of need, she sought refuge in the book. She opened to the page which contained the *memorare* and recited the short prayer to the Blessed Virgin.

Kate looked up and saw that O'Toole had entered the room. "Mrs. Riordan," he said quietly, "we've received a note. Chief Dolan wants you to have a look at it."

Kate grasped it eagerly. It was a single piece of white paper with blue lines, the left edge was ragged like it had been torn from a child's composition book. Kate stared at the crude lettering done in what looked like Magic Marker:

TO THE MOTHER OF THE ALTAR BOY
DON'T CALL THE POLICE OR ELSE
YOU WILL BE CONTACTED
HAVE $50,000 READY

She looked, worried, at O'Toole. "My God, what does this mean?"

"It may not be genuine. We haven't ruled out

the possibility of a crank, a sick mind who wrote this and sent it. We found it in a milk bottle by your back door. We really have no idea how it got there. Carl Burke of the FBI has already looked at it. He'll be coming by in a few minutes to talk to you about it."

"And what does Brian have to say about it?"

O'Toole's imperturbable face gave her no clue. "Officially, he's not sure." He took the note gently from her hand. "We're going to give it to the FBI for more analysis."

As soon as he left the room Kate decided to call Jerry Manning. Now she would have to take him up on his offer. She dialed his private line. "Jerry, we got a note about Danny. We found it about half an hour ago."

"What did it say?"

"They want $50,000."

"I'll get it for you. No problem."

"Jerry, they say the note might be bogus, but I can't take a chance. Can you really lend it to me? I don't know when I can pay you back."

"Don't worry about it, Kate. The only thing that is important is your son's return."

"I don't know how to thank you." Her voice choked.

"Don't say anything. I'll be by to see you later."

Brian and Carl Burke came into the room as she hung up the phone. Brian spoke first. He looked nervous. Kate's heart sank. Did they have bad news? "Kate, this note has us puzzled."

"That's right," chimed in Carl Burke. "No one goes to all the trouble of stealing a kid and then asks for only fifty thousand."

Brian was surprised by the man's crudeness. This was a woman whose only son was missing. "What Carl is saying is that probably some crank did this. Did the writing look at all familiar to you?"

"I just don't know," Kate said. "For all I know it could have been a child's writing."

Carl Burke spoke up again. "We have our mobile lab down at the station house. Our people are looking at it there. We're hopeful they can give us more background on it."

"What do we do now?"

Carl Burke looked at Brian and back at Kate. "We wait, I guess. That's what we do."

Monday, 10:30 a.m.

SISTER VANESSA stood in the hallway of St. Dominic's school watching as the children ran to make third period class.

"Good morning, Sister," said Kathy Carroll. "I'm really enjoying that Marjorie Rawlings book you suggested."

"That's nice," Sister Vanessa said, but she wasn't really paying attention to Kathy. Instead, she was watching the janitor's room, a brown door near the chemistry room. If her bet was right, a little after 10:30, two figures would sneak around the corner, look up and down the empty hallway, and quickly open the door. Once inside, they would take out a pack of cigarettes and start smoking up (and in the case of Skeeter Bannon, coughing up) a storm.

Sister Vanessa folded her arms and waited. She was just around the corner, the perfect place to spy on them, and when she nabbed them she wouldn't wait to see the look on their faces.

The halls cleared and she waited. Her class would just have to wait today, because she was simply not going to tolerate Skeeter Bannon and

Billy "The Horse" Conley coming in one more
day with some pathetic excuse like they forgot
their books in the gym. She waited, hunched up
in the doorway, when suddenly someone
touched her on the back.

She turned quickly and stared into the eyes of
the Mother Superior. They were not pleasant
eyes to stare into, either. Businesslike gray.

"Sister Vanessa," the Mother Superior said
archly. "What are you doing standing outside of
your classroom? I should think you would be
inside."

"Yes," Sister Vanessa said. She didn't want to
explain what she was doing. She wanted to catch
Billy and Skeeter and give them a good talking
to, but she didn't want to turn them over to the
Mother Superior. That would be too rough.

"I was just going into class," she said.

"I see," said the Mother Superior, running her
tongue across her lips. "Well, you won't be
teaching class today, Sister. Father Feely from
the Archdiocese has come to our school on
behalf of the Pope's World Hunger Campaign.
He wants to talk with you for a half-hour. I've
sent for Sister Diana to come down and take
your class. I'd appreciate it if you'd come along.
There she is now."

From the stairway, Sister Vanessa saw the li-
brarian walking toward her. She had no choice.
And it was a shame, for she knew—she was
positively sure—that the two little devils would
be along any minute.

"Certainly, Mother Superior," Sister Vanessa
said.

She walked inside her class, introduced Sister

Diana, and instructed them to be good and work
quietly. Then she joined the Mother Superior,
and walked down the long green hallway toward
the office.

Precisely fifteen seconds after Sister Vanessa had
been forced to give up her vigil in front of the
janitor's office, two boys made their way down
the south stairwell, crept around the corner like
a couple of double agents, furtively looking to
their right and left, tried the janitor's door,
repressed giggles of delight when they found it
unlocked, and quickly slipped inside.

"Just like I told you," Billy Conley said. "Sam
ain't around. He got to polish the lavs around
now."

The thought of old Sam the janitor out polish-
ing the toilets cracked the smaller boy up. Skeeter Bannon giggled hysterically, and finally had
to shove his fist in his mouth so he wouldn't
laugh out loud.

"This is really neat," he said to Billy, in a tone
that suggested idol worship. "But what if we get
caught? I mean, Sister Vanessa could come
around here and if she does, boy we . . ."

"Ah," Billy said, "would you stop worrying?
You're getting to be like a girl. Always worried
'bout everything. Look, you wanta have a
smoke, doncha? We have to take a few chances.
Besides, it's fun in here. It's like our own secret
place, you know?"

"Yeah, I suppose so," Skeeter said. "But like
I hope we just don't get caught 'cause if my mom
ever thought I was smoking cigarettes, that
would really be it."

With his forefinger, he made a slicing motion across his neck.

"Relax," Billy said. He took out one of the Parliaments and put it in his mouth. Then he went over to Sam's old cracked mirror and stared at himself in it.

"Awright youse guys," he said. "Om the boss here see."

Skeeter Bannon began to giggle, and came up behind Billy.

"Give me one of those cigs," he said. "I seen an old Beatles movie on TV the other night and the guys in it called them cigs."

"Sure," Billy said. He turned and offered one of the cigarettes to Skeeter who took it, lit his match with a fanfare, cupping his hands around it, though there was no wind inside the room.

Nervously, and with a little cough, Skeeter took his first few puffs.

"This is . . . ahem . . . great," he said.

"Sure," Billy said. "And we're doing it right under the school's nose. Isn't that the neatest part? If they knew. Can you picture Merja? He'd really go nuts, huh?"

"Yeah," Skeeter said, but suddenly it didn't seem all that neat any more. The thought of Monsignor Merja catching them was a lot worse, a whole lot worse than being caught by Sister Vanessa, or even the Mother Superior.

"Look," Skeeter said, "I think we better get to class. We're already ten minutes late."

"Relax," Billy said, scrunching up his face like a muscle with eyes. "We're not even half done with our butts yet."

He had just learned the word "butts" on a

Starsky and Hutch rerun the night before. He had been sitting there watching it while his parents were having a terrible fight upstairs. He tried to listen real close to every car squeak, every line, and that way he would drown out his mother's crying and his father's yelling.

"Well, look," Skeeter said, "I'm going to put out my cigarette and like, maybe have the rest of it later, over by the swings or something."

"You know," Billy said, flexing his big biceps and blowing smoke at his own reflection in the mirror, "this is chill."

"Yeah, well, it won't be so chill if Sister Vanessa finds out," Skeeter said, really scared now. It was almost fifteen minutes into the period.

"Go ahead if you want," Billy said. "I'm staying here and finishing my smoke."

"Okay, see you later, after class," Skeeter said. There was a touch of regret and guilt in his voice. A pleading. He didn't want to get on Billy "The Horse"'s bad side. Like Danny Riordan had done. That would be a big mistake. And where was Danny Riordan, come to think of it? He was never out of school, and now everyone knew he'd been kidnapped or run away or something. Boy, that was something and it scared the hell out of him. But he couldn't worry about it now. He had to get out.

"See you later, Billy," Skeeter said, dropping the stubbed-out Parliament into his pocket and heading for the door.

"Chicken," Billy said. "Chick chick chick."

"Hey come on," Skeeter said. "I just don't want to get caught."

"Suit yourself, little girl. If you're afraid of them, suit yourself."

Billy watched as Skeeter slipped into the hall. He sat down in Sam's red plastic-covered chair and blew smoke up at the ceiling.

He thought of his mother, Arlene, sitting in the living room late at night crying to herself, and how he had gone upstairs and taken his big new transistor, like one of those ghetto blasters, only not quite as big, and how he'd put it under his pillow and listened to the tunes, and how pretty soon the words and the music and the disc jockey's talk drowned out the terrible feeling he had inside. He wanted to smash things. He wanted to get up in his room and pick up the chair and throw it through the mirror, just to see if it really would bring him seven years bad luck. He wanted to smoke in bed and fall asleep just to see if he really could start a fire. He wanted to walk under ladders and step on a crack, and he wanted to rip his pillow to shreds. But there was no use of thinking of all that. He felt good in Sam's room, safe, and he smoked and he felt, he almost felt like an adult. He almost felt as tough as he pretended to be with Skeeter and Danny and what others.

And what had happened to Danny? The Little Brainiac. The kind of kid who got 95 right on his tests and felt bad 'cause he didn't have his holy 100. Boy, Billy Conley had received 32 on his last spelling test, and he just dared anyone to say he was a dummy. He just dared them. It was just 'cause he couldn't concentrate around the house. If anyone knew. . . . He started to light another cigarette, but the truth was he was feeling kind of dizzy and weird from the first one. He felt a little cold in the temples. He thought that maybe he'd go use Sam's bathroom, run some cold water over his face before he made his grand entrance into Sister Vanessa's English class. Boy, they would look up to him. He didn't take anything off of anybody.

Billy got up and walked over to the bathroom door. He went inside and ran the tap water. Put his head down and let the water run over his hands. It was cold and he cupped his hands catching it, and bathed his face. He did it again and again, and then he looked up in the mirror. Something moved behind him and he froze. Could Sam have come back early? Jesus, Mary and Joseph. But then he relaxed a little. Sam was a good old guy. He wouldn't tell Sister if Billy asked him not to. He reached down to turn off the water, and then turned around.

"Sam," he said, grabbing a paper towel and wiping his hands on it. "Sam, is that you?"

Billy "The Horse" Conley, the strongest kid in the fifth grade, took one step outside the bathroom and felt a powerful pair of hands clasp him around the throat. There was something being stuffed over his face. Billy had seen enough TV shows to know what it was. Ether. It had to be. If he breathed in . . . but by the time he had had time to think about it, it was too late. He had already breathed in, and in his head he could hear a little bell going off like the bell in a department store when the lady on the elevator would call out "Third Floor." He saw a whirlpool in front of him and he was stepping into it. And then he was sailing down, down, and beyond the pool there was only blackness, thick, creamy, like icing. He plunged into it and disappeared.

Monday, 12 noon

EVEN O'TOOLE seemed nervous. He paced the small house listlessly. All morning long there had been no calls. All was silence. An unearthly silence. Kate had spent most of that time in her bedroom, praying. To take her mind off the events at hand she had been reading from Devine's *Liturgy of Holy Week*. It was almost perverse but as she read through those sad events somehow she felt better about her own situation. Misery loves company, she thought to herself.

There had been no call after the note and that had bothered her tremendously. When she went out to discuss it with O'Toole, he begged off, asking her to table all discussion until Brian came back again with the FBI. Did the fact that there was no call mean that it was a hoax? That Danny was already dead? God, she needed to ask somebody, anybody.

Maura prepared endless pots of tea for anyone in the kitchen who would drink them. Kate went in to see how she was doing. She also had been strangely silent the last few hours. Kate wondered if she had been told something she was to keep to herself. "How are you doing, dear?" Kate asked.

"I'm fine," Maura said, trying to smile. "And yourself?"

"I'm just so restless. I can't stand all this waiting."

"Patience is the virtue of a soul in heaven."

Kate looked at her strangely. "Maura," she said, "what does that mean?"

"Just an old Irish proverb said in time of need. Want some tea?"

Just then Kate heard the front door open and Brian and Carl Burke came in. She studied their faces. She could tell nothing. They came through the living room into the kitchen, each taking a chair around the table.

Brian spoke first. "Kate, we've got some potentially good news. Agent Burke, why don't you tell her—"

Carl Burke looked straight at Kate and began calmly. "We've thoroughly analyzed the handwriting on the note. We feel it's clearly that of a child. In short, we feel it's a fake. Whoever sent this definitely does not have Danny."

Kate was unconvinced. "That's it? How can you say for sure it's a child, not some deranged adult? Are you sure?"

"Our experts say the penmanship is that of an immature individual between nine and twelve. Believe me there are thousands of these in the files in Washington. You'd be amazed at the kids who pull things like this. I've personally seen a half dozen of these in the last ten years myself. In a child disappearance case that gets wide publicity invariably one or two of these show up. But they are almost always red herrings like this one."

"Where do we go from here?" she said wearily.

Brian spoke up. "We're going to maintain phone surveillance and see if anything does turn up. There's always the outside chance that an adult put a child up to this and that an adult is the actual kidnapper."

Burke broke in. "That's highly remote, I want to emphasize, Mrs. Riordan. And I might add, just a speculation on Chief Dolan's part. The Bureau's official position—"

"Wait a minute, Burke," Brian said angrily, his neck reddening, "her kid is missing. I don't think she cares what your official position is. All she wants is her kid back."

"Tea's ready again," Maura chimed in. Kate scanned the tense faces and broke into tears. "I wish you would all begin working together." She got up from the table and went into her bedroom.

For the first time, Kate felt ready to face the possibility that Danny might not be coming back. Certainly, if the police hadn't a clue about where he was, how could she be expected to find him?

She heard a light knock on the door. "Come in," she said quietly.

It was Jerry Manning. He was a gray-haired bear of a man, nearly fifty. He came in, sat down on the bed next to her and put his hand on hers.

"Kate," he said, "I have the money here with me. Have hope. We're going to get him."

She turned and looked directly into his eyes.

"Jerry, they tell me the ransom note may be a hoax. So I guess you can take your money back now."

"No, I think you should hold onto it, just in case."

"Jerry, you please keep it. I'm afraid of that much money in the house. If we need it, I'll call you. Oh, Jerry, I'm so afraid. I don't know what to do."

He put his arm around her. "Danny will be found soon. I'm sure of it."

"He's got to be," she sobbed.

They sat on the bed, her head on his shoulder.

HE SAT in the room, sweat pouring off of him. His hands were shaking and he fumbled with the bottle of cheap bourbon. The beauty of it, the incredible ease with which he took the Conley boy. This was better, much better, than the first one. He drank the bourbon, and sat down heavily at his desk. There had been a period, he thought now, caressing his leg, noticing the muscle in it, the strength—there had been a time when he had been about to give up. For what they had done. There was no doubt it had ruined things for him. But that was when he had felt that there was only one way to go with things. Only one way to build his life. The narrow proper channels. That was before he realized that a man can make his own rules. Now he had them where he wanted them. In his own game. The strong men make their own rules, and he was stronger than anyone. And the reason was he had the willingness to wait—to wait forever if necessary. He picked up the pen, and began to copy a sentence from an old book. Chapter 61 of *The Spiritual Combat*. The lines read as follows:

Among other things necessary for succeeding in the spiritual combat, perseverance is justly reckoned. It is vain to think of putting an end to this war. It cannot end but at our deaths. Whoever ceases to fight must give up his liberty or his life.

He sipped the bourbon and copied the lines in a handwriting that was tight, small, precise. Yes, he had perseverance. He had never given up, even when it looked like his dreams were crushed. What he had learned was that he had to have new dreams. Dreams which were his own. Dreams which didn't depend on anyone else. On understanding, or kindness, those false emotions which were only the cover for man's greed, and endless capacity to hurt his fellow man. He had to be strong, strong and alone. But meanwhile he had to be one of them. A good fellow in the community. Go to all the games, smile at all the right people, cut the lawn. He had to appear as normal and natural as the rest of them. But soon he would live another life. He would be stealing their futures from them, taking away the children, sucking all of the uncaring bastards dry.

Monday, 1 p.m.

ARLENE CONLEY could hear a screaming inside her head. It was as though a small woman had climbed inside her ear, and had fallen into a pond and she could hear the woman screaming, "No helphelp help I'm drowning." She could shut her eyes and see the woman in a black dress, with a single strand of pearls around her neck and high heels, and she was going down into the water by a frozen lake, over and over again. The image wouldn't stop, though she was wide awake, her eyes open, watching as the police went through Billy's locker.

"Listen," her husband George was saying, holding her hand. "They are going to find him. Don't worry. It's going to be all right. Somebody just couldn't take him right out of school like that."

She nodded her head and said, "Yes, dear," and she smiled at George. But she could not turn off the screams of the small drowning woman. Even through the Valium she could still feel the reverberations of the screams in her temples, and all the way down to her chest.

She saw Brian Dolan walk into the classroom and look down at her. She was suddenly very, very afraid of him. She tried to look past him, but when she did she could see the locker being opened out in the hall, and she thought if she saw Billy's baseball cards and the new Ted Williams glove she had bought him, she would really start to go mad. She held her temples and tried to talk.

"It's like I told you," she said. "First he was here and then he wasn't. Sister Vanessa got worried. They thought he might be playing hooky. Oh God, Brian."

"It's possible that he is playing hooky."

"Come off it, Chief," George Conley said. "When a kid plays hooky he doesn't go to school at all. It's not like any fifth grader I know to go to school and then take off."

"But it has been done before," Brian said. "Look, I don't want to softsoap this. We've called in Skeeter Bannon. They're out in the hall. I'm going to ask him some questions. I want you all to hold on here. Try not to panic. We'll get to the bottom of this."

Skeeter Bannon was trembling. His mother and father, John and Nancy Bannon, hovered around him as though they were afraid to let him out of their sight even for a moment. Skeeter held on to their hands tightly and looked down at the floor.

Up above him he saw what looked like a jury of all the adult world. The Police Chief, Brian Dolan, was standing there giving him a tense smile, and behind him was Sister Vanessa, looking as though she could rip the bricks out of the walls. And in the classroom to the left were Mr. and Mrs. Conley, though he guessed he wasn't supposed to look in there at her while she cried.

"Hello, Skeeter," Brian said. "Listen, you can be a very big help to me. But more important, you can help your friend Billy. Don't you want to do that?"

"Sure," he said, though he doubted any policeman could help Billy. If they knew how he broke windows at the school sometimes after his mother and father had fights, they might want to put him in jail. Maybe that was what happened today, in fact. Billy had known they were going to put him in jail, so he ran away. He wasn't going to say anything. Nothing at all. They weren't going to make him into any stool pigeon.

"Now you and Billy skipped study hall today, didn't you?" Brian said.

"Maybe we did and maybe we didn't," Skeeter said, remembering that was the way James Cagney answered the cops in a gangster movie he'd stayed up late to see.

"What kind of answer is that, Skeeter?" John Bannon said. "This isn't a joke. I want you to answer the Chief's questions."

He held Skeeter's hand hard and Skeeter shut his eyes and pretended that it wasn't his father at all but a dirty screw from the prison.

"I don't really remember, is all," he said.

"Sure you do," Sister Vanessa said, coming forward. "And I know *where* you were. I saw you."

Skeeter held his breath for a second and tried to think of Sister Vanessa as a mean policewoman, but he found it difficult. Because she was beautiful and she was incredibly kind and patted him on the head a lot and he was kind of in love with her.

"Well, okay, we skipped," he said. "So?"

"Then what did you do?"

"Went outside?" Skeeter asked.

"No," Sister Vanessa said. "I don't think you went outside. I think maybe you did something else."

"No, we didn't," Skeeter said. "You can't say we did anything else 'cause you don't know. We went outside and we played some soccer."

"Yes. And was Billy with you the whole time?" Brian Dolan said.

"Yeah, sure he was," Skeeter said.

"Then how come he wasn't with you in class?" Brian said.

"I don't know," Skeeter said. "I mean, when I left him in the . . . I mean outside."

"Wait a minute," the Chief said. "You said *in the.* 'I left him *in the.*' So you were back in the building when you left him. But *in where?*"

Oh shit, Skeeter thought, how the hell did that happen? It was just like Perry Mason. He had made a fatal slip or something.

And now his parents would find out about his smoking.

"You better tell him, son," John Bannon said. "This could be really important."

Skeeter looked around and shook his head.

"Let me tell you then," Sister Vanessa said. "You came up here and were smoking in the janitor's room over there. Isn't that right?"

"No. We weren't," Skeeter said, but he was

starting to cry a little. He took a deep breath and tried hard to hold back the tears.

"Yes you were," Sister Vanessa said. "Look, you must tell us about it if you were. If you saw anybody, a man or a woman lurking about the janitor's room. You see, somebody may have taken Billy."

"Taken him where?" Skeeter cried out in despair. The thought shook him badly. Billy Conley was the strongest kid in the fifth grade and maybe the whole world, and the idea that anybody could just take him off was inconceivable.

"I didn't smoke any . . . Well, maybe a little."

He began to cry a lot now. He was looking up at Nancy Bannon, who shook her head and stared at him fiercely.

"I'm sorry, Mom," he said. "I didn't mean to smoke. It really wasn't my fault. Billy said it was chill. . . ."

"That's all right, son," Nancy Bannon said in a distant, pained voice. "You must tell them everything. Your friend's life could depend on it."

His life, Skeeter thought. Now he felt afraid, very afraid. He began to blurt out everything at once. How they waited there and how they sneaked off to the Medical Center Drug Store to get the cigarettes, which they had a man buy for them.

"A man?" Brian said. "What man?"

"An old man named Mr. Todd," he said. "He's just an old bum and we gave him a couple of cigarettes to get 'em for us. One day I gave him some of my candy bar. I'm sorry, really, I'm sorry."

"Can you pick this man out for us?" Chief Dolan said.

"Sure. But what if he sees me?" Skeeter asked.

"He won't," Chief Dolan said. "But you've got to tell me what happened today."

"Well, we came in here and we started to—" He looked up at his mother, who now looked as though she too were going to cry.

"Go ahead, Skeeter," she said.

"Smoke. I mean, I just smoked a little, and then I was afraid we were gonna be late for class. So I left. And Billy stayed behind. He wanted to finish his butt."

John Bannon gave his wife a long, pained stare.

"And he never came to class," Sister Vanessa said. "That's when I looked in the room. You know, I'd heard rumors kids were smoking in there and I was watching today, but I got called away at the last minute. I can't help but think if I had just . . ."

John Bannon and his wife both reached out and took the Sister's hands.

"Don't blame yourself," Nancy Bannon said. "Please."

The Sister gave a weak smile and shook her head.

"All right," Dolan said, turning to O'Toole. "I want that janitor's room closed off. I want it dusted for prints. I want everything in there gone over with a fine-tooth comb. Don't stop until you've gone over every surface, looked in every crack. You understand? Now, Mr. and Mrs. Bannon, please come with me for a minute."

He took them off into an alcove and talked to them in a low, urgent voice.

"Listen," he said, "I need your permission to take Skeeter up to the William's Crossing Mall, right now. We'll keep him well out of sight. But I want to pick up this Todd guy right away."

"You're sure he'll be safe?" Mrs. Bannon said.

"Absolutely."

"All right, Chief," John Bannon said. "But we're going to be with him. I don't want my son any more scared than he already is."

"You got it," Brian said.

He shook Bannon's hand and motioned to O'Toole to bring Skeeter along. They started walking briskly down the hall.

They waited by the video games section of the mall, Skeeter staring longingly at Space Invaders. He wished suddenly that he could climb inside the machine and hide from them all.

He waited and watched as the familiar faces strolled by in the mall. There was Erin the Shopping Cart Lady. She waddled through with her three shopping carts and looked for refuse to put in them. There was old Jake Flood, the town drunk. He sat on the fake marble bench by the potted palm and sipped a drink of whiskey from his brown paper bag. Other people went by. Skeeter waited, feeling more and more nervous. Finally he saw him, standing over by Williams Liquors. It was Mr. Todd. Skeeter looked again to be dead sure, then touched Brian's raincoat.

"That's him," he said, "over there."

Brian looked across the mall and saw a man of

about fifty in an old pair of tattered and torn her-
ringbone wool pants a couple of sizes too large
for him, a cigarette hanging out of his mouth.
His hair was gray and stood up in uncombed
spikes on his head. He had a three-day growth of
beard. Brian could feel his pulse race. He hadn't
seen the man before. He must be new to William's Crossing. Maybe, if they were lucky, this
was it.

He signaled to his men across the mall by
touching his head. Suddenly three men moved
for Mr. Todd swiftly and grabbed him from the
front and behind. He offered no resistance,
except for a surprised yell.

"Hey," he said, "what the hell's going on? I'll
call a cop!"

Monday, 4 p.m.

KATE RIORDAN and the Conleys were down at the William's Crossing Police Headquarters with high hopes. Police Chief Dolan had someone, a stranger in town, a man who bought cigarettes for the children. Maybe he had taken them. Maybe they were at his house. People did that now and then. Took children and pretended they were their parents. Kate had convinced herself of this fantasy. Of course, he had been good to Danny. He had to be. She tried to keep the panic and fear down in the back of her brain. She didn't allow herself to articulate the words *dead, torture*. They were just impulses inside of her, which filled her with dread.

She waited on an early-American bench, alongside the Conleys, while Brian Dolan interrogated Mr. Todd in the station's back room. She worked on her knitting, a scarf she had been working on for no real reason. She comforted Arlene, who had lost her businesslike facade and seemed paralyzed with fear. She waited for O'Toole to tell them. To tell them all that Todd had confessed and that the children were safe and sound.

Only Todd didn't confess. Chief Dolan had him sit on a hardbacked chair in front of a hot light for a while. But all that did was make him sleepy. Then Dolan had tried the opposite tack. Kindness, the kind of loving father whom you can tell all to. He tried his gruff voice, the one which made people jump. He tried his conspiratorial, it's-you-and-me-against-them-all voice. None of them seemed to work at all. Todd had a story. He was a drunk from Toronto. He had had a mail-order business out of his home but his wife had split on him, run off with his partner, a man named Owen Glass. Owen and Thelma were living in Montreal somewhere. There were no kids. Todd regretted that. He'd always wanted kids. But there weren't any, and there weren't any friends either once they realized that he'd been swindled out of most of his money. He'd always had a drinking habit, and now he was really going at it night and day. He had driven down to the States. His plan was to get somewhere South, where the sun shone, start up his mail-order business again.

"I sell St. Christopher medals," he said. "I got a bunch of 'em back at the house. About ten thousand. I can get more if I get some capital. And I'm gonna get it, too. Real fast. If I can just get off the booze. Jesus got to help me."

He smiled the smile of the perpetual drunken loser, and Brian's heart sank. There didn't seem to be any way this little man could be a kidnapper. But he kept on grilling him anyway, making him tell the story over and over again and asking the man what he was doing in William's Crossing. And why did he buy kids cigarettes?

"I don't know, Cap'n," the man said. "I guess 'cause they asked me to. I felt sorry for 'em. They don't have nobody to take up for 'em, kids don't. So I buy 'em cigarettes. I only did it a couple of times. It was just something to pass the time. I get a kick out of seeing the little guys light 'em up, thinking that they're adults. They ain't, though, you know. They ain't got the troubles adults have. Know what I mean? Besides, Jesus tells you to help your fellow man."

"That sounds wrong to me," Brian said, walking behind the man and staring down at him. "That doesn't sound right. I think maybe you liked those kids. Maybe you took them home with you."

"No," the man said. "I just bought 'em cigarettes 'cause I like to see 'em smoke."

He threw Todd in the cell and went out to the foyer and talked to the parents.

"It's still going on," he said. "We don't have anything yet."

There was something about the man's story that was off-center. The idea of liking to see children smoke was too strange, offbeat. Brian called the man's ex-wife in Montreal.

"Hello, this is Thelma Glass."

Brian told her who he was and asked about Barton Todd, the seller of St. Christopher medals.

"Yes, I left him. He's a drunk. He blew all our money on booze. You picked him up in the shopping mall? Yeah, that sounds about right. He liked to go down there and chat with folks. He's real helpful. Likes to help old ladies and kids, and mothers with their shopping carts. He says it makes him more like Jesus, helping out people. But he didn't want to help around the house at all. Or to help keep any damned money in the bank. His helping stopped there. Kids? Sure, he will buy anything anybody wants, help women with their bags. When he is drunk he is most affable. Old Barton Todd is the living example of the affable drunk."

Brian felt his heart sink a little further. What had seemed to be so promising was turning out to be a bust.

They had been to his rooming house and printed it. All that was found was a trunk full of genuine gold-plated St. Christopher medals and two thousand Jesus calendars.

His landlady, Maude Gone, explained that Barton Todd was with her all day Sunday, listening to gospel on the radio.

"He sings real bad," she said. "Real loud and real bad. And he cooks awful, too," she said, smiling. "But you people shouldn't go and run him out of town. He's the first interesting man we've had around these parts for many years."

Brian thanked her and went back to the station.

"Never come back into this town again," he told the man.

"I don't believe I will," Barton Todd said. "I believe I will find the Kingdom of Heaven in Fort Lauderdale."

He left that afternoon, and his landlady cried most of the night.

Monday, 5 p.m.

"CANCEL THE MASS!" Brian's voice ordered.

"You're the Police Chief, not the Pope, I may remind you," Monsignor Merja said, his eyes filled with gray fury.

"With all due respect," interjected Carl Burke, "I think Chief Dolan is right. We've got a real public safety problem here and we've got to start dealing with it, right now."

Monsignor Merja turned to him. "Don't you think I'm aware of that? I'm not a fool."

The small rectory parlor seemed uncomfortably stuffy all of a sudden.

"Look," said Brian, "Monsignor, the evening Masses must be cancelled. We just don't have the manpower to protect the children. I don't know how much clearer I can make this. I'm responsible for their safety and I won't have you jeopardizing it."

Merja was unswayed. "And I'm responsible for their souls. I ask you who has the greater task?"

"Monsignor," Burke cut in, again assuming the role of pacifier. "Perhaps your parishioners could stay home and we could get the local cable system to televise the evening Masses this week. I've checked and they have local origination power. They could set up right over in the church."

"Media. I am sick to death of the media, young man. Those boys would still be here if it were not for the media. There will be no more talk of the media in this rectory. Please."

Brian was furious. "We've got other things to do, Carl. We just don't have time for this nonsense. It's on his head now."

"There is a greater law," Monsignor Merja began ponderously, but Brian Dolan was not listening, he was already halfway out the door.

Monday, 5:30 p.m.

JOHN AND Nancy Bannon were beside themselves. The children were all upstairs. Skeeter had been through quite an ordeal and although he had not been as forthcoming initially as they would have liked, they understood his desire to protect his friend and camouflage his own involvement.

But they had no understanding of a madness that takes two little boys. Two out of three altar boys from a Palm Sunday Mass. Why would anyone do anything like that? It was unspeakable as far as they were concerned.

"I want to keep him in the house until this is over," said Nancy Bannon tearfully.

"Nancy," John said softly, "Skeeter has suffered a terrible shock. He may not seem that way, but I know that he has. His friends are missing. His teachers and the police have given him the third degree. I don't think we need to add to his trauma. The town is crawling with police and reporters and vigilant parents. Anyone who *talks* to a kid is going to get a funny look."

Nancy shifted her considerable bulk on the

sofa. "Maybe you're right John. But I'll keep an eye on him. I promise."

John reached over and took her hand. "That's my girl. Now let's call the family down and all say a rosary for the safe return of Danny and Billy."

He went over to the stairs and called up. "Skeeter, bring your beads and tell the others to bring theirs."

Upstairs, Skeeter Bannon's disposition brightened. He was going to get a suspended sentence, he knew it. He'd beat the rap. Dad never whacked him when the family said the rosary. He was home free. Everything was going to be A.O.K.

Monday, 6 p.m.

THE PHONE was ringing as Kate opened the front door. Where was Maura? Where was O'Toole? Damn, they were supposed to be watching this place when she was out. Impulsively, she picked up the receiver.

"You aren't even interested in where to leave the money," a high pitched voice began. "You didn't answer my call, you didn't, and you'll pay." Then there was a loud click in her ear.

Kate became hysterical. O'Toole and Maura, who had been in the back yard for a moment, heard her screaming and came running into the small foyer. She began upbraiding them. "Where were you? Someone called while you were out to say where to drop the money. They just called back. How could you have missed these calls? You're supposed to be paying attention. What's wrong with you?"

They calmed her down and she explained it again. O'Toole put in an immediate call to Brian. Maura sat quietly sobbing on the sofa.

O'Toole called Kate to the phone. "Brian wants to talk to you."

"Kate, hold on tight," Brian said. "If this was really the kidnapper, he'll try again for his ransom. And we'll be ready for him next time. But remember this could all be part of a hoax."

Kate hung up and sat across from Maura in the Kennedy rocker. She scanned the newspaper headlines for the umpteenth time. The electric headlines of the Boston papers were in stark contrast to the understated "BOY MISSING" that appeared in the William's Crossing *Transcript*. They'd all have a field day tomorrow with two altar boys missing, she was sure of that. Suddenly she couldn't stay in the house waiting to see whether another call came. "Lieutenant O'Toole," she asked, "do you think it would be okay if I went for a drive? I really need to get some air. Just to clear my head for a while."

O'Toole looked at her gravely. "I think it would be fine if you wanted to go out for a minute. I promise I'll be here. Just don't stay too long in case Chief Dolan wants to get in touch with you. Where are you going?"

"I think I'll just head downtown."

It was good to be behind the wheel of the yellow Fairmont again. She felt herself drawn inexorably toward St. Dominic's. I'm just going to have one more look, she thought to herself. Maybe there is something I've missed. Some clue. Some shred of evidence I haven't found and the police have also missed.

She circled the rectory on foot, paced off the perimeter of the parish parking lot and found nothing. She drew one quick breath and decided to search the church one more time. She made

her way into the main sanctuary. Jimmy Lawlor
was sweeping out the center aisle.

"Evening, missus. Terrible, terrible, isn't it?
Still can't find the lad?"

"This is not a great time," she said benignly.
"I'm here to have one more look around."

"Ah, suit yourself. I'm just leaving. I'll be out
front sweeping off the steps if you need me for
anything."

"Thanks, Jimmy. I appreciate it."

The lights were off in the sacristy. She could
see the priests' garments hung neatly on racks
and beside them the frocks that the altar boys
wore. Her heart sank as she fingered the small
garments. Would Danny ever wear one again?

Back in the church Kate heard a sound. The
scrape of metal on marble. Someone was trying
to move the votive candle rack. She went to the
door of the sacristy and saw Sister Vanessa val-
iantly struggling with the heavy rack. She was
having a hard time because of its weight and she
had to be careful because all of the candles were
lit—the parishioners' offerings for the two lost
little altar boys.

Wordlessly Kate crossed to where the nun was
working. "Let me help you, Sister," she said.

The nun's face turned toward her. "I'd appreciate that. It's heavier than I thought."

When they had finished moving it, they both
genuflected in front of the altar and headed into
the sacristy. Sister Vanessa was very solicitous.
"Poor dear, how are you holding up?"

"As well as can be expected," Kate said. She
felt nervous, like a little girl who has done something wrong. And she felt out of place in the sacristy, the sanctuary of priests and altar boys.

"Is there any more word?"

"No, nothing in the last hour." And then, because she felt compelled to explain her presence, she added, "I came back because I had the feeling we might have overlooked something here."

Sister Vanessa looked sympathetically at her and took both of Kate's hands in hers. "I understand, but you must rest."

Kate thought she heard a noise. Footsteps. "What was that?" she asked sharply.

"Hush, child," said Sister Vanessa. "Your imagination is on overtime."

"No. No, I heard something. Please, over there. The cellar door."

Sister Vanessa looked at Kate quizzically but crossed to the door. Boldly, she cracked it open wide enough to lean her head down the stairway.

More sounds. Footsteps. Both women heard them.

"Perhaps it's Jimmy Lawlor," Sister Vanessa said, but she didn't sound like she was even convincing herself. She opened the door fully. It creaked like in an old horror movie. Stealthily, the two women made their descent down the narrow stairs. Now they both heard the receding footsteps, echoing in the passage. At the bottom of the stairs they stared long and hard. Nothing. The dim and musty passage disclosed no one.

"I think we're imagining things," Sister Vanessa said with a nervous laugh. "I guess we're spooked."

Kate was not so easily put off. "Look," she said sharply, "we both heard something and you know it. Let's go down the whole passage."

"Oh, that would be foolish."

"Are you scared?" Suddenly, Kate felt like a brazen teenager.

"No, of course not."

They made their way, hand in hand, in the near dark to the double oak doors at the end of the corridor.

Something was different from last night. It was the large boxes in front of the oak doors. That was it.

"Look," Kate said, "someone's been down here."

"Yes," said Sister Vanessa, "Mother Superior marched over some of the seventh-grade boys today and brought those. They're outdated Baltimore Catechisms. Behind the manger scene in this room is the furnace and Jimmy Lawlor was to burn them today. I see as usual he's slipped up."

Just then there was a loud bang in the corridor behind them. Kate's heart started racing as she whirled. It was Brother Charles.

When he saw he had startled the women, he was apologetic. "I'm sorry if I scared you. I didn't know there was anyone else down here. I was just putting the gardening equipment away."

Sister Vanessa let out a giddy laugh of relief. Kate stared intently at the man. She looked deep into his eyes but saw nothing. He returned her gaze innocently enough, she thought, but there was something she didn't like about the man.

Tuesday, 9 a.m.

THE KIDNAPPER—if that was who he was—had not called again. Brian had asked Kate to meet him at the Conleys' house to go over the disappearances in detail. It was nearly nine when they all met there. Brian did a lot of the talking.

"I know you're all disappointed that it wasn't Todd, but there's something we've got to be missing here. Is there some common thread, something that connects both kids we're not focusing on? Do you have any idea if there's anyone with a grudge against both families?"

George became agitated. "Are you serious?"

"Possibly Arlene and her finance committee?" asked Brian. "A lot of people . . . I'd suppose it's possible."

Arlene looked thoughtful. "No, there's really no one with overt hostility I can think of."

"Kate?" asked Brian.

"No. I'm drawing a blank. There's no one."

The doorbell rang and George admitted old Mary Murphy, who had a casserole in her hands. "I've brought you your dinner," she said. She put the casserole on the table and turned to Kate.

"I'm sorry for the loss of your son."

Kate looked at the old woman and tried to be civil. But the words cut through her and, before she knew it, she was answering bitterly.

"What do you mean, 'the loss of my son?'"

"I only meant that I was sorry. I mean . . ." Mary Murphy looked confused. She started to leave.

"You tell me what you meant," Kate said. "You think my son is dead, don't you? Well, I can assure you, he's not. So I don't need your patronizing comments. I'm going to get him back, do you hear?"

Mary Murphy stared out at the little group of people.

"I only meant to help," she said.

She looked down at her feet and Kate felt ashamed of herself.

"Thank you for the food, Mary," George Conley said. "We're all a little tense here."

"Yes," Kate finally managed to say. "We are. I am. I apologize, Mary."

"No need for that," Mary said, but she sounded hurt, and then she turned, walked past them and out the front door without saying another word.

There was a brief silence after she left, and Kate felt a new fear taking hold of her. She couldn't seem to control her emotions. She had to watch herself, or those who were willing to help would be cut off, driven away. And she didn't want to kid herself. She needed people. She needed them more than she ever had in her life.

"Now," Brian said, picking up the thread,

"let's talk about possible enemies. Perhaps we've been looking in the wrong place. Is there anybody who would possibly have something against both boys? Or the families of both boys?"

Kate felt her heart sink. Because no one came to mind. She looked over at Arlene and George and found them staring at her for help.

"I just can't think of anyone," George said. "It just seems impossible, totally impossible."

Kate shrugged and threw up her hands. There was another long silence, and Brian tried to hold back his greatest fear: that the crimes were committed by a psychopath. With no easily indentifiable motive. With no history in the town. Yet, he wasn't ready to go that route yet. Whomever had done it knew a lot about these kids, that was for sure. He knew when they'd come out of church, and he knew about their school. He had to have watched them, made notes.

"Okay," he said. "We're going to talk about what I know here, and we're going to go over this for as long as we have to. Until we come up with something. We've all got to dig a lot harder."

Kate looked up at him and nodded her head. He was a good, strong man, she thought suddenly. Not the unhappy boy she had known as a teenager. He would help her.

DANNY FELT himself coming out of a deep sleep. He was cold, so cold that he had wakened, and he wanted to cry out, but he wasn't sure why. Then he remembered. It was clear to him. He wasn't home and it wasn't a dream, not even a nightmare. It was real. A man had come and taken him somewhere and the place was dark and cold, and over in the corner was some kind of box, and he didn't want to think about that. And the man had worn a hood so he couldn't see who he was. The man must have knocked him out with some kind of drug, and checked his knots too, because his arms and legs were still tied up tight. But the tape over his mouth was a little looser. Maybe when he had fallen asleep, some spit had come out of his mouth, like it did when he was home and he'd wake up with a wet spot on his pillow. He had to try to get out of here. He had to. Then he remembered something else. Before the man had knocked him out, he had said something to him. Something about his mother paying. Maybe he was being held for ransom, but where was Mom going to get the money? She had complained about not having enough collateral to buy a new car, and then she had explained to him what collateral was. You had to own so much stuff, so in case you didn't pay, the bank could come get it and take it away. And that had scared him, because what if they used him for collateral? What if they took him away if Mom couldn't pay? He tried not to think too much about that, because his heart would start beating again and he would panic and it would be harder to breathe.

Then he heard something. Someone.

Was it the man come back to get him again?

He looked to his left. That was where the man had come from the last time. But the sound came again, and it didn't sound like the man's low raspy voice. It sounded more like a moan. And it seemed to come from across the room, near the boxes.

Maybe something was coming out of the boxes.

Danny fell on his belly and began to scrape toward the wall. He wanted to be as close to it as he could get. Maybe then the thing wouldn't see him.

Though his heart was beating so loud that he could hardly hear anything else, he waited for the sound again, and then, sure enough, it came.

"Ohhhhh . . . hmmmmm . . . hmmmm."

It was somebody trying to speak. But they couldn't. They couldn't because . . . because their mouth was taped. That had to be it. The man had put somebody else in here with him. Who? Who could it be?

Danny tried to make himself heard.

"Who is it" formed in his brain, but the sound same out muffled, strained.

"Mmmmmmmmmmsssscrrrrr?"

"Brrrrre . . ."

Danny couldn't make it out.

"Mrrrrr," he said, not even trying to make words, but just a sound to show where he was.

He looked over toward the boxes. He had to get close enough to see who it was. If there were two of them in there, maybe they would figure out where they were, and who had gotten them. Maybe they could escape.

He began to crawl on his belly slowly, across the ice-cold floor. His shirt ripped open, and he remembered his new dress jeans, and he got scared again. But still, he had to get over there. He felt cold and hot at the same time, and then he felt like he was going to get sick. He could feel the perspiration dripping from his forehead. He was tired, so tired, and his arms and legs were still bound together, and he could feel the bumps in the concrete floor cutting through his shirt, ripping his skin. But he had to get there and see who it was. Only it was such a long way away in the pitch dark. It was so long, and he didn't know if he would ever make it.

Then suddenly he hit something, and when he looked up, he realized what it was. A shoe. Oh, he was scared now. The person didn't move, didn't move at all, and he was so scared that he didn't know what to do. Maybe it was the man after all. It had been a trick to get him to come over there, and he was going to put him in the box. He almost started to crawl on his belly back to the far wall when the shoe moved and the person made a noise.

"Hmmmmmmmm."

Then Danny crawled up next to him and looked through the darkness. He waited until the dust cleared, and then he saw Billy "The Horse" Conley.

"Billllerrr," he said. "It's Dnnn . . ."

He put his face right on top of Billy's, until he could look into his eyes, and then suddenly he saw Billy's eyebrows rise, his eyes light up.

"Dnnnn," he managed to say.

Danny nodded. He had never thought he would be glad to see Billy "The Horse" in a dark alley. In fact, he used to have nightmares about the idea. Billy would hold him down, put his knees on Danny's arms and say, "What's the matter, Brainiac, does it hurt, huh?" But now, now . . . he was glad, he had never been so glad about anything. Billy was tough, the toughest kid. Whoever was kidnapping kids had made a bad mistake, because Billy was a fighter and he would figure out some way to help get them out of here. For the first time since his ordeal had begun, Danny felt almost deliriously happy.

He was going to get out. He had to now, with Billy here.

He looked up at Billy. He had to communicate to him that the first thing they had to do was get themselves untied. Then find the doorway. There had to be a doorway somewhere, or else how would the man get in?

He moved close, and then he heard the whimpering.

Billy was crying like a baby.

Danny couldn't believe it. Billy "The Horse" Conley, who could hit a softball three miles, and who beat up little kids on the playground for hitting him with the dodgeball when they were supposed to, Billy, who called him the "Brain" and knocked him down and accidentally on purpose stepped on his glasses, Billy Conley was crying like a baby.

What's more, he seemed to be backing away. Like he didn't want to do anything but go over in the corner and just curl up and cry. And die too, for that matter. 'Cause that was what was going to happen. The man might let them go if Mom paid, but what if she couldn't get the money? And even if she did? Would the man want a kid around who might be able to recognize him? Of course, Danny couldn't. But did the man know that? Could he be sure?

"Bieeeee," Danny said fiercely, sliding toward him.

He was trying to tell him that they had to help each other. They couldn't just stay there, tied up, and hope the man would let them go. Then it occurred to Danny. The man had told Billy the same stuff about letting him go when the money was paid, and Billy was frightened to try and escape because they might make the man mad.

Billy "The Horse" believed the man. But that was wrong, completely wrong. They had to stick together and fight him.

Danny crawled toward Billy, who was moaning now, and moving backwards. He was heading toward the boxes, and Danny felt the fear inside of him again. Billy was backing toward them, mumbling through his tape, scared. Billy Conley scared stiff.

Danny moved toward him again, but Billy was

backing off, crawling awkwardly in total panic. He was heading toward the boxes and now, for the first time, Danny could see what they were.

It was as he had feared. Coffins. And Billy didn't see them. He backed into them, smashing up against them, and when he felt them, he tried to twist and turn, and, with all his brute strength, he managed to half stand, and then he fell, and the coffins fell on top of him. Danny watched in horror as the lid slid off the top coffin. He watched the contents spill out on Billy, and he screamed beneath the tape.

Bones were spilling out on Billy. Dead man's bones, and Billy gave a high-pitched wail and fell back.

Danny watched a human skull land in Billy's lap. Arms, legs and hands clattered to the stone floor.

Danny could go no farther. He was paralyzed. Numb with fear. And Billy "The Horse" Conley didn't move. He didn't move at all.

Tuesday, 12 noon

THE SUNLIGHT streamed through the window. Kate drank a cup of coffee and stared at the maple tree in front of the house. She fought hard to hold back the memories but they came anyway, each of them more painful than the last. She recalled the day Paddy, Danny and she had gone to their first baseball game in Fenway Park. The Red Sox had played well, and Fred Lynn had hit a home run to win the game. That was when Paddy and Danny were the happiest she had ever seen them. She could still recall Paddy picking the boy up, holding him up in the sunlight and bouncing him up and down. Sometimes he would toss Danny up in the air and she would be terrified that the child was going to drop. "Be careful," she would yell then, but Paddy would laugh and tell her, "It's all right. Don't worry. As long as I'm alive nobody will ever hurt this kid." God, the way fortune mocked people. It made her furious. It was almost enough to make her lose her faith in God. But as soon as she had had the thought, she squelched it guiltily. She had to keep herself together, and she couldn't

129

risk offending the Lord. She was beginning to be one of those kooks who looks at the way the tree limbs are bent for portents of the future. Who stares at the ground to find a lucky penny. Anything, anything which will tell her that her son is coming back again.

She stared out the window at Mt. Olive. All the tourist traffic that ascended the narrow winding road which led to the mountain top passed her door. But today no one was going to the mountain top. They were perched just outside on the lawn.

Among the throng were the print reporters, the TV reporters, and a few curious neighbors. Kate had often seen on television these gatherings on other people's doorsteps—an astronaut's wife, a policeman's widow, a crooked politician's mother—but she had done nothing to deserve this notoriety, and she wished with all her heart that they would all just go away and leave her in peace. Buzzards, she thought, eager for any scrap of information that might become available in the case. Every so often she felt like walking to her front door, throwing it open and screaming, "Think if it were your child. Would you want all these strangers around? Leave us in peace. I can't think. Please, you've got to give us time to collect our wits."

She also felt that the continued presence of all these people would prevent the kidnapper from calling again. He'd want to make his bargain in a secret way; all the media scrutiny could do was reduce his odds of getting away with this crime.

Each of the television stations had requested an interview with her which she declined. Brian had counseled her to consider it.

"As loathsome as you may find it, there may be someone out there who knows something or is in a position to contribute to our investigation. The more we have to go on, the sooner we get them back."

"I'm sorry, Brian, I just can't. I'd be too nervous. I'm afraid I'd break down on camera."

"How about speaking to a print reporter?"

"I just can't. I'd fall apart. I couldn't bear to see a piece about the distraught Mrs. Riordan."

"I understand, Kate. Don't worry. We can make it up in other ways. From the looks of the group on your doorstep, I don't think we're going to have trouble keeping this case in the news."

Kate had been upset at that.

"Brian, that sounds so cold."

"Listen," he said gravely, "a little boy was lost in New York a couple of years ago. You may have read about it. They just couldn't keep the trail warm long enough to get all their homework done. As soon as interest fades in a case, that's it. There's no putting it back in the public consciousness. There's no second chance to have people come forward with clues, because they're just not thinking about it. That's a police judgment, Kate, and not my personal feeling."

She was mad at herself for getting upset with him. He was the one person she was sure was desperately trying to get Danny back. He was decisive and caring. Not like the mechanical FBI men attached to the case.

"Perhaps Arlene could do the interview," she said to him. "She's so resourceful. She's been on television before, you know, and she always looks so comfortable, so at home. That might solve your problem."

"No, it would only complicate it. Arlene can come across cold and hard. Viewers wouldn't respond to her. The attitude would be 'Too bad she lost her kid, but from the looks of it she deserved it.' No, you've got to have someone who'll create sympathy in the viewer's mind. They've got to have a reason to call in with any information that they have. The only response that Arlene could provoke is a negative one. She could hurt our case. She'd turn people off. If we can't make the media exposure a positive thing, I'd prefer we didn't do it at all."

And that had been the end of the discussion. Brian was forthright. He seemed to know the right thing to do at all times. He was altogether a more impressive man than she had ever imagined. She felt the stirrings of something that her Irish Catholic background would not let her acknowledge.

O'Toole was still on duty with her at the house this afternoon. Nothing ever seemed to faze him. He was always cheerful, and yet considerate of her. He loved to talk, but he seemed to know instinctively when she needed silence. Now he sat silently drinking endless cups of Melitta coffee dusted with Sweet-n-Low.

The phone rang and O'Toole answered it. Kate was seized by panic. The kidnapper again? O'Toole's grave manner gave no clue.

"Yes, she's right here. I don't know if that would be proper. That could create a problem for all of us. That's not really something we should be getting into at this time. I'm sure the

Chief would back me on this. Well, I don't know if she wants to talk to you right now."

Kate could stand the suspense no longer, so she motioned for him to give her the phone.

"Mrs. Riordan, you don't know me," began the male voice on the other end. It seemed faint, a bad long-distance connection. "But I'm concerned about the events of recent days in William's Crossing. They are evidence of a disturbing malaise gripping this country." Kate listened in fascination. Was this a crank call? "My name is Jay Herbert and I'm a citizen like you. My job? I'm a studio producer for World International Pictures. We'd like to make you an offer on the rights to your story. It's receiving national press and . . ."

Kate groaned and handed the phone back to O'Toole. Here someone may be trying to get in touch with her with news about her son, and this clown was on the phone trying to sew up the movie rights. Kate grew angry. She snatched the phone back from O'Toole.

"I don't know, sir, whether you have any children of your own, or if you will. But I suggest that when and if they disappear, you film your own story. That'll show everyone a true measure of your concern. Until then, do me a favor. Leave this line free so we can get on with the business of finding my son." She slammed the phone down. The outburst had done her good. She felt a partial release of the tension she had felt during these last few days. She looked at O'Toole, who said nothing. She moved to fill the void.

"I'm sorry I acted that way. But the man had

no right. That's not my usual self," she found herself apologizing.

"That's quite all right, Mrs. Riordan. I can understand your dismay. Please don't give it a second thought."

What a curious man, she thought. He doesn't seem to get upset over anything. She had a feeling she could dump his cup of coffee over his head and he would be just as solicitous of her. It was clear to her why Brian had sent O'Toole to run operations at the house.

From the kitchen Kate heard a commotion at the door. As she walked into the living room she saw Maria Venuti. Maria was a short woman in her early thirties with frosted blonde hair. Her claim to fame was that she had the stigmata. On stressful occasions, she began to bleed from wounds in either hand that were not apparent at any other time. Kate herself had always been dubious. She knew that Maria's father had been a leading magician in the forties, and she sensed that Maria's "powers" were an outgrowth of her father's instruction. But Maria got serious attention from the diocese, and Kate knew that documents attesting to Maria's "miracles" had been forwarded to Rome and were being scrutinized by Vatican experts. Kate and Maria had met a couple of times, but Kate had always shied away from Maria, who was an effusive woman with a very cogent sense of public relations. It was just like Maria to present herself when all the reporters were camped out on Kate's doorstep. Maria was not one to let opportunity go knocking.

"Kate," Maria said, crossing the comfortable living room and embracing her. "How are you, my dear? I must talk to you. In private, of course."

Kate gave her a puzzled look. In her present emotional state, the last thing she wanted was a scene with Maria.

"All right, Maria," she said. "Please come into my bedroom. No one will disturb us there."

Maria seated herself on the bed. Kate sat on the little stool which was in front of her vanity. Maria spoke first in a low voice.

"Kate, I have important news for you. I have been in touch with Danny."

Kate gasped involuntarily.

"When . . ." The sound scraped from deep inside her.

"In the last twenty-four hours he has contacted me."

"How?"

"That I cannot reveal."

"Oh Maria, you must tell me. You must tell Chief Dolan."

"It cannot be. I only know this. My bleeding has stopped in the last hour and that is a good sign. I bleed continuously during Holy Week from my hands."

Kate grasped the woman's hands and turned her palms up. There were small crusted scars, recent ones, it seemed to Kate, on both palms.

"Maria, this isn't a time to go mystical on us. We need hard information. What do you know and how do you know it? Every hour the boys are gone increases the chance they won't be found unharmed. Please, please, Maria, as one mother to another, I beg of you to be straight with me."

Maria's eyes blazed back at Kate.

"You must have faith, Kate. Your son is involved in a miraculous undertaking. He is part of God's special plan. Indeed, your faith is being tried, but all of this will come to a good end. I have word of it."

Kate was beside herself.

"Please, Maria."

"Kate," Maria began in earnest again, "I have been aware for some time that you don't believe in my special powers, the gifts that God has given me. You are not aware of my part in His plans. I am used to dealing with people of little faith. Maybe you could say it was an occupational hazard. I am not deterred by this, and I want you to know that I take no personal offense. All I ask is that you have patience during this hour of your trial."

Kate shook her head.

"Maria, I'm not getting through to you. The boys are lost in this town, in this time, in this space. Can you comprehend that? Do you know of their whereabouts?"

"I have already told you, Kate. I bring you word of your son."

"Oh Maria, let's stop this game. Where? When?" Kate screamed.

"Last night in my dream," Maria began.

Tears began streaming down Kate's cheek. Maria clearly knew nothing that would help get Danny back.

Tuesday, 3:30 p.m.

CANDY HIGGINS, William's Crossing High School's finest long distance runner, and a hopeful for the Boston Marathon, was out training. Her route took her up and down the hills of the city, a twenty-six-mile course, which ended on the slopes of the mountain itself. She loved it up there among the dogwood and clover and honeysuckle. The mountain was a magical place where she could unwind and look down on her beloved town. Like so many of the other residents, Candy never wished to leave William's Crossing. At least she had never thought of leaving until recently. Now things had changed. It was Tuesday, and two children were missing since Sunday. And fear had spread through the streets. Candy could feel the tension in the air as she ran. Though the sun shone brightly, and there was a nip in the air, she felt, for the first time in her life, that William's Crossing was not exempt from the troubles that she heard about in Boston on the six o'clock news. Terror had struck the community, and Candy wanted to hide from it, wanted to run as fast as she could, as hard as she could until there was nothing left but muscles straining and the wind blowing in and out of her lungs. So far she had gone fourteen miles, and she was still unable to banish the thoughts and fears. There were too many reminders. Police cruisers, and silence on street corners where kids used to hang out.

Candy kept running, hoping to reach the almost mystical transportation the runner feels, but it was not happening. She crossed Dogwood Lane, and saw Skeeter Bannon delivering his *Pilots*, the weekly diocesan newspaper. The only kid on the street. She waved to him and he waved back. But there was a strange, isolated look on his face. She cut across the park which bisected the town and started her run around the outside of it. Because the town was only twenty miles across, she had to race around the outside of the park to make up the full distance. Now she strode hard, looking for kids on the swing and seeing none, used to hearing the sound of laughter from teenagers hanging out at the basketball courts. But today only two or three were there. From what she could see, they were shooting the ball listlessly, as though there was really no point to their effort. Candy ran on, trying to make her bones flow easily, trying to lighten her step, pushing, but the effort seemed insurmountable somehow. She wondered as she rounded the outside of the park for the second time, just how she was going to make it up the mountain today. It wasn't going to be easy—she felt drained, something vital had been cut out from under her. She went around the park again and saw Skeeter Bannon approaching. A good kid, she thought. How did he feel with Billy and Danny missing? He must be scared. All the kids at St. Dominic's must be scared. But Skeeter was out with his *Pilots*. She started her third run around the park's edge, beyond the seven-foot hedges which were the pride of the Park Board. Not many old towns could boast such a lovely spot. The city had never let it become the commercial building some developers wanted it to be. Candy loved the city for that as well. She ran, trying to keep her mind on the darting of bluejays, the sight of a squirrel hopping in front of her. The simple things that gave her pleasure. Finally she turned and started across the park. She would run up Woodview Avenue, which eventually turned into William's Crossing Drive, and then she would start the long climb up the mountain.

She never made it past the centerpiece of William's Crossing Park, the fountain.

There, beneath the arching, sparkling water, she found a pile of fifty drenched *Pilots,* Skeeter Bannon's shoulder bag, and one tennis shoe.

Without saying a word, without calling his name once, Candy knew that the worst had happened. Right under her nose, without anyone seeing a thing, Skeeter Bannon had vanished.

Then she began to scream. She screamed his name, and she screamed for the police, and she screamed her own mother's name. Later, when she had been given a shot and sent home, she said that she supposed it was a combination of the shock of the thing and her exhaustion from running. Candy was a proud athletic girl who didn't like to picture herself as an hysterical female. But at that moment, the moment Skeet-er Bannon disappeared—when she was not twenty-five feet away, right on the other side of the hedge—she had screamed, and torn at her own hair, and felt that she had been touched by a madness from which she would never escape.

Tuesday, 5:30 p.m.

KATE RIORDAN met Brian Dolan at the fountain. The police had cordoned off the actual fountain itself, but just outside the police ropes a huge mob was growing. There were TV cameras and sound trucks and Boston reporters somehow magically appeared on the scene. There were newspaper men from the *Globe* as well as from the William's Crossing *Transcript,* whose head-line read "THIRD ALTAR BOY GONE!" And there was a group of mothers who had with them a banner saying "Save Our Children." Their leader, a tall, thin woman named Margaret Fine, talked through a loudspeaker and urged people to come to a meeting which had been hastily called in the William's Crossing High School.

"You must come to save our children," she said. "My husband, Roy Fine, is signing up peo-ple as of right now to start a street patrol."

Chief Brian Dolan didn't like what he heard. Margaret Fine looked hysterical, and there was no doubt in his mind that the situation could turn into vigilante justice and end in tragedy. Already the comments of the crowd were turning vicious.

"Maybe the cops really can't protect us."

"Hey Chief, you good for anything but making speeches?"

"Maybe we ought to get a real police chief instead of this idiot."

The police held the surging crowd back and Dolan tried to ignore them as he watched the fingerprints expert complete his work and tried to talk to Monsignor Merja. But conversation was nearly impossible, as Merja was being severely hassled by another parent, Ted White.

"I want to know what's going on, Father. And don't just stand there and smile at me. What I want to know is why these kids are getting taken? And is the church going to do anything about it?"

Before Merja could answer, someone else was thrusting forward in the crowd and yelling at him. The priest was keeping his poise, but it wouldn't take much, Brian was sure, to turn the whole show into a riot.

Kate Riordan stood by with her arm around Nancy Bannon, who looked as though she could barely stand.

"It's my fault," she said. "It's my fault. I should never have let him go out there. I told him not to—told him to stay home. But he begged me. Said he'd lose his job, and that he'd be in broad daylight. And everybody knew him. Oh my God, my God."

She began to cry hysterically and stare down at his tennis shoe. Finally John Bannon fought his way through the crowd and took his wife in his arms.

"We're going to find him," he said. "It's going to be all right."

But the words were a monotone, and lifeless.

Kate watched as Nancy was led off by her husband. She felt as though she were in an endless dream of terror. When would it end?

"Brian," she said, just so she herself wouldn't scream, "have you found anything at all?"

"Still checking," Brian said. "The FBI is all through the neighborhood. Everything is being done that can be."

"You didn't answer my question," she said stubbornly.

"I respect you too much to lie to you, Kate. We have reason to believe that there is a suspect."

"Who?"

"I don't want to say here. May I drive you home?"

"I've got my own car, Brian."

"All right. Let's take a walk then."

Brian put his hand on the small of Kate Riordan's back. They walked along the edge of the park, and around the hedge where Candy Higgins had run.

"There's a couple of things. First of all, Father Joe. You know him?"

"Father Joe? Of course. He's on vacation."

"No, he's not on vacation. He's been missing for several days. I didn't tell you in the beginning because I wasn't sure he was missing. The night Danny disappeared I talked to Monsignor Merja and he told me Father Joe was a day late getting back, that he had called from Baltimore and he said he had some family business. At the time it seemed harmless enough, but now . . . he's two days late and two more kids are missing. Can you tell me anything about Father Joe?"

Kate Riordan was stymied. "Father Joe? He's tremendously popular. But you must already know about him, Brian. He's the one who started the Folk Mass in the early seventies. He's the priest the kids most respect. He takes an active interest in social issues. He plays the guitar, even writes his own songs. He was giving Danny music lessons. Danny and all the other kids are crazy about him. You don't think there could be any connection?"

Brian stared Kate Riordan directly in the eyes. "I'm more interested in what you think," he said.

Kate hung her head and shook it. "I don't want to talk about . . . that kind of thing," she said, obviously deeply troubled.

"What kind of thing?" Brian pursued.

"Well, when Father Joe came here many years ago, the Mass was still said in Latin. There were some old-timers who really resented the modernization. And they took their bitterness out on Father Joe, although it was hardly his decision or responsibility. Anyway, people said things about him. Because he was charismatic, interesting. You know how people who are jealous can be."

"You mean, they said he was gay?" Brian said.

"Well, not outright," Kate said. "But in so many words, yes."

"And were there any rumors that mentioned who his partner might be?"

"Partner?" Kate said.

"Lover," Brian said. "If he was gay, perhaps they said he was getting it on with someone in particular."

Kate frowned. She suddenly felt sullied and dirty. Father Joe had taken an especial interest in Danny. He had understood the problems a bright child has among his classmates. He had counseled him, almost acted like a therapist when Kate desperately needed help. Now she felt like a traitor for even suspecting him.

"No," she said honestly. "No one ever suggested he was actually gay. That he really had a lover. It was just bitter, provincial talk. You know, comments like, 'Oh, he likes folk music and long hair, next he'll be dressing like a girl.' Mean, but really silly things. Even those who said them didn't seem to mean them. It was just a difficult time. No one could ever suspect Father Joe. He's too good a man. He's a great friend of Danny's."

"How great?" Brian said, though he knew the question made him sound like a hardnosed cynical cop. He hated talking this way to her.

"Don't make it sound like there was something awful between them. He took an interest in Danny."

She went on to tell him how Father Joe had helped Danny realize he was gifted, and that some boys might feel confused about that, and that Danny would have to live with it for now, but that in the long run it would make him happy.

"I'm sorry to sound like a cop," Brian said, "but it's odd. He said he'd be home soon. Yesterday. And he hasn't called and now two more kids are missing."

"A man who takes children has to hate them, doesn't he?" asked Kate. "Or hate somebody.

Father Joe was respected, for the most part, loved."

"Yes," Brian said. "I know that. But, all the same, there is still a conservative group who doesn't trust him. And there was pressure from within the church. It's well known that he and Monsignor Merja have never agreed on the new casual style of the church. Maybe something slipped—resentment for the church, being unappreciated, perhaps an unconscious desire for worship from the children. Look, I know it's a slim lead. But the fact remains he's not back yet, and the kids are missing. It's our only lead, the only firm lead we've got."

Kate Riordan looked into Brian's blue eyes.

"I still can't believe that Father Joe is the man we want. He wasn't that frustrated, that . . . *type* of person. I know that doesn't sound very scientific, but I'm a very good judge of people, Brian."

Brian Dolan rubbed his tired eyes. He smiled wearily and found himself taking Kate Riordan's hand in his.

"I believe you are, Kate," he said.

"So? Where does that leave us?"

"I want to have a talk with Billy and Skeeter's parents," Brian said. "You too. Maybe there's something we have all overlooked. Meanwhile, I'm putting out an APB for Father Joe. I've already called the other parents. We're to meet at the Conleys' tomorrow night at seven. Can you make it?"

"Of course," she said. "And I'm sorry if I was short with you, Brian. I know you're killing yourself over this."

Brian Dolan smiled and said nothing. But he pressed Kate Riordan's hand once again.

Yet as he walked away, Brian Dolan felt himself a failed man. He had failed his family, his country and his God. He only hoped he would not fail Kate Riordan. But the truth was, they had absolutely nothing. Not even a good working hypothesis. And he wasn't sure where to go from here.

Tuesday, 7:30 p.m.

TOMMY GLEASON and Johnny Blake readied the altar for Mass. Three of their friends were missing and it made them feel very creepy. One had disappeared from this very church and one had disappeared from school and one had disappeared on his paper route. There was no place a guy could be safe.

But at this moment they both had to concentrate on how to get the altar and all the things Monsignor Merja would need for tonight ready. Neither of them had ever served a Holy Week Mass. They sort of had an idea how it went but they usually served with one of the older boys— Danny, Billy or Skeeter. Those guys had the whole thing down cold. They were pros.

"Let's see," Tommy said to Johnny, "the water and wine cruets are ready. Is the bread in the ciborium?"

"I dunno," Johnny frowned. "Do they do that during Holy Week? Do they do that at evening Masses? I never served neither before."

"Okay," said Tommy, sounding like an airplane pilot ready for takeoff, "chalice, paten, purificator and corporal are in place. How about the bowl and finger towel?"

"I guess," said Johnny hazily.

"We're all set on the Sacramentary and the Lectionary. And I saw the incense and boat around here somewhere on Sunday."

"Candles," mumbled Johnny. "Danny said something about candles, you do something special with 'em in Holy Week."

"Naw, listen, they light that big white paschal candle out there between Easter Sunday and Pentecost. But this week just the regular candles are okay. Remember to genuflect when you pass in front of the tabernacle. You didn't the last time we served together. And make sure Merja's mike is on, he goes nuts if you forget."

"I know. I caught hell the last time I forgot."

Tommy Gleason shook his head. He was the whole show tonight and he knew it.

"Now remember," he said to Johnny, "we're sticking together. If there's a weirdo out there, he can't grab both of us at once."

Johnny Blake got the picture, he was a head shorter than Tommy anyway. "I'm staying with you, Tommy. Nobody gonna mess with us."

"Yeah, just remember we're the toughest of all the kids who are left. That's why Merja chose us. You can't fool with us and everybody knows it."

Mother Superior stood in the doorway of the sacristy as they returned. "Now boys, you must be very alert. Call for help if *anything* should go wrong. Don't be afraid to call. Do you understand what I'm saying?"

Johnny nodded. "We can take care of ourselves, Mother. But thanks for the good words."

Carl Burke had been standing nearby and heard this conversation. As the altar boys returned to their pre-Mass duties, he approached Mother Superior. "We don't approve of this Mass, Mother," he said forthrightly. "No way to cover all the exits. I told the Monsignor this was a bad idea but he wouldn't listen."

Mother Superior gave him a sympathetic look but then said, "You must remember in this church that his word is law. There have been Holy Weeks for two thousand years. The Church goes on. Always."

Carl Burke's tone turned sarcastic. "I guess the Church is more important than its young altar boys."

Mother Superior's face tightened. At this point Jerry Manning joined the proceedings. He was just putting on his vestments to serve as deacon for the Mass. "Mr. Burke," he said, "I don't know how they do things in Boston. But this is a small town where everybody knows everybody else. My son is out there. If I thought for one moment it was a risk for him to be there, I'd keep him home. We're going to put an end to this by sticking together, not by fighting among ourselves. Cancelling the Mass would serve no useful purpose."

"The Church, after all, has its traditions," said Mother Superior.

Carl Burke remained unconvinced. "I sure hope you're right. I wouldn't want to be the one to explain to those people out there why another kid disappeared, would you?"

"I take your meaning," said Jerry Manning, struggling into his long white alb. Tonight, he put on a dalmatic over it, a small chasuble he wore in preference to his usual stole. "But I'd appreciate it if you spent more time, Mr. Burke, on your investigation and less time complaining. There are a lot of professional second guessers out there on the church steps with TV cameras and microphones. Let's not give them a chance to be right, okay?"

Carl Burke was speechless. Mother Superior had known Jerry Manning a long time and had never heard such vehemence in his speech before. The situation was getting to everyone now.

The Mass began promptly at 7:30, and the church was packed to overflowing. Monsignor Merja seemed determined to keep the pace up. Jerry Manning thought it reminded him of one of those 6 a.m. Masses priests often said alone. Merja's performance was elliptical and had none of the exaggerated ceremony that usually characterizes a priest's performance in front of an audience.

But the Mass turned out to be one of the most affecting Jerry Manning had ever attended. As he sat in the deacon's chair at the side of the audience and looked out over the faithful, which included his son Mike, he reflected on the grief that Kate and the Conleys and the Bannons must be feeling.

As Merja read the gospel, Jerry Manning felt fear inside himself. It was the gospel of John and it related how Jesus had been betrayed by Judas. He wondered if there was a Judas in the audience in front of him. And in the same passage, Jesus said to Simon Peter, "I tell you

before the cock crows three times you will have
disowned me."

Where the traitors were, Jerry Manning did
not know. All he knew was that something that
had always been wonderful for him, his faith,
was enduring a severe test in the last few days.
Jerry did not know where to look for this traitor
before he struck again. All he could do was wait
and suffer. But as he looked from Tommy to
Johnny and back to his own son Mike, he knew
one thing, the traitor would get no one else. Not
if he, Jerry Manning, as powerful as he knew
himself to be, set out to stop him.

Now it was communion time. He bowed his
head and knelt at the side of the altar to receive
the Host. Tommy put the paten under Jerry's
grizzled chin, Monsignor Merja's consecrated
fingers placed the Host on Jerry's tongue and for
a moment, everything in the universe was right.

Wednesday, 8 a.m.

THE CARS poured into William's Crossing High School. One of the teachers, Fred Myers, stood out in front watching and feeling as though he were inside a nightmare. People walked in a determined, plodding way, the fear obvious on their faces. They talked in a low hush, nodding their heads as if they had finally agreed on a course of action only to fall silent a few seconds later. Helplessness, Fred Myers thought, was a terrible thing to see. It gave rise to a wild, irrational anger. Myers had been teaching *The Ox Bow Incident* to his students and he thought of that novel now. Maybe someone would come out of all this as the scapegoat. Maybe the whole town wouldn't survive, the fabric of community would be ripped apart forever.

He walked inside and sat down in the back, and watched.

Up on the stage, Margaret Fine was tall and commanding in her tweed jacket and glasses with the gold chain dangling around her neck.

On the dais with her was the Mother Superior of the elementary school, Monsignor Merja,

Brian Dolan and a faceless brown-suited man.
The FBI, Myers thought.

Margaret Fine beat her gavel on the lectern
and called for quiet. The room quickly became
silent.

"I don't have to dramatize the deadliness of
this situation," Margaret Fine said. "We are
being attacked. And we must share our information, pool our knowledge and our human
resources, and save our children."

In the third row Kate Riordan held her hands
in her lap, and tried to keep herself together.
She could barely stand to hear words like "We
must save our children." For her child was gone,
already out of her control. It still didn't seem
possible. If only he hadn't been in church that
day, he'd be safe now, safe and with her. She
looked around at Meg Thomas, and her husband
Rollie. They had a twelve-year-old daughter,
Megan, and suddenly Kate felt a wild irrational
anger. Why not Megan? She was an annoying
child anyway, always whining, and not half the
student Danny was. Why not Megan? She shook
her head and felt an intense stab of guilt. She
had to remain rational. She had to think, and to
put things together. She couldn't give in to those
mean-spirited emotions. She had to stay sane.
She turned back into the crowd. People were
already interrupting Father Merja, who was
appearing on the stand, looking visibly older.
His hands, always firm, shook a little, Kate
thought.

"I must insist," Monsignor Merja said, "that
we not give in to panic. Everything that can be
done is being done. We must go on with our
lives. School will stay open."

People shot out of their seats as if propelled by rocket fuel.

"That's great," Jack Smalley said. "But you can bet on one thing. My child isn't going to be there. You say we ought to go on with our lives? Well that's exactly what Mrs. Bannon did. She went on with her life and allowed her boy to deliver papers per usual, and look what became of him. God help me for saying so."

"That's right," Claire Woodruff said. "And you say everything that can be done is being done. Well, we'd like to know just what that is."

"That's right," someone else said.

"Let me answer that," Brian said, walking to the lectern. "We have every available man working on this case. We've got a close alliance with the FBI. We have the streets patrolled, and we are working with Roy Fine getting together citizen street patrols. Now I want to say something to all of you."

"Talk away," a man yelled. "It's only our kids."

Brian looked in the direction of the man and pointed his finger.

"George Dowson, I want you to sit down and listen to me. I mean it."

The man sat down heavily and shook his head.

"I don't want," Brian said, shooting a look at Kate, "I don't want our fears to get the best of us. We do need help patrolling the streets. I am for people staying up, watching. But I want it understood that no one will attack anyone he thinks might be a suspect. You get information, you call the police. I mean you call right away. I don't want anybody trying to be a hero or an avenging angel. The law is not on a holiday here. Anybody who tries to play sheriff will be prosecuted, and I am completely serious. We have everyone working full tilt, night and day, and we are going to bring those children back, so help me God."

The incredible gravity of his speech, the forceful way he presented it, shut the audience down. Some people actually smiled, and one man raised his fist in a salute to Brian. From the stand Brian stood tall, looking every inch the defender of right and justice, but inside he was shaking. He knew that this speech, however strong it sounded, was going to hold people for no more than a few hours. If the kids weren't found soon, he could have a compound tragedy on his hands.

"What the hell is the FBI doing?" Clarence Moss yelled.

"Let me introduce you to Mr. Burke from the FBI," Brian said.

"Many things are being done," Burke said when he reached the lectern. "I can't say exactly what they are because we don't want to leak anything. But you must have faith that I have men working on this job night and day. It's our top priority. You are not alone, and we are going to get your children back."

Brian watched as the crowd stayed quiet. He wasn't sure of everything Burke was doing and he suddenly felt an intense pang of jealousy. He knew that computers were being used, and that information was being sifted. Burke would probably try and take over, and maybe he had a right to.

But then he thought it through. It was his

town, and his people, and he meant what he said. He was going to get the kids back.

He had to comb the town, use the knowledge he'd acquired, knowledge no computer could match. He was this town and he had to find the link that would put him there. In the kidnapper's mind.

The meeting went on, but people seemed less frantic and in the back Fred Myers relaxed a little. There wasn't going to be any hanging tonight. But he felt a fear anyway. The panic in his fellow citizens made him wonder about human nature.

Who would be the first to crack?

He thought of Kate Riordan, and he had to admire her guts for showing up. The other parents hadn't come.

How could they stand it? he thought. How could anybody stand losing a kid?

He thought of his girlfriend, Sandy. She was always talking about having a kid. He had been feeling ambivalent about it, but no more.

There was no way he was having a kid now. No way.

Then it occurred to him. It wasn't like *The Ox Bow Incident,* not that bad—yet. But all the same, somebody had already died. His kid, his heir. He just couldn't go through with it. He couldn't bear it.

He felt like a kidnapper himself suddenly.

He had stolen his own dream. And was busy burying it in a dead weed lot somewhere in his mind.

Wednesday, 4 p.m.

ED DEVLIN smiled up at the perfect day through the windshield of his Ford pickup. The sun was shining brightly and there was just enough of a chill in the air to make him feel good about his work, which was woodcutting. It was nearly 4 p.m., when he finished chopping down shanks of oak, and the back of the pickup was stocked full. Down in the little town below, he would quickly sell the logs, because people shut their furnaces down and used their fireplaces this time of year. By tonight, he'd be at the Wishing Well Tavern on Fulton, playing shuffleboard with Ernie and Sonny and the rest of the guys. He'd have a couple of hundred in his pocket and hell, maybe he'd even stand the boys to a round of drinks or two. Ed chuckled to himself. There were some guys who worked all day in those new office buildings the town had erected over on Dorset Street, and his girlfriend Marge always bugged him about showing a little ambition and getting a "real job." But he was happy. After all, as Monsignor Merja himself had said, you were really only here a short speck of a time, and it's a wise man who knows his limitations. He'd never become one of those guys who developed ulcers, or got heart disease trying to make some kind of big deal. No, Ed thought, a little vainly, he was a simple man, and given to a good, healthy simple life. Oh, he supposed he did drink a little too much of the Old Bushmill when he was flush, but every man has to have some vices. But right now, he was enjoying bumping along the dusty old road on top of Mt. Olive, carting his bolts of wood down. The sun was shining, he'd worked up a good sweat, and life itself seemed all right, though down below, he knew things weren't the same. Those missing kids. The town had never experienced anything like that before. Still, that wasn't his business. No sir. He stayed away from things like that. Some people now, they dwelled on the subject. Like his friend Ernie at the bar. He was morbid about it, always talking about those poor missing kids. Well, Ed was as sorry as the next man, but it was none of his business. He didn't want to think of it. He didn't really want to think of anything that would change his happy carefree life. But of course, some people. They were always going to be ramming it down your throat. Like Marge. She was always talking about poor Mrs. Riordan and poor Mrs. Conley and poor Mrs. Bannon. Why couldn't people just let the police take care of it?

Ed got a little irritated at himself. Here he was dwelling on it. Better not to think about it. He could ruin his whole day, and what good would come of it in the end? Not a bit.

Ed turned the truck to the left, down Mt. Olive Pass. It was a steep grade here, and he had to be careful, take it slow. The brakes weren't what they used to be, and he'd need help from the gears. You didn't want to get rolling too fast on this grade, or you could go right over the edge. That had happened once back in the fifties. Old Tod Manning, Jerry's brother, had been drunk, fooling around at the top of the mountain and his brakes had either given out or old Tod had been playing chicken. Whatever happened, he went sailing over, a flaming wreck. You had to be careful if you wanted to stay alive. Stay out of other people's business, stay fit, enjoy the simple life, and you'll live a long, long time.

Ed turned yet another steep grade, carefully braking down, when he thought he saw something in the woods. He turned his head to the left and looked again. There wasn't anything. He was certain of it. Ed let out a sigh and kept going. Still, he had thought for a second there that he had actually seen someone in the woods. A man in a black robe. A priest. What else? There was something on his face, something like blood. No, that was just his imagination. He hadn't seen it the second time. It wasn't any of his business anyway. He ought to go down and sell his wood before it got too late. He didn't want to miss his time at the Wishing Well tonight. They might have a local country and western band, the Hard Riding Boys. He and Marge would maybe dance a few. He let the truck roll on a few more yards, then, almost in spite of himself, he found his foot involuntarily hitting the brake.

"Dammit all anyway. It's none of my business."

But again, almost as though someone else had taken over possession of him, he found himself shifting into reverse, and backing the pickup carefully and slowly up the hill.

He rounded the bend, and just prayed that no one was coming down. Like one of those crazy teenagers from over the high school who used the top of the Mount for necking or whatever they called it these days.

He turned the bend and looked into the woods. Nothing. What a waste of time. He started to gear into first, when suddenly he saw it again. There was somebody in there all right. He saw a flash of black, and a man's face, and then saw him stagger against a tree and fall. Jesus, Mary and Joseph!

Ed pulled on the emergency brake and jumped out of his truck. He moved quickly through the trees and the dense underbrush, and felt stickers hitting him in the face. He cursed as they scratched him. Then he was walking across a field of blue flowers and into a deeply fertile, shaded opening, and there, behind a fallen rotting log, he saw the priest staring at him wide-eyed. He moaned and moved toward him, and Ed felt a cold flush of fear.

"Father Joe," he said, astonished. "Father Joe."

Ed raced over and picked up the young priest. He was still dressed in his cassock and he looked at Ed Devlin as though he were a perfect stranger when, in fact, they had known each other for five years. Not well, of course. Ed wasn't a regular communicant. But still . . .

"Let me help you, Father."

Ed reached down and picked up the younger man. He put the priest's right arm over his shoulder and attempted to help him walk. But the priest collapsed on the ground.

Ed knelt over him.

"Father," he said, "it's me, Ed. You don't remember."

It was then that he saw what looked like a bright patch of blood on Father Joe's head. A wound of some kind. It looked like it had been caused by a pipe. He realized now that Father Joe was in deep shock, that he shouldn't be moved at all. But there was no time to waste either.

Ed cursed the fact that his CB was out of order. He could radio for an ambulance. But then again the William's Crossing medics weren't exactly like the guys on *Emergency*. They might not even make it up the mountain at all, the way they drove. No, he had to get the priest down himself.

"It's all right, Father," Ed Devlin said.

Then, summoning up all his strength, he picked the priest's body up like he would a child's. He began to sweat profusely. His heart beat furiously. God, he hoped his back wouldn't go out. He still wanted to get down to the Wishing Well. He'd have something to tell them down there tonight. That was for certain.

Taking each painful step slowly, he carried Father Joe through the forest toward his waiting truck.

Wednesday, 6 p.m.

KATE RIORDAN walked through her living room, straightened up the magazines on her coffee table, picked up a pillow which had fallen onto her blue rug, and tossed it on the couch. She sat down heavily in the old leather chair that Paddy had bought—a recliner. Paddy had sat in it with his feet up, reading the baseball scores. She remembered getting angry at him for tracking mud through the house after one of the American Legion softball games. Then Paddy had begun to lose weight, lose his terrific appetite, and soon, so soon, he was gone. She could still feel the anxiety that had screeched through her. She had thought for a while that she wasn't going to be able to bear it. But she had to, for herself and, more importantly, for Danny. There was no telling what effect it would have on him, especially if she fell apart too. So she stayed strong, kept busy, showered her love and affection on her son. And now . . .

Kate got up and walked across the front room, up the three steps toward the back of the house. She stopped in front of his bedroom and looked in. There in front of her was his baseball glove sitting on the toy box. She felt her knees buckle and her breath seemed to be sucked out of her. She went into the room and looked down at his unslept-in bed. How many times had she yelled at him about learning to keep his small room neat? The day he had disappeared he had cleaned it up. And what would she do now if he were here? God, she would help him mess it up. They would celebrate by throwing toys around the room. Afterwards, she would take him out for ice cream. It was silly, she had to get hold of herself. But the sight of his Star Wars curtains, his bookcase with his Winnie the Pooh books, his Roald Dahl books, *James and the Giant Peach, Willy Wonka*—how he had loved those books when he was little. The sound of his laughter when she read them to him, doing the voices differently, making her voice deep to play the villain, and then putting him into bed, hugging him, his strong little arms hugging her. She knew she had to stop, this was not going to get her anywhere. She had to be over at the Conleys' in an hour. And she had come in here ostensibly to think. Was there any relationship between Father Joe and Danny? Was there something she didn't know about? She looked around the room, saw his model case with his carefully constructed models—Dracula, Frankenstein, the Werewolf, King Kong, Mothra. How she loved him. It astonished her really. Even before this, after Paddy had died, she had been afraid of her love for her son, for, late at night sometimes, when she had stared down at his sleeping body—when he looked most an-

gelic—she would feel a terrible fear. If anything
ever happened to Danny . . . The thought was
unbearable, simply unbearable.

And now, she thought, something has happened. Somebody had taken him. Some man or
woman had her child. It seemed almost impossible to believe one woman could do that to another. Still, it happened, it happened to women
who hadn't had kids, or who had lost their children like Monsignor's housekeeper, Mrs.
Mullen. But surely it couldn't be her. Babysitters
who became too fond of the child, and one day
simply picked one up at the park. None of it
made sense in Danny's case. She reached into
her pocket and found her rosary, and then she
knelt down next to the bed, his bed, with a couple of his Marvel Comics on it—the Fantastic
Four and the Hulk—and she started to say the
rosary, then put it aside and appealed to God
directly.

"I know I haven't always been perfect. I know
I've done things to offend you. But if you have
any mercy, any mercy at all, please don't let anything happen to him. Take me if you want. Take
me. But not him. He's so young and bright. He's
got so much to give."

Then she began to cry and the fury of her
tears, the depth of her sorrow and feeling, surprised even herself. For she found herself grabbing at his bedspread, bunching it in her hand,
half in grief and half in an anger and rage that
she didn't know she possessed.

And then her prayers seemed to change. She
wasn't asking God any more. It was as though
(and the fury of this, the sinfulness of it, overwhelmed her) she were threatening him.

"You better bring him back. You better. If you're anything at all. If you care at all. If you're not just some illusion we've made up. If you're not some cruel, crazy . . ."

She let go of the bedspread and breathed in deeply. Her entire body shook. And when she looked over at the picture of him riding a pony, a picture he had brought home years ago, with the man who had taken it asking for four dollars, she felt herself crumbling.

Yet she could not fall apart, she dare not let herself get any more out of hand.

The meeting was in an hour and she was likely going to have to help Brian console the others. She hoped this meeting would be more productive and less hostile than the general meeting that morning. She was sensible, bright, capable Kate Riordan, the smart girl, the one who was going places. She was the woman who could raise a child alone, who didn't complain about extra work, who was still able to be a good neighbor and got to church as well.

What a lie. What a lie that all seemed now.

She felt like jelly, like simply a mass of fear and panic and rage. Those emotions swept over her as though they came from the outside. They possessed her and she was incapable of stopping their tide.

But she must. She must.

Danny was alive.

"He's alive," she said defiantly, making a fist. "He's alive and I'm going to find him, do you hear?"

She was practically screaming. But at whom? At God himself?

Quickly she got up and looked through the room. Through his drawers with his t-shirts. There was his Red Sox shirt, his Patriots jersey. Don't think about it, don't let it get to you.

She went through his underwear, his socks, she moved to his closet and, after sorting through everything, she found herself once again sitting in the room, this time in the middle of the floor, surrounded by his toys and sports equipment.

Her forehead felt clammy. There was a numbness and icy feeling in her fingers.

"Nothing," she said.

She began to focus a little more clearly. She thought of Danny and Father Joe playing guitar together. The smile on Father Joe's face as Danny picked up a difficult run or played a new lead. Was there anything more in that look than mere pride, friendship, love for the boy? Was there something perverse and twisted just beneath the surface?

And now, trembling, feeling nauseous, she could no longer say for sure.

All she knew was that she ached and hurt. A pain like no other she had experienced. And she didn't know how long she could stand it. That was the truth.

When the phone rang in the hallway, Kate nearly jumped out of her skin. Dazed, trembling, she got up and walked toward it. Where was O'Toole? She dreaded having to answer it herself.

"Please, God," she said as she picked it up. "Forgive me for my anger."

"Kate?"

It was Brian. She tried desperately to read the tone in his voice.

"I've got some important news."

"What?" she said breathlessly.

"We've found Father Joe. Ed Devlin, the woodcutter, found him up on Mt. Olive."

"Does he know where the children are?"

"I don't know, Kate," Brian said. "He's in shock. He's suffered from some kind of wound to the head, and from exposure. You know how cold it gets up on the mountain. Well, Dr. McGill said he's been up there for maybe three days. He's in something like a coma, though it's not a deep one. They think, though nobody can be sure, that he'll come out of it. I've got men waiting in his room, and, of course, both our men and the FBI are up on the mountain right now hunting for the kids. So far, though, I have to tell you, nobody has found a thing. I've got to get back in the room now. There are a few things I want to check. I'll still see you at the Conleys' at seven. I'm not sure of anything, Kate, but maybe this is the break we've been waiting for."

"Yes, Brian," Kate said. "Maybe it is."

She set the phone down gently in its cradle. What did it mean? Up on the mountain? Father Joe in a coma? How could that happen? The neat, ordered, continuous existence she'd grown so fond of had been blown away.

But she had to hold up. Perhaps, perhaps this was the break.

"God," she said again, "let Father Joe lead me to my son."

HE SAT in his room surrounded by newspapers and the headlines made him laugh. It felt good to be laughing. He hadn't laughed out loud in fifteen years. But there was no way he could keep it back now. The Boston headlines were wonderful: "TOWN PRAYS FOR MISSING ALTAR BOYS." Oh, it felt good to see them writing about him. He had dreamed of it when he was young. He had been a smart kid, too, like the Riordan child. But there had been a different world in those days. In those days you were taught to be a team player. And he had been one. Everything he had done had been for the good of the team. Always the team.

But then they had taken it away from him. And it had taken him until today to get even. He dropped the papers on the floor, and thought about what power he had. Everything in the town now was flowing right from him. The reporters were there because of him. The FBI was there because of him. The mothers were giving their pathetic little cries for help because of him. The entire state of Massachusetts was gripped by fear because of him. One man. One man whom they had thought was finished. It all flowed from him, and yet here he was sitting peacefully in his apartment, relaxing, taking it easy with a foot up on his desk and a can of beer open in front of him. It was incredible. But it was nothing compared to how they were going to react when he finished the project. He worried about the children a little. They were smart little brats. He had to get down and drug them again soon. But first, first he would read from *The Spiritual Combat*. There was a section he had once taken seriously, so seriously. But now it had a new meaning for him. It read like a comedy.

From Chapter 26 he read:

When you perceive yourself wounded, that is, fallen into any sin, whether through frailty, or deliberately through malice, be not too much cast down. Do not abandon yourself to God, say with a humble confidence: "I am now convinced, O My God, that I am nothing; for what can be expected from so blind and wretched a creature as I am, but sin and folly?" Dwell on this thought, in order to stir up a lively sorrow for your fault.

To think he used to believe such stuff. To think of the nights he fell on the moonlit floor and looked up at God, begging him for forgiveness for his sins. And the irony of it was, the laughable irony of it, that back then he had been GOOD. So damned GOOD. He had cared about his fellow men and all he had ever gotten was a kick in the teeth. He had cared about the community and no one had ever really appreciated his contribution, and he had cared about the Church, and what had that gotten him? Now, now he was BAD—very, very BAD—but again, ironically, he felt wonderful. He felt powerful. Perhaps that was the great unspoken secret of evil. That it was wonderful, that it was fun. Perhaps those who knew it guarded the secret so that other people would stay in their places. Judges and police and politicians and bishops— they were all doing evil every day, toying with people in ways that were much more profound than his. And they didn't stir up a lively sorrow in themselves. No, they laughed and had women and drank, and enjoyed themselves. They all knew the secret he had only just now discovered. That to do evil, to defy God himself, was pleasure, pure and simple. Where was the conscience that was supposed to wrack him and deny him sleep? Where was the pain that was supposed to cast him into Hell? He felt none of it. Only joy and power, and the promise of more and more power.

There were still small details to fulfill before his plan could go forward. No one could stop him now. One man had tried and he lay dead upon Mt. Olive.

Wednesday, 7 p.m.

As KATE RIORDAN got into her Fairmont and
headed for George and Arlene Conley's house,
the rest of William's Crossing was reverberating
with a fear and terror which mirrored her own. It
was only 7 p.m., but mothers had pulled their
children off the streets. Only two blocks away
seven-year-old Sherry Dillon was receiving a
spanking from her mother for leaving the back
yard. And one block away, four boys in Danny,
Skeeter, and Billy's class were arming themselves with baseball bats for a trip down to the
local soda fountain. One of the boys' fathers,
Dan Loughery, was explaining to them that until
the missing boys were brought back, he didn't
want to see any of them out alone—ever. They
were to stay in groups of threes, they were to
wear whistles around their necks, and they were
to carry their bats at all times. He felt foolish,
even a little crazy, telling the solemn ten-year-
olds such things, but he felt that he had no
choice. The boys themselves agreed completely.
Two blocks away a little girl, Amanda Lane, was
waking from a terrible nightmare in which a

huge man in a black mask was trying to smother her. She screamed for her mother, who came running into the room, quickly followed by her father, holding a Colt .45 he hadn't used since his days in the service. The three of them looked at one another, as Mrs. Lane held onto her daughter tightly, afraid of something she couldn't see, something that had pervaded the town like a poisonous odor, the odor of fear. At the local radio station, newscaster Jim Terry gave reports on the status of the investigation every hour, and handled an endless succession of calls from the Boston media. Indeed, the little radio station had never seen such a response to anything—not even the blizzard of '78—and they were ill-prepared to deal with it. At the Wishing Well Tavern, Ed Devlin was a hero for bringing in Father Joe, and he was asked to tell his part in the drama to his pals over and over again, which he did over a steady diet of Old Bushmills with Miller chasers.

Little League games had been canceled, Boy Scout meetings were patrolled by parents in teams of twos. Vigilante-like groups rode up and down the streets. Kate Riordan saw Tom Hale and Bill Busby going by, their bats and crowbars plainly visible. She looked at the local 7-Eleven store, where kids usually hung out on the bench. Now there was no one. She rode by Wendy's, where teenagers prowled, but she saw very few cars. Older kids were staying home watching their brothers and sisters, waiting for the news. And the newsmen, TV and print media people from Boston were everywhere. It seemed now that the only people on the streets were people

who were making a living off of the kidnapping.
The city had been overrun with them. Carl
Burke of the FBI sent men everywhere, asking
questions, digging, but as of yet nothing had
happened. The town was unnaturally quiet, and
the effect on Kate Riordan was shattering. She
felt as though she wanted to scream out loud as
she approached the Conleys' house. But once
again, she told herself she must keep herself
together. She must.

She sat in the front room with the four other parents.

Arlene Conley's beauty was not apparent
tonight. There were dark circles under her eyes.
It was obvious she had been crying. It was also
obvious she was embarrassed about it. Never let
anyone get too close, Kate thought, even in
times as bad as these. George Conley, usually
thoughtful and polite, was shaken. It was easy to
see how he would respond to his son's loss. He
would simply remove himself to a vague distant
place where nothing hurt. Kate remembered that
he had become that way when Paddy died. God,
she thought, how can they stand it?

Sitting on the camel-back couch across the
room, the Bannons fidgeted nervously. John
Bannon, in one of his ill-fitting blue serge suits,
polished his glasses and bit his lower lip. From
time to time, he nervously looked down at his
watch, as though he were in a hurry to get the
meeting over with so he might get back to the
store. Kate knew that he wasn't cold and heart-
less. But, like George Conley, he didn't seem
able to deal with the problem emotionally.

Though Nancy Bannon too looked as though she had been crying, she at least seemed ready to talk, to deal with the problems directly. Kate took a deep breath. It would be up to her and Brian, who joined them now from the kitchen.

"I'll tell you what we know," Brian said, pacing back and forth in front of the fireplace. "Father Joe has been out there in the woods for several days. He's suffering from deep shock—and from something else. A blow on the head. It looks as though he's been hit with a hammer. I want any of you to think of anything Father Joe might have against your children. Something they did to him perhaps. I mean, let's say, for example, the three of them got together and played a joke on him. Now let's say he's suffering from a certain imbalance, and to get even he snatches the boys. Do you follow me? Anything that would link these particular boys . . ."

Arlene Conley, as always, was the first to speak.

"I don't understand the reasoning here," she said. "You tell us Father Joe has been out in the woods for several days, suffering from exposure. You say he's been hit on the head, Brian. Now, does a man who kidnaps children hit himself over the head? Stick himself out in the woods? That doesn't sound like very good detective work to me, Brian. Perhaps we ought to listen to that FBI man, Mr. Burke."

"I'm working closely with Mr. Burke," Brian said. "Naturally we've thought of those things. We don't know that Father Joe is involved in this. But let's say for now that somehow he is. Let's say that he had an accomplice. The two

men were going to ask for a ransom, only,
whoever Father Joe was working with decided
why split the ransom? He grabs the kids, hits
Father Joe over the head, thinks he's dead, and
leaves him in the woods. Only Father Joe isn't
dead. I admit that it puts the Father in a dark
light, and Kate here has told me what a good
man he is, but right now it's all we have. We
know the Father lied about being on family business in Baltimore. He never even got to Baltimore. We called his family there. Why did he
lie? No, the thing we have got to concentrate on
is this: Your three boys were taken. What's the
pattern? Is it money? If so, why you three? I
don't have time to be polite here, but of the
three of you, it's no secret that only Arlene's
family is really well off. So why Skeeter and
Danny?"

"Well," said Kate, following Arlene Conley's
line of reasoning, "if money is the case, why am
I the only one who has gotten a ransom note?
And you're not even convinced about that one—
despite the call I got."

"I don't know," Brian said. "I was just using
that for conjecture. But let's say there is another
motive, one that's not based on money. Which
gets me back to my first question. Is there something the kids share against the Father? Or
against somebody else, somebody the Father
may know, for example. Something that would
make this person want to take the kids. You
have to help me here. But supposing there was
such a thing, Father Joe and his accomplice want
to get back at these kids. Or let's try some other
lines of reasoning. Maybe Father Joe is mad at

the Church. Getting even by taking these symbols of the Church—the senior altar boys. Why else *would* someone take your children? Is it to get back at the Church or because of something the kids did? Or is it to get back at you? For something you did?"

Brian looked around the room, intently gazing at the Conleys and the Bannons and finally at Kate. When his eyes met hers they softened some, as though he were apologizing for having to be this direct. She smiled at him. He was a good man. Strong and compassionate. But his questions stirred something in her. What if the person *had* something against all of them? The families? After all, it was the families who would suffer if any harm came to the children. The thought sent a pain through her chest, and she felt such a deep anxiety that she wanted to get up and run from the house. Suddenly it seemed there was no air at all in the room. Yet she had to stay, had to force herself to think.

"My Skeeter loves Father Joe," Nancy Bannon said in a choked voice. "He's always liked him. I'll admit I've had some reservations about his Folk Masses, and his closeness with the kids. I mean, at one time he seemed like a kind of hippie to me. There was even talk, a while back, that Father Joe used marijuana, but that was a couple of years ago. Since then he's become a respected member of the community. I mean, why would he have anything against my Skeeter?"

She started to cry, a deep sobbing that threatened to become uncontrollable. John Bannon reached over and awkwardly held her hand.

"There's something else here," Arlene Conley said. "Since Billy and Danny have never really gotten along that well, the likelihood that they teamed up to do anything to Father Joe or to anyone else is extremely remote. Wouldn't you agree with that, Kate?"

"Yes," Kate said. "I would. But that brings us back to one of Brian's other theories. That whoever has done this is trying to get back at *us*. Now, Nancy mentioned how she felt about Father Joe. I have to say in the beginning I had some reservations also, but I never said anything. I only discussed them with one person. Paddy. And he never mentioned anything to anyone else, to my knowledge."

Finally George Conley coughed and spoke up.

"Well, I've never been particularly fond of Father Joe. I mean, he's kind of a performer, I think. I've often thought that some of his so-called modern advice, to teenagers especially, has been almost blasphemous. He's been very 'modern' on birth control, things like that. The truth is most of Father Joe's opposition has come from parents of teenagers. Not from parents with kids around ten."

There was a long, awkward silence. Brian looked around the room, then shook his head.

"All right," he said. "I don't expect anyone to come up with the answer this second. I want you all to think about one more thing in relation to Father Joe. Perhaps he tried to interfere with the kidnapper. Maybe he caught him in the act? Keep thinking about that.

"Now, if you could all think back to the past, and not necessarily the recent past, is there anything that binds you in this room? Anything that happened between you? I mean, as far back as you can remember. Before you were married, even, if that's the case. Something, anything that someone would hold against you?"

John Bannon wrung his hands, then shifted uneasily on the couch. He looked up at the gold American eagle mounted over the fireplace. He got up and absentmindedly straightened it.

"Listen," he said, turning around. "I think . . . I think we're wasting valuable time sitting here rooting through the past. The truth is, our kids are missing. Shouldn't we be turning every possible hiding place—basements and warehouses and abandoned buildings, whatever— upside down instead of sitting here playing games? I just don't think this is a very businesslike way to get things done."

Nancy Bannon looked up at her husband and held his hand. He looked down at her and meekly sat down.

Brian nodded his head.

"I assure you that, while we are sitting here, both the town police and the FBI are doing exactly that. Every possible hiding place, including the woods where Father Joe was found, is being combed once, twice, and again. But we have to try to establish a motive. Now stick with me, please. Is there anything, anything at all in your common pasts that could have caused someone, not necessarily Father Joe, but anyone, to want to get revenge on you? Please think."

"Well, I can think of one thing," George Conley said. "It's probably not important, though."

"What is it?" Brian said. "It doesn't matter how trivial it seems."

"Well, it has to do with Mick Shea. Maybe you remember, John?"

"You mean the football team?" John Bannon said, crossing his legs. "Surely you can't think . . ."

"Just tell it," Brian said. "I'm sorry, but we don't know how much time we have."

Kate felt Brian's words cut through her.

"Well, it was back when we were in high school at Mercy High. Mick was the football coach then."

"I remember now," Brian said. "He was pretty successful too. But then he suddenly quit and started working with the Optimist Leagues."

"Only he didn't quit," George said. "Back in those days we had a code. Whatever went on with the team—well, it stayed within the team. Not like today, with athletes running to the press. I guess we were really kind of afraid of our coaches. They seemed like gods. At least Mick Shea did. The problem was he thought he *was* God. He was brutal on the field. He slapped Paddy once for missing a tackle, and another time he asked me for my helmet and then hit me across the face with it. I guess young people today would have gotten together and told the school, but we didn't do that. Instead, we just agreed to quit the team. Paddy quit, and John and I, and quite a few of the other boys. The word got back to the higher-ups pretty quickly. Paddy, John and I were called in and we told them, though we felt bad about doing it, just how brutal he had been. Mick was allowed to resign quietly, but with that resignation ended his real dream, which was to coach Boston College. He called me and told me that. He was plenty angry, and drunk, and I still remember his words. He said, 'Someday I'm going to end your dreams just like you little fairies ended mine.' I was scared for a while, but then I forgot all about it. But we haven't talked to one another since. Still, I can't believe that he'd . . ."

"Very interesting," Brian said. "All right, I'm going to have another talk with him."

"It's going to stir him up," Nancy Bannon said, with tears in her eyes. "I hate to have all our neighbors think we're digging up their pasts."

"I know," Brian said. "It won't be pleasant, and there will be some ruffled feelings. But we have no choice. Was there anything else?"

"Yes," John Bannon said, "though I really hate to tell this. It's about Monsignor Merja."

"John," George said, "we've never talked about this."

"I know," John Bannon said, "but maybe it's important. Paddy, George and I were seventeen. Monsignor Merja still had high hopes. He was one of the bright young priests of the diocese. He'd always been a member of the Chancery in Boston doing administrative tasks, the safest and surest way to make Bishop. He'd been sent to St. Dominic's to gain pastoral experience, but the word was that he was soon to return to diocesan headquarters in Boston. He never got back, I'm afraid, partially because of us. We were all altar boys, though we were a little older than our sons. Anyway, we were all influenced by the modern ideas that were taking shape in the Church, and we had been having a running debate with Monsignor Merja about Transubstantiation. We argued that when you drank the grape juice, and ate the wafer, it was merely a symbolic ritual. How could anyone believe that the grape juice and the wafers would actually become the blood and body of Christ? It seemed preposterous to us, and I suppose the three of us were rough on Merja, whom we thought, to be perfectly frank, was a pompous old fool."

"John," Nancy Bannon said, "I'm shocked."

"Not as shocked as you're going to be," John said, looking ominously over at George Conley. "Well, this debate became quite a cause for us, I'm afraid. And Monsignor Merja began to take his anger out on us. He took our offerings—the few dollars we got as altar boys—and made us donate them to the Church. He constantly got on our backs, and generally made us furious. We finally decided to give him a living example of why he was wrong. One weekend we heard that Bishop Speaks was coming in for an Ordination. There was to be a lot of pageantry and the three of us decided to teach Monsignor Merja a lesson. If the wine was transformed into blood anyway, why not put some real blood in the cup? After all, if the man was drinking blood due to hocus pocus, he shouldn't notice the difference."

Arlene Conley's mouth dropped open.

"You didn't," she said.

"I'm afraid we did. We stole some blood from the Red Cross, though later we donated some to make up for it. But I'll never forget the look on the Bishop's face when he took a sip of the 'wine.' His cheeks puffed out, he turned and looked at Monsignor Merja, and spit the stuff right out on him."

"My God," Kate said. "I recall that incident. But they said that the Bishop was taken sick. No one ever mentioned anything about the blood."

"Not to anyone in town," John Bannon said. "But privately, Monsignor Merja was enraged. Not only embarrassed, but deadly angry. He told us that we were the spirit of the Devil. God, he would have liked to have had us excommunicated. It was a long while before our apologies—and we did feel terrible about it—began to sink in. You see, that was why I was so surprised that he allowed our children to become altar boys. It seemed like the ultimate act of Christian forgiveness, because I suspect the day that the Bishop spat out the blood was the last day anyone ever thought about bringing Merja back to the Chancery. In short, I think we ruined his career. Now, I have a question for you, Brian."

"Yes?" Brian said.

"Does Merja seem like a forgiving and kind man? I mean, forgetting the fact that he's a priest?"

"Not particularly," Brian said. "But just because he's stern and rather rigid doesn't mean he couldn't find it in his heart to forgive you. Sometimes stern men, especially priests, fight their own worst impulses and are capable of acts of generosity simply because they want to prove to themselves they can change and act in a Christian way."

"That's true, I suppose," John Bannon said. "But if you're looking everywhere, I thought you should know."

He looked down at his feet. His wife, Nancy, sat still next to him. The story had obviously shocked her and Kate wondered whether she could take much more.

Yet now Kate recalled something too.

"I remember another time," she said. "Paddy told me about it. It was the accident the three of you were involved in. I guess this story reminded me of it. It was when you broke Retreat."

"I recall that night very well," George Conley said.

"Tell us about it, please," Brian said.

George Conley nodded his head and began to speak. There was a tension in his voice as he recalled the night Paddy, John and he had gone over to the Mt. Barrow Passionist House in Fleming, New Hampshire, on Retreat. High school seniors at the time, the three of them had been full of high spirits, and after two nights there they had started to go a little crazy from the diet of religion and solitude. On the second day, they met three boys from Dorset with similar feelings. Boys named Billy Riley, who was a high school halfback, Thomas Flannagan, and Gus Coppazano. By the third night all of them had worked up a powerful thirst for some excitement and some liquor, and by eight o'clock that evening they had broken Retreat and gone back down into town for some serious drinking. It had been a good night, filled with Irish whiskey, town girls and dancing until 2 a.m. Just the kind of night to thrust out the rigors and sadnesses of Retreat. Everything had gone well and as they climbed into the Chevrolet, George felt that it was one of the best nights of his life. He felt clear, with that particular clarity alcohol brings just before it drops you off the edge into chaos and confusion. Which was why he wanted to drive. He felt as though he could steer the car back as though it were on tracks. Nothing could stop him now. But Bill Riley wanted to drive more, and he was a very big halfback from Dorset. He was also very drunk, too drunk George knew to get behind the wheel. But then so had he been many a time, and nothing had ever happened. They started off up Route 17, back toward the mountain, and for a time everything had been fine. Then Riley had started to show off. He could drive with one hand, see? He could drive without any hands or knees, because the car knew where to go all on its own. They veered—just for a second—over the second line and hit head on with a bread truck headed for Dorset. Rolls, white bread, and English muffins shared the road with the bent and injured bodies of the boys. Luckily for the boys from Mt. Olive, they were in the back and at the last instant Bill Riley had managed to steer to the left so the crash wasn't dead center. When they found Riley, the steering column had gone through his chest. Coppazano had a broken arm and bad facial injuries. Flannagan's face too was badly burned and his right arm smashed. George came away with a badly broken arm but nothing more. John Bannon got a broken leg and contusions on it. And Paddy—always the lucky one until the disease struck him down—came out of the whole thing with nothing more than a bad bump on the head.

"The guys in the front really took the brunt of

the accident, but if you're looking for some connection there I wouldn't think of it. We all went to the hospital to see the injured boys and they had nothing against us. As for Riley's relatives, well, we went to the funeral and saw his parents. They were two sweet old people and they were deeply hurt by what happened, but certainly they wouldn't be capable of kidnapping. They're probably dead by now, anyway."

"Did Riley have any relatives, or a girlfriend?" Brian asked.

"Yes, he had a sister. She was younger than he. Just a kid. I don't think he had a girlfriend. I don't remember anyone like that at his funeral. But then, I didn't know him very well. He was a popular boy at Dorset High School, so maybe there was someone who had a crush on him or something. I just wouldn't know."

"John," Brian said, "can you remember anything else?"

"Nothing else. Just that Flannagan had to have surgery, but he came out okay, I recall. I talked to him when he was recovering. He was scarred some, but he said he would be okay."

"Was he bitter?" Brian said.

"No," George and John said in unison.

"I wonder where they are now," Brian said.

"I heard something about him. Flannagan, I mean," Kate said. "He went on to St. John's Seminary in Boston. Perhaps by now he's a priest. Wait, I remember something else, too. Coppazano *was* bitter about what happened. His legs were hurt. I don't know what happened to him."

"That's all?" Brian said, slightly deflated.

"Yes," George Duncan said. "He wasn't so happy to see us, but then, we were lucky and he wasn't. I didn't take it seriously."

"God," Arlene Conley said. "Must we suspect everything?"

"I'm afraid so," Brian said.

"Then I don't know where to start," Arlene said. "My Billy is out there. God knows where or who's got him. My baby."

Arlene Conley began to cry. Kate got up from her chair, ran across the room, and hugged Arlene Conley tightly. Arlene's hands clutched her back, and then Kate felt her own tears coming.

"It's all right, Arlene. It's all right. We're going to find them. We are. They're alive, and we're going to find them. I swear it."

She turned and looked at Brian.

"I mean it," she said. "We are going to find those boys. We have to. Whatever you think has anything to do with it, look it up. Do whatever you have to, Brian. And we'll help you. But we are going to find our sons."

Wednesday, 11 p.m.

It was late when Brian drove Kate home. He felt she was too upset to drive and so Brian had insisted on taking her. She looked out the window as though she were dead. Hearing the stories the men had told had made her feel even worse. The thought that people she knew, respected, even loved—people like Father Joe, Mick Shea, and Monsignor Merja—could be suspected of kidnapping and, possibly, hurting Danny and the other children, threw her into a deep depression. Was it possible that all along she had deluded herself about her townsfolk, the people she saw every day? Was it true what they said about small towns, that behind the smiles, the kind gestures, there was resentment and frustration that would one day burst forth in an act of monstrous irrational violence? Was she so naive that she simply hadn't seen it? And, if she was, then wasn't she really guilty of not protecting her own son? She should have known, she thought, how frail human beings are, how resentful they were, how they could harbor grudges for years and years, and she should have protected him. Brian looked over at her and seemed to catch her mood without the exchange of words.

"I can see you sitting there blaming yourself," Brian said. "Well, don't do that to yourself, do you hear me? There was no way you could know these things. Listen, you're a wonderful mother."

"If I'm a wonderful mother," Kate said, "what's my little boy doing kidnapped? Oh my God, Brian, I'm falling apart."

She reached over and held his hand. Brian felt the pressure of her fingertips. His desire to protect her, to hold her was so immense that he almost stopped the car. But that wouldn't have been right. She needed his support now because of her son. Nothing more.

"Listen," he said, "there is something I have been holding back from the others. But I want you to know. We looked at all of Father Joe's things and found something curious—on his shoes."

Kate took a deep breath. "What was it?" she asked, surprised that her voice was so composed.

"It was a kind of mold. Now that might not sound like much, but it was a mold that you wouldn't get out in the woods. Not up there. It was as if he'd been somewhere else. You know, mold grows in dark, damp places. We're checking it out. Listen, I know you're upset, but you can help on this case. I want you to get over to the hospital tomorrow, and talk to Father Joe. Just keep making contact with him. He liked you, right?"

"Yes. I think," Kate said. "After tonight I don't know anything. I feel . . . I . . ."

Tears came down Kate's face, and Brian held her hand more tightly.

"It's all right, Katie," he said, using the old term of endearment from so many years ago. "Go ahead and cry. It'll do you good."

But she shook her head, took out a handkerchief and wiped her eyes.

"No. I'll get over there. I'll talk to him. If he can hear anything at all, I'll reach him somehow."

"That's just it," Brian said. "You may reach him. And if you do, maybe he can tell us something. If he did try to stop the kidnapper, then he's the key."

He turned down her street and looked up at Mt. Olive in the moonlight. They had parked up there, he thought, so long ago.

"Get some sleep," he said. "And believe me, we're going to find Danny. I mean it."

Kate nodded, and then suddenly reached over and kissed Brian on the cheek.

"I don't know how to thank you," she said.

"Good night, Kate," Brian said. "I'll call you tomorrow. First thing."

Brian felt the weariness in his bones. When had he last gotten any sleep? Two nights ago. Yet, he was wired now. There was no time to worry about sleep. He sat in front of St. Dominic's Church, and stared at the dark rectory. It was a shame to wake up Monsignor Merja, but on the other hand, it was sometimes best to conduct interrogations in the dead of night. A man coming out of sleep was less able to construct an on-the-spot alibi.

Slowly Brian got out of the car and headed up to the stone house.

After the bell rang twice, the door was opened by an exhausted-looking Brother Michael.

"Good evening, Brother Michael," Brian said. "I'm terribly sorry to call at this hour, but I need to talk to Monsignor Merja."

"But Monsignor Merja is asleep," Brother Michael said, scratching his full beard.

"No, I'm not," said a voice from behind Brother Michael. "Let him in, please."

Brian walked in as Brother Michael moved out of the way. He gave Brian a resentful stare as the Chief walked by.

"Good evening, Monsignor," Brian said. "I must have a talk with you. It's about the children."

"I hope you haven't come here at this hour to get me to reconsider my feelings about the church's stand on this matter. I haven't and I won't get the church involved in such a matter. I stated my feelings very strongly at the town meeting—you're aware of that."

"It's not about that," Brian said. "May we have some privacy?"

Brother Michael turned his back to the men and disappeared down the hall.

Brian took a seat on the deep leather couch and watched as the Monsignor sat down in a highbacked leather chair across from him. His lips were pressed together tightly. He looked severe, Brian thought, perhaps like a man under pressure.

"I'm here to ask you about an incident that happened a long time ago," Brian said. "An incident involving the fathers of the three missing boys."

Slowly, and with a measure of detachment, as though he were reciting a laundry list, Brian recounted the story of Monsignor Merja's greatest humiliation. When he was done, he sat back and, for effect, pulled out a cigarette.

"What do you want me to say?" Monsignor Merja said. "Do you want me to break down like some television criminal and confess that I have always harbored hatred for the three parents, and, to get even with them, I stole their children? Well, I hate to disappoint you, Mr. Dolan, but I anticipated this a long time ago. As soon as all three of the boys disappeared, I knew that eventually the story would come back to haunt me. It was a terribly embarrassing moment for me, and I was quite angry. Quite angry. I was also a good deal younger. I was also rigid. No, let's say that I was a highly traditional thinker, and still am. I see very little in the new theological wisdoms and don't mind saying so. Perhaps . . . perhaps sometimes I am a snob. You look surprised. But do not think that because I am of the old school that I am not capable of reflection, that I am not capable of kindness or regret. When the incident happened, those few who knew about it assumed that I had been passed over, but in fact, nothing could be further from the truth. Though I was at first upset, I knew that the incident itself was unimportant, only an embarrassment. In time I came to understand better my relationship to William's Crossing. You see, I had grown to love it here. I speak personally now, which is not usual for me.

People think that I have no personal feelings, but this is not true either. I found that I was happy here. I realized I loved St. Dominic's, that I cared deeply about serving God here. I realized that all the tests life had to offer could be found right here. In some ways the boys' trick on me turned out to be a blessing in disguise. For it gave me a chance to examine myself, my own anger, my desire for advancement. I thought about it long and hard. What would it mean if I could not go back to Boston? I found that it meant very little. I had become happy here. So when the time came for them to consider me, I told them I was happy where I was. After all, the Bishop was a forgiving man. He never held the incident against me. If you don't believe the story I've told you, please check my facts. I have come to believe that the day Paddy Riordan, John Bannon and George Conley made the Bishop drink the blood was my own small test of character and faith. I never told anyone else this before. I am not the kind of man who believes in public confessionals. But I tell you now, because I want you to understand why I made Danny, Billy, and Skeeter senior altar boys. It was my own sense of irony, my own way of thanking God for helping me find the right place to serve him. I would never have been happy as a Bishop. Lucky is the man who knows his own limitations."

Brian smoked the cigarette slowly, and nodded his head.

"All right, Monsignor. That's an interesting, even a moving tale. But I need to know your whereabouts on all three of the days the boys disappeared."

The Monsignor smiled wearily.

"That's easy. When Danny Riordan disappeared, I was standing outside the church. The day Billy Conley disappeared I was attending a lecture in Boston, and I have half a dozen witnesses to say so, and when Skeeter Bannon was taken I was here in the rectory. I found out about it from the radio. Brother Charles was here. Michael Shea, too. I'm afraid I'm going to be a poor suspect, Chief Dolan."

"Yes," Brian said, rising. "Sorry to have bothered you."

"I will pray for the children," the Monsignor said.

His tone was once again formal and slightly cold. He had hidden, Brian thought, hidden behind the mask of formality. It would be nice, Brian felt himself thinking, if you could equate that formality with coldness. But, after hearing Merja's tale, Brian knew that it wasn't so. Unless he was very very wrong, Monsignor Merja was not their man.

Thursday, 2 a.m.

BRIAN DROVE the broken-down Dodge to McDonald's on North Main. The restaurant had recently gone to twenty-four hours and he was grateful there was someplace in this sleepy town to get something to eat. A light drizzle had started coming down, and Brian felt the rain cool on his face. It brought him around a little. He was beyond sleep now, he thought, and perhaps beyond good detective work as well, but he had to move on. He had to push himself. He walked into the neon room and stared at the clown's face smiling up at him. Suddenly he had a terrific urge to smash it. It seemed to be mocking him. How long did they have before whoever had taken the kids decided to kill them? Maybe at this very moment they were being tortured. He tried to push the thought from his mind. He ordered two cheeseburgers and two cups of coffee, and sat like a zombie in the cold plastic seat, picking listlessly at the food. Was Kate asleep? God, he hoped so. You could only go so long without sleep, especially when you were under such pressure.

In spite of himself Brian recalled the past with Kate. Seeing her again, being next to her, and worrying with her through the ordeal had brought them close, perhaps closer than they had been as kids. Though that barely seemed possible. He remembered the way she had looked at him the first time she had met him—in the high school library. She had been looking for a reference book he was using. Something about the Great Spanish Empire. When the earnest, pretty girl in the plaid dress came over to see him about the book, he had started a conversation about a subject of which he knew next to nothing. In a few minutes she was rattling off the names of the principals in the Spanish Armada, names Brian still dimly recalled—Henry of Navarre, Prince Philip, and Sir Francis Drake. He loved her excited and enthusiastic voice, the good, clean, innocent strength in her eyes, and, in what seemed like one minute, Brian found himself entranced by Kate McGraw. He had walked her home that day on the pretense that he still needed to look over the book, so why shouldn't they have a soda while he finished taking his notes? It was a weak ploy, and she smiled at him as if she was all too aware of what he was really interested in. Yet, there was an immediate rapport betweeen them that was strange, for Brian was known as one of the quieter boys in the school.

Now Brian stared down at his soggy hamburger, and shook his head. Paddy had been going out with Phyllis Prevas, a tall girl with giant breasts. It never occurred to Brian that Paddy and Kate would hit it off so well. But they had right from the beginning. For a while, the four of them had gone everywhere together. The four of them went to movies and dances and fairs together. They drank their first beers, bought their first cars (Brian's a great-looking Mustang). No, there was no end to their happiness, until one day Paddy came by and told him that he had to talk with him.

"Hey, pal, I wish this hadn't happened, but, well, Kate and I have decided to get married." Brian had been flabbergasted. He adored Kate, was wild about her. He drove furiously over to her house to talk to her, find out it wasn't true. But it was. Oh, she had been faithful to him. She was deeply distressed by what had happened, perhaps almost as much so as he. It was just that Paddy had started calling her, and they had talked, and then he had stopped by again, just as a friend, and pretty soon something had happened. Brian had planned on screaming things at her, but what was the use? There was something so straight about her, so honest, that he came to understand it almost at once. Of course they were going to fall in love. Paddy was the most popular guy in the class, and Kate the smartest and most attractive girl. He had always suspected back then that she was somehow out of his league. He had been deeply hurt and, in the end, they had moved away. He had finished school, and then suddenly, without even knowing why, he joined the police force. It had seemed like a whim at first, and he wasn't sure at all he would go through with it. But in the end he had surprised even himself. He was a classic late bloomer. For in no time it was apparent to everybody that he was born to be a cop. He was one of the few cops whom ordinary citizens could relate to. He had good instincts and was resourceful. In a few years he had made detective and then suddenly, when old Chief Thomas died, he was made Chief. It was a tough life sometimes, long hours, low pay, and it had robbed him of a chance to have a real homelife. But he loved it. And he knew that few people worked at things they loved. At least he had that. After Kate he'd never found another woman he wanted to marry.

Now Brian looked at his watch. There were more stops to make. No time to rest now. He thought of the three boys. Were they able to breathe? Were they being fed? Slowly he got to his feet and threw the trash into the clown's-mouth trash can. Mick Shea. He remembered him from high school. Outside the eastern sky was lightening. Sunrise was not far off.

Mick Shea's bachelor apartment was in a lower-middle-class area of town. The apartments were called the Lan Lea, and there was a black rose outside on the sign, which time and the weather had worn away. It made the rose look as though it had wilted. Brian stared at the white stucco walls, the black iron railings. The place was post-war vintage and looked more like a motel than an apartment complex. He wandered around, past a soda machine which glowed almost supernaturally in the pre-dawn. Finally he found the right bell. He had to ring three times before Michael "The Mick" Shea turned on the light and growled, "Who's there?"

Brian gave his name and the door slowly opened. Mick Shea looked and smelled as though he had been drinking hard for a long time. His hair was mussed, and the deep lines in his face seemed put in by a machine.

"I've got to talk to you, Mick. It's urgent."

"Jesus, Brian, I can barely walk. Or see. Had a little party tonight. Our softball team won a big one. Jesus, what time is it?"

"It's 3 a.m. I'm sorry," Brian said. "May I come in?"

"Oh yeah, sure. Place is a little messy though."

Brian walked into a barely furnished room. There were beer cans and whiskey bottles scattered all over the place.

Mick Shea walked to the little kitchenette and opened the refrigerator.

"Care for a beer, Bri?"

"No thanks. Listen, I'm here about the children. My time is short, Mick."

"Oh, the kids. They find . . . I mean, you find those kids yet? Good kids. That Billy Conley is going to be a hell of a ballplayer. Good in all sports. You should see him play football. Kid's a natural athlete."

"Like his father was?" Brian said, staring Mick Shea in the eyes.

"Yeah," Mick said. "Like his father was."

It was as if someone had thrown a bucket of cold water in his face.

"You didn't like his father a whole lot, isn't that right?" Brian said.

"Did his father tell you that?" Mick Shea said. "Did he? Hey, wait a minute, you don't think

that I, the old Mickeroo, had anything to do with
those kids disappearing, do you?"

"Why not?" Brian said. "The three kids had
three daddies. The three daddies didn't like your
brutal methods of coaching and got you booted
from the high school which, I understand,
knocked you out of the Boston College coaching
assignment and consigned you to a lifetime of
CYO ball. That could make a man pretty bitter.
Bitter enough, for example, to call George Conley and tell him that someday you would kill his
dreams like he killed yours. I think those were
your words?"

The Mick slammed his beer down on the for-
mica table. He started to approach Brian, but
tripped on a whiskey bottle and tried to regain
his balance by grabbing onto a table lamp which
he knocked onto the floor. The bare bulb made
the place brighter than the McDonald's Brian
had just left. Mick staggered, but righted himself
and reached down and picked up the lamp.

"I never said anything like that. Never."

"He says you did. Both he and John Bannon
know you hate them. They also know about your
drinking. And they didn't have to tell me about
your run-ins with parents over the years. You're
legendary for pushing around twelve-year-olds."

"Hey," said Mick Shea. "I got my methods
and they work. Ask me, too much of this namby-
pamby shit around. I'll tell you straight. Mothers
and fathers are worried if they're being too harsh
on a kid. I say spare the rod and spoil the child.
You look at this whole country. It's weak,
Bridey, it's very weak. Iranians push us around
and the Africans push us around and the Mex-

icans. Hell, we're just a buncha sitting ducks. I
teach kids character."

"Does that include smashing them in the face
with their football helmets?"

The Mick waved his beer around, slopping
some of it onto the rug.

"Oh I know where you got that all right. You
got that from John Bannon. That's a story he's
made up and told for years and years. I never
done anything of the kind to him. I don't see him
out there coaching. They leave it up to the Mick,
but when the Mick has so much as a harsh word
for their little darlings, then they scream child
abuse. Well, we're raising a whole world of sissies. That's the truth."

"Maybe you like beating up on kids," Brian
said, suddenly out of patience with this loud-
mouth. He walked toward Mick and grabbed
him by the collar. "Maybe, tough guy, you want
to try and play Vince Lombardi with me, huh?"

"Hey, what's this?"

"Maybe you decided that those three kids
should learn how to have strong moral fiber.
Maybe you decided to take them off somewhere
and teach them privately."

"Let go of me, Bridey. I don't have to talk to
you. I haven't done anything."

"Let go? Sure."

Brian put his foot behind Mick Shea and
pushed him down on the floor.

"What the hell are you doing? I play hard, but
I wouldn't hurt a kid. You ask anybody. I like
kids. I wanted to have some myself, but . . .
but . . ."

"But what?"

"But my wife, Sheilah, she left me years ago. She couldn't stand this town. She wanted Boston. She left me, and went off to Boston and then to New York. I was pretty bitter about it. But I got over it. I just think we got to be tough. We're America."

"Where were you when the boys were taken?" Brian said.

"I don't know exactly. Was it during the last three days? Well, that's easy. I been down to Connecticut playing softball. I got my whole team to back me up."

"You're going to need them," Brian said, suddenly feeling the anger flare up wildly in him again.

He reached down and picked Mick Shea up by his collar.

"I don't like guys who abuse kids, trying to make them pay for their own goddamned mistakes. You hear me? I ever hear that you hit, or even touched, one more kid, I'll have your ass in jail for the next ten years. You think I'm kidding, try it. Save the rah-rah shit for your buddies down at the bar."

"I don't have to take this," Mick screamed as Brian pushed him back up against the wall hard. "This is police brutality. I can get a lawyer. Come barging in here—you got a lot of nerve."

"Get a lawyer," Brian said. "I'd love to have you in court. The judge would love to hear your story. You understand?"

Brian didn't wait for Mick Shea's reply. He walked over the littered floor and let himself out.

Back in the car, he gripped the wheel with both hands and took several deep breaths. They were getting to him now. All of it was getting to him. There was an anger, a monstrous anger rising in him he was struggling to control.

He thought of Kate. Of Danny. Where the hell could he be? Where?

He gunned the motor and started the rainy morning ride back to the office. No time for sleep. There were phone calls to make.

Now that he was on his own, everything came easily. All things made sense. Take the passage in the *Rule of St. Benedict*, Chapter 37:

Let them . . . receive compassionate consideration and take their meals before the regular hours.

When he used to read that line, when he was studying hard to be the way they said he must be, then it seemed silly, a useless line of drivel to be memorized and forgotten. But now, now that he was God himself, yes, now that he was making the rules, it seemed to be written just for him. It seemed to fit. Everything fits when you are God. You know what to do and how to do it. All things flow from you.

He smiled and fixed the sandwiches.

"I will be your mother," he whispered. "I will be your father. I will come to you, little children. Yes, sweet, dear little boys. Boys who shall be my body, my life. I am coming to see you now. With food, with the staff of life. I am coming. You will be glad to see me, very glad, at last."

Thursday, 6 a.m.

BRIAN PULLED the Dodge up to a large A-frame unit on the northwestern edge of Mt. Olive. It was here in the winter that the trendy skiing crowd descended down the sharp pine-covered "A" trail of the mountain, and it was here that Mike Baines lived.

O'Toole had tried to interview him twice but hadn't found him home. So Brian had decided to try an early-morning visit.

There was something about a ski instructor that seemed so out of character for Kate. She had explained that she had met Mike Baines at Filene's Basement one day, while she was having a terrible anxiety attack. She had thought she had lost her wallet and all her credit cards, and she had been in a panic. He had helped her find the wallet (she had left it on the counter), and, in gratitude, she had joined him for a drink. He was sympathetic, a good listener, and soon she had come to depend on him. At first he had been great with Danny too, but after a while it became apparent to her that they were not right for each other. Baines was a bit of a prima donna. He had been an Olympic skiing star and was used to women doing his bidding. He was not used to independent women, and he had grown angry at Danny for monopolizing her time.

Brian stopped at Unit 42 on the Northwest Ridge. The condos were ugly, soulless-looking buildings with orange iron rails and poured concrete. Brian walked up the steps and rapped on the door. Inside he could hear Bruce Springsteen playing on the stereo.

The door opened and a blonde in a bikini stood before him.

"Hello," she said. "You here to go on the sunrise swim?"

"No. I didn't even know there was one," Brian said. "I'm here to see Mr. Baines. Michael Baines. Maybe he's getting his trunks on inside?"

"You sound like a cop," the girl said, laughing.

"My name is Dolan. I am a cop," Brian said. "Is Mr. Baines around?"

"Yes," a voice said. "Right here."

From the bedroom Mike Baines appeared. He had on a pair of tight black swimming trunks, and his body was perfectly muscular. He had short clipped hair and a good, solid face. Brian thought he looked like the Marlboro Man. Images of Kate naked in bed with Baines tortured him. He tried to keep to the subject at hand.

"I'm here to talk to you about. . ."

"About Danny Riordan," Mike Baines said. "Cindy, this is Officer Dolan, I take it?"

"Yeah," Brian said, "but it's Chief Dolan. I have a few questions I want to ask you. Alone."

"Oh wow," Cindy said, holding her head. "Cops are such a drag. We're trying to party. Up with old Sol . . ."

"Go ahead out to the pool, Cindy," Baines said. "I'll join you in a minute."

The girl rolled her eyes and grabbed a towel, then left.

"You want a drink, Chief?" Baines asked.

"No," Brian said. He knew his tone was abusive.

"You find me distasteful," Baines said, pouring himself a drink. "You're wondering what a woman like Kate saw in me."

"Let's forget about that," Brian said. "Do you know why I'm here?"

"Yes," Baines said. "But I do wish you would sit down. Over on the couch there is quite comfortable. You'll have to pardon me. Cindy is a student here, and we're having a little fun. I've been having a few drinks."

Brian nodded and sat down. He looked around the room. It was painted stark white and had a couple of director's chairs and one Eames chair in the corner. On two walls were blowups of Baines in a USA Olympic Skiing Team outfit. He looked good going down the slopes.

"You're here because you are a savior of the middle class, a watchdog of society, a public servant. And you'd like to think that I am responsible for Danny Riordan's disappearance. Let me guess about that one too. Kate mentioned to you that I was jealous of her with the child. You thought, aha, spurned lover and child hater. I just go over to the good old ski area, pick up both the kidnapper and the kid. It's a charming idea, but the problem is, I've got alibis. On Sunday I was working all day setting up my sporting goods store here, with three witnesses, Cindy among them, to back me up. On Monday and Tuesday, more of the same."

"What did Kate ever see in you?" Brian said sarcastically.

"A sympathetic ear, perhaps?" Baines said. "Maybe she liked me because I'm good at having fun. A lot of women find me attractive for a time, and then . . . unfortunately, they get to know me. After that they like me less."

Brian got up and walked around the room.

"You did have fights about her son, Baines?"

"That's right. I wanted her to get out a little more. I wanted her to enjoy herself, see the world a bit. She's a wonderful girl, but she's so straight. I thought I could loosen her up, make her enjoy life a little."

"Do you enjoy life, Mr. Baines?" Brian said.

"Hey, I'm the life of the party," Baines said. He set down his glass and attempted to do a handstand.

"Do you realize we're talking about a kid that might not be coming back?" Brian said.

"I do," Baines said, giving up on the handstand and sitting back down in the chair. "I also realize that he's a wonderful kid and that he was lucky as hell to have a mother like Kate. I didn't dislike the kid. I disliked what the kid did to us."

Brian was jarred by Baines's words.

"Look, when I met Kate she really was on the rebound. She was deeply distressed by Paddy's death, and she needed somebody. I came along at the wrong time. When we got to know one another a little better, we realized we came from two very different worlds. I thought for a time I could make the switch. You know, maybe I'd marry her and live in William's Crossing and wear leather patches on the sleeves of my jackets and have a CountrySquire Station Wagon and a dog named Buster, and me and the kid would go to Little League, and there would be pinochle games and barbecues. Things like that. It was a mistake, Officer Dolan. *Chief* Dolan. I'm not ca- capable of that kind of thing. For a time I didn't want to admit it because I had fallen in love with her. It was the damndest thing. I didn't love Wil- liam's Crossing, or that tight little church scene there. God, I felt strangled by it. But I did love her, and in some weird way I loved her because she was part of it. You see, in spite of everything I just said, I really grew to respect, well, people more because of Kate Riordan. She made me see that living for the moment isn't the only way to go. But, in the end, well, I'm just not a domestic scene kind of guy. I like the fast track too much. But Kate had me for a time, Chief. She had me doing laundry and fixing meals, and, worse, I was even liking it. Christ, I didn't care if I ever looked at another snow bunny. It was strange, Chief, not the way Mike Baines is used to going, I mean, I was turning into a real Fred MacMurray. I wish to hell I'd been able to cut it, because she's a great girl."

"And her son," Brian said, liking Baines in spite of himself.

"Her son," Baines said, "is a wise-ass little kid

who gets himself kicked around by one of the other kids who was snatched—Billy Conley. But he's a wonderful little wise-ass. I miss the kid, if you want to know the truth. I got to thinking I was his father for a while. Hey, I'm the Gold Medal kid. I didn't need that. I used to yell at her about him so I wouldn't feel too much, you know what I mean? I was getting to care about things too much down there. That is not Mike Baines's style."

"You have any idea where he is?" Brian said, walking toward the door.

"No," Mike Baines said. "I don't. But I'll tell you this. You ought to find that kid pretty soon."

Suddenly Mike Baines looked as though he was going to cry. He held up his glass and drank it down in a hurry and fell back in his chair.

"I love both of them. I wasn't like this when I was with her. But it was too much for me, you see? It was too confining, hemmed me in, cut out the action. But you better find that kid, Chief. Because, to tell you the truth, I haven't slept good one night since he was taken. Which is why I have been drinking. You see, I got this crazy idea that it was my fault. Is that weird?"

"How's that?" Brian asked.

"Because if I had stayed around and taken care of the little bugger, he might be here now, you know? So you find him, huh, Chief? And when you do, give Mike Baines a call."

Brian nodded and looked once again at the poised Olympic skier on the wall. Then he went out the door. From down below he heard a yell and saw the girl in the bathing suit waving and calling to him.

"Hey," she said, "tell Mike to hurry out. The water's great for April!"

Thursday, 10 a.m.

FATHER JOE was in a private room on the third floor at Holy Redeemer Hospital. He had intravenous tubing in him because he had been very dehydrated when Ed Devlin found him.

He was still not conscious, though he responded to certain stimuli like light and sound. Dr. Wheeler, the neurosurgeon, had arranged for Kate to spend time with Father Joe, but had told Kate it might be days, even weeks, before they could be sure as to whether he would make a full recovery.

"We know he's had some trauma injury. A blow to the head. But whether this was a fall or he was hit, it's still too early to know. Judging by the configuration of the injury, it could have been either. He has some peripheral consciousness, but that waxes and wanes. For some reason, it's a little better in the morning."

Since the blinds were drawn, Kate was forced to sit in semi-darkness. All she could focus on was the steady sound of his breathing, which was interrupted by periodic tossing and turning, as if he were having a bad dream.

Dr. Wheeler had said to her, "Try talking to him in a low voice. People think that unconscious people can't hear people talking to them. Our experience has been that they can and that they find the sound of other human voices soothing to them."

Kate had felt silly at first. Sitting in the dim room talking to someone she felt probably could not hear her. But as she spent the first hour talking to Father Joe, she felt he might be responding a bit. He seemed to move slightly in the bed. At one point she thought she heard a moan. She put her fingers to the side of his throat to see if she could feel any speech vibrations. She wasn't sure but she imagined that he was actually trying to talk.

Then Nancy Simpson, the charge nurse, entered the room. She checked Father Joe's IV, took his pulse and temperature, and emptied his catheter.

"How's he doing?" she asked Kate.

"He moved slightly, and I thought he was trying to talk. But he just looks so completely out of it."

The pretty, auburn-haired young nurse took Kate's hand.

"Don't be afraid. We call this path back to consciousness 'lightening up.' It can be kind of spooky. I've seen them out cold and then they pop awake, cursing a blue streak. It really can freak you out. If that should happen, just stay calm and ring for me. I'll be just down the hall. Don't be upset, it's not uncommon after one has had injuries like he's sustained."

Kate sat there thinking. I would like to talk

him awake. I would like to have a long conversation with him at the end of which he opened his eyes and said he was fine and told me what had happened to Danny. Why can't this nightmare be over? Why can't Father Joe just wake up and help me? Isn't that what priests are for? They are supposed to help you in your hour of need. Not the other way around. No one ever helped a priest. What kind of a lousy trick is this? My doing all the work and Father Joe just lying quiet as death.

She put her head down in her hands, determined to wait out Father Joe. He had to come around sooner or later, didn't he? She started all over again to plead with him, quietly, as she had been instructed.

"Father Joe, this is Kate Riordan. I know that you've had a hard time in the last couple of days. You've suffered a head injury, but you are going to be all right. Please believe me. I know that this is so.

"Now something terrible has happened. Maybe you know something about it and maybe you don't, but I really need your help. I'm going to try to explain to you what has happened. If you can help, if you hear me, please try to talk or move your head for yes or no. Please, this is a matter of life and death.

"You know my son, Danny. You know Billy Conley and Skeeter Bannon. Starting with Danny last Sunday, and the other boys on the following days, they've all disappeared.

"We have reason to think that you might know where they are. Why they have not come back. If you do, please tell me. Try to answer this question: Where are the boys?"

A low moan came from Father Joe's lips at that instant, almost like a whistle. Kate drew back in alarm.

"What?" she pressed on. "Do you know where the boys are?" Could he actually be responding? It was like a miracle. Sounds poured from the priest that were unintelligible. Kate put the question to him one more time.

"Where are the boys?"

No more sounds this time. Just one word that she heard distinctly as she tried to repeat it.

"Unner . . . unda . . . underr . . ."

Excitedly she pressed on.

"Under *where*? Under *where*, Father? Please tell me under *where*, under *what*?"

But it was no use. He was back in the deep sleep again. But he knew. If he could just be roused one more time to complete the sentence. Kate talked to him for another fifteen minutes without success. There were no sounds, no words, no movement.

Thursday, 11 a.m.

BACK AT the police station, Brian bit into a doughnut and stared at the pile of papers on his desk. Suddenly the phone rang.

"Dolan here."

"It's O'Toole. Nothing more on the ransom note—no more calls—but I found Billy Riley's sister. She's a hooker in Boston now. She's garbage."

"See if you can run her down tonight, O'Toole."

"Wait, Chief. There's about twenty more names of ex-girlfriends. Maybe one of them has harbored a grudge."

"I don't know," Brian said, dropping his guard. "I'm worried. By now there should have been a real ransom request."

"How are the mothers taking it?"

"Mrs. Conley is back to acting like a marine sergeant. I'm afraid if she gets any harder she'll turn brittle and crack into a million pieces. Mrs. Bannon is loaded up with so many tranquillizers she can't move at all. And Kate, well, she's got a lot of guts."

"We'll break it yet," O'Toole said.

"Yeah," Brian said. "Get back to me. Soon."

He hung up the phone, picked up the coffee, and sipped it. It was cold and tasted worse than the inside of his mouth.

"Coppazano," he said, trying to fight back the urge to fall down on his desk and just pass out.

He picked up the phone and tried Celia Coppazano's number again. The truth was he should get over there and see her, but there was no time. He had to try the phone. The phone rang again and again and echoed in his head. Again there was no answer. Christ, she had to get home sometimes. He was about to put down the phone when someone picked it up.

"Hello," he said, "is this Mrs. Anthony Coppazano?"

"That's right. Who is this?"

"Mrs. Coppazano, this is Chief Brian Dolan of William's Crossing. I'm calling about your son, Gus."

There was a sudden intake of breath on the other line.

"Wait a minute," she said, "I have to go get Tony."

"Mrs. Coppazano," Brian said, "wait a minute."

"Tony, they're calling about Gus. Tony, come here."

"Mrs. Coppazano . . ."

"You found Gus? Oh, thank God. Is he all right? Tell me he's all right."

"Mrs. Coppazano, I don't understand. I'm calling about . . ."

"You're not from the army? You said you

were a . . . I don't remember, who did you say you were?"

Brian could feel his hands get sweaty. It was something he had never gotten used to in police work. The moment when you ran into someone who had gone over the edge, who was lost. It could happen like this on the phone, or it could happen when you least expected it—at the end of an alley, or as you walked into the neighborhood bar. For the last time.

"Celia, give me the phone. Please."

"Hello, Mr. Coppazano?"

"Yes."

"My name is Chief Dolan. I'm over at William's Crossing. I'm trying to get in touch with your son."

"You are?" There was a bitter laugh at the other end of the line.

"What's wrong, sir?" Brian said, trying to offset the panic he could sense in the older man's voice.

"It's just that we've been trying to get in touch with our son too, Chief Dolan. For ten years. You see, he's missing in action in Vietnam. They told us they think he's dead, but we don't believe it. My wife, she held up for a long time, but the past few years, all the false hopes, and then the disappointments. It's worn her down."

"I'm sorry, sir," Brian said.

"Why did you want to see my son?"

"Well, it's about his accident at the Passionist House Retreat many years ago. Let me ask you, sir, how badly was he injured?"

"He broke his leg. But it healed. It wasn't bad."

Not bad enough to be turned down by the service, Brian thought. Missing. What if he had come back? Hadn't let anyone know? The thought seemed unlikely. Brian knew that ninety percent of those missing were dead, blown into bits so small that no one could ever find them. Still, there was the possibility.

"How did he respond?" Brian said.

"He was all right," Mr. Coppazano said. "He was bitter for a time because he was a swimmer. He wasn't able to swim so good after that. When the war came he coulda used his legs to get out. Like so many of those bums. Instead he knew a guy down at the draft board. While other kids were pulling strings to get out, Gus pulled some to get in. He told me he didn't want to see this country go communist. He wanted to fight for what's right. I think he's still alive, Chief Dolan. Listen, why are you calling me now?"

"Well, it's just a routine check," Brian said. "I'm sorry to bother you, sir. As you have undoubtedly heard, there are three missing kids in our town, sir. We have to check everybody who ever knew the families. Gus was in an accident with all of the fathers of the kids."

"And you think, you think my Gus is involved in kidnapping. Goddamn you, he's out there in the jungle somewhere, Dolan, and you think he's involved in taking kids?"

"No, sir," Brian said, "I don't. But I have to check. You said he was bitter. Perhaps his bitterness got to him."

There was a long breath on the other end of the line.

"I'm trying to control myself, Chief Dolan.

I'm trying to put myself in your shoes. Let me tell you this, though. If there was anybody you ought to investigate, it was that crazy one who became a priest. Flannagan. He's the one. He used to call us when Gus first disappeared. He used to say crazy things."

"What kind of things?"

"I don't remember exactly. Wait, he used to say that Gus and he were alike. That the accident made Gus join the army and that it was what made Gus go AWOL. It didn't make any sense. He said he knew why Gus went AWOL. But Gus didn't go AWOL. No sonofabitch is ever going to say that, not about my Gus."

"That's all he said?"

"That's it. But Gus wouldn't go AWOL. No way. Don't you see that?"

"Yes," Brian said. "I see it. Have you heard from Flannagan in recent years?"

"No, and I don't want to. He was crazy. Accusing my Gus. Gus would never . . ."

"Yes, I see," Brian said. "Thank you, Mr. Coppazano. I'm sorry to have bothered you. I'm sure that your son had nothing whatsoever to do with the disappearance of the children. I just had to check it out."

"Check out that crazy one that wanted to be a priest," Mr. Coppazano yelled into the phone. "My boy, he's a good boy. And he's alive. I don't care what they say."

"I'm sure he is, sir. Thank you."

Brian hung up the phone. He took a deep breath and stared at the pile of papers in front of him.

"Flannagan," he said. What the hell did they

know about Flannagan? Just that he wanted to
be a priest, that he had gone on to the diocesan
seminary in Boston. He looked down at the file,
opened it and found the number of the seminary.
He dialed the phone quickly, sipping cold coffee.

"Hello."

"Hello. Let me speak to the priest in charge,
please."

"You mean Father Lowery? May I ask who is
calling, and what this refers to?"

"It's Chief Dolan in William's Crossing. It
refers to the kidnapping."

"I've heard all about it, sir," the man's voice
said. "We've seen it on television. I'll put you
through."

There was a strange static, a buzzing sound,
and Brian waited what seemed like an eternity.

"Hello, Chief Dolan. This is Father Lowery.
Is there some way I can help you?"

"You had a Thomas Flannagan there in the
late sixties. I want to know if he is a priest today,
and if so, where he is."

"I wasn't here then, sir," Father Lowery said,
"and that's information I'm not allowed to give
over the phone."

Brian nodded in disgust. He was ready for
this.

"We don't have time for that. Three children's
lives are at stake. I can have the FBI over there
asking, if you want. Maybe some of the reporters
who are practically living on my doorstep will
find out and come along."

"Are you threatening us, Chief Dolan?"

"No," Brian said. "It's simply that I have to
know this within the hour. I'll expect you to call
me back."

"I don't like this kind of treatment, sir. We have nothing to hide here. I'm not intimidated by the FBI or anyone else."

"I know you're not, Father, and I wouldn't want them to foul up the atmosphere over there. I'm not too crazy about them myself."

There was a pause and Brian could hear the priest breathing.

"All right. I'll look it up. I'll call you as soon as I get it."

Brian thanked him and put down the receiver. He sighed and picked up a pencil. Priests. So many of them were like Merja. They didn't want to be involved. When he was a kid, he had thought that priests were the true messengers of God. They could do no wrong. Now he found himself making a conscious effort not to dislike them. God's work, God's way. Somehow it didn't leave room for man. Brian bit his lip and tried to think of the next step. He went over his meetings with Merja and the Mick. Neither one of them was completely clear, especially the Mick. He'd have to get somebody on the softball alibi immediately. Yeah, that was the next move all right. He started to pick up the phone when it rang. He picked it up, hoping that Lowery in Boston had gotten the Flannagan information for him. Instead, it was Dave Roberts, an FBI kidnap specialist who was in on the case.

"Brian?"

"Yeah, Dave."

"I got some news."

Brian didn't have to hear the words to know that it was bad. Roberts's voice sounded flat, a monotone of disappointment and pain.

"I just found something. A Thom McAn loafer. We don't know who it belongs to. And there was a notebook, too. I've already called Skeeter Bannon's parents and they've identified it as his. The sneaker isn't his or Billy Conley's. I'm afraid it might be Danny's. We've been trying to get in touch with Kate Riordan, but she isn't home. Somebody said she was at the hospital. We're trying to reach her there."

"Where did you find the stuff?" Brian said, running his finger around the inside lip of the coffee cup.

"Near the Merrimack River, about a mile out of town. Near Shady Landing."

"I know the spot," Brian said. "Have you started dragging yet?"

"Just getting going now."

"I'll be right there," Brian said numbly. "I'll stop by the hospital and pick up Mrs. Riordan."

"We can still hope," Roberts said.

"Yeah," Brian said. He hung up the phone and got up from his desk. Outside the sun was beating down brightly. The newsmen were hovering around on the grass, waiting for the story. And at the hospital, Brian thought, Kate would be praying for a miracle.

Thursday, 12 noon

KATE DECIDED to follow her feeling. She got in
the Fairmont and shut the door automatically, as
though she were in a trance. She felt too silly to
tell anyone what she was doing, so she set off
alone. They'd lock me up, she said to herself, if
they knew I was out here driving around trying
to connect with Danny. It didn't sound rational,
she had to admit. But still there was that feeling,
that intuition. Not much to go on. Only that and
Father Joe's mysterious "under."

It was a clear spring day, sunny and cloudless,
when the earth was springing to life again. Ordinarily the kind of day that Kate loved, but now
one she was not concentrating on as she drove
through the center of town. Past the municipal
building, past the McDonald's and Brigham's on
North Main that Danny dearly loved. There was
that dumb feeling again. She couldn't shake it
and yet it wasn't anything she could connect
tangibly.

St. Dominic's school was two blocks away on
the corner, and the church was tucked in behind
that.

I feel so like a fool, she thought, and yet there was something pulling her on. Something stronger now, something that made the traffic swimming around her, the people walking across the street at McPhail's Lane, seem unreal. The only real thing was this feeling that somehow Danny was calling to her. Tugging at her. What? Wait. Nothing so ridiculous as a voice, but just that feeling. He needed her. Somewhere he was *under*. Jesus, what did that mean? She felt her hands loosen on the steering wheel, she felt her entire body go slack. It was almost as though the car was driving itself.

Suddenly a red Dodge van was in front of her. Kate gripped the steering wheel again and slammed on the brakes. Too late. There was a sickening crunch as her fender smashed into the van's side. Kate screamed and shielded her eyes. Behind her someone else piled into her rear and she was knocked forward, smashing her head on the windshield. There was a shot of pain in her neck. And she felt herself getting sick. Then she was out cold, falling over like a doll in the seat.

Brian drove down Center Street. He had called Kate at the hospital with no luck. Now at the corner of North Main and McPhail, he saw the accident in front of him. A couple of local hippies were getting out of the van. They looked stoned and dazed, but they didn't seem to be hurt. Then Brian saw Kate's car. Quickly he pulled out his flashing red light and placed it on top of the car, then hit the siren button. He pulled around the long line of traffic and parked his car on Mr. Ruth's lawn.

"Hey, like, wow, she just plowed into us, Chief," said Bobby Palumbo, the town's resident hippie.

"All right, Bobby," Brian said. "Is your van still running?"

"Sure, man."

"Then get it out of the intersection."

"Right."

Bobby and his friends got back in and moved the van across the street into the Dunkin' Donuts parking lot.

The man behind Kate was screaming about women drivers. Brian pushed him aside and got to the door. Kate was trying to pull herself up. All the color had gone out of her face, and she looked frightened and dazed.

Brian opened the door and gently took her hand.

He saw the nasty bump on her forehead.

"Kate," he said, "you're all right?"

"I think so. Oh, Brian, I feel like such a fool."

She began to cry then, putting her head on his shoulder. The tears came in long, deep sobs, letting out all the tension and fear which she had been suppressing.

"We've got to get you out of here," Brian said. "Here, come with me."

Two more police cars sped to the scene. Brian waved to one of the officers, who got out and came over.

"Chambers," Brian said, "move this car out of here. Get the license of the man behind. Kate, do you have your license and your registration?"

Kate fumbled in her bag and gave Brian her wallet. Brian opened it and got out the necessary cards.

"Chambers, take care of this and move her car out of here. Mrs. Riordan is coming with me."

"Yessir," Chambers said. "Here, let me help you, Mrs. Riordan."

He helped Kate out of the car. When she started to stand, she felt her legs give way a little and she had to lean on Brian.

"You all right?"

"Yes," Kate said. "God, I've caused a real wreck here. I'm sorry, Brian. It's just that I was up in the hospital and I talked to Father Joe, and he woke up for a second. I asked him where the kids were, and he said something. He said, 'Under, under,' and I felt like Danny was drawing me to him. It was the strangest thing. But I've had the feeling before. It does exist between mothers and their children sometimes, Brian. Oh, I know it sounds ridiculous."

Brian blanched.

"He said, 'under?' Kate, I know you're upset, and this is a terrible time to tell you this, but we've gotten a lead on the kids. It's nothing definite but I'll be frank with you. It doesn't look good."

Kate gripped his arm and steadied herself on an oak tree by the side of the road.

"Tell me," she said.

"They found Skeeter Bannon's collection book—his newspaper route book, I mean. And one other thing. A child's loafer. A black Thom McAn. Size seven."

"Oh God," Kate said, biting her lip. "That's his, Brian. It's Danny's. Where did they find it?"

"Down by Shady Landing, near the river's edge."

"Oh God. Mother of God," Kate said.

"I was on my way to the hospital to get you," Brian said. "They're dragging the river right now. It doesn't necessarily mean . . ."

But Kate squeezed his arm.

"Don't patronize me, Brian. I can't stand that coming from you. We both know what it might mean. If anyone else talks to me like I'm going to fall apart, I think I'll scream. Just take me there. Now, please."

"All right, Kate," Brian said.

She took a deep breath, held on tightly to his arm as he helped her get into his car.

Thursday, 1 p.m.

BY THE time Kate and Brian reached Shady
Landing, a media circus was underway. Television and newspapermen raced toward the car,
their cameras clicking and whirring and their
microphones pushed out in front of them.

"The meat eaters are here," Brian said. "Just
stay by my side. We'll get over to the pavilion.
We've got it roped off. They won't be able to
bother you."

They drove across the lawn toward the shingled pavilion. Kate remembered coming out here
with Kevin for a church picnic, with Danny and
Paddy. Now both of them might be taken from
her.

She wanted to scream out, to smash her hands
on the cameras, knock them to the ground. She
wanted to kick them, smash them to bits. But
instead she got out of the car, took Brian's arm
and walked quickly, her head down, toward the
pavilion.

Around her she could hear what sounded like
the speeded-up jabber of monkeys.

"Mrs. Riordan, do you think your son is
drowned?"

"Any comment, Mrs. Riordan?"

"Just one or two questions, Mrs. Riordan?"

"Do you have any idea who may have done this to your son?"

Suddenly Kate stopped walking. She could feel Brian tugging at her, but she felt she had to make a statement.

"No one has proven anything has happened to my son and until they do, he is alive."

"What about his shoe?" said a hard-looking woman with a lacquered smile. "Didn't they find his shoe by the river?"

Kate looked at the woman and said nothing. Quickly she turned to Brian and kept walking toward the pavilion. Four feet away from the pavilion were the police ropes and a sawhorse roadblock.

"In here, Mrs. Riordan," said Carl Burke as he opened the door to the pavilion.

Kate looked across and saw a nurse standing next to Nancy Bannon. Nancy was sitting in a wicker chair and staring down at the floor. Next to her John Bannon was standing with his hand lightly on her neck. He looked as though he were from another planet, Kate thought.

"Mrs. Riordan," Carl Burke said, "we've found a shoe. I need to know if it's your son's."

"Where is it?" Kate said, her voice sounding as though it were on a cassette somewhere in her body. This couldn't be her talking about Danny. It was impossible, and yet, there in front of her now was the shoe. There was no doubt about it. It was the same black loafer Danny had put on Sunday morning. Oh, Danny, Danny . . .

"It's his," she said. "It looks like the ones I bought him. God . . ."

She turned and put her head on Brian's shoulder. He patted her head lightly and led her to a chair. But Kate indicated she wanted to go see the Bannons.

Somehow she walked across to them. As she went she was aware of the eyes of police and of the medical team and two skin divers, who were preparing to go out and search the river.

"Nancy," Kate said, "we mustn't give up hope."

Nancy Bannon looked up at Kate. Her eyes and her face were puffed from crying. Her hair was uncombed.

"But they found Skeeter's collection book. Down by the river. Oh God. God, Katie, I can't stand it."

Then she was up and hugging Kate. Kate held on to her, and somehow together, sharing their grief made it slightly more bearable. It was as if there was no one else there. Only Nancy Bannon could understand and share her grief. They were in a select and terrible club, and Kate knew if her son was found in that river by the men in black rubber suits, she would never come out of it. It was as though a glass dome separated them from everyone else. John Bannon too, Kate thought, but John is so lost he doesn't know what he feels. Suddenly Kate began to worry about him. John was unable to get any of his feelings out. He was locked in.

"John," Kate said, "John . . ."

She left Nancy and went over and hugged him. But it wasn't the same. He was stiff and formal.

"Look," he said, "here come George and Arlene."

Arlene had on dark glasses and Kate suddenly felt a hostility toward her. It was as though Arlene had already given up. She had started grieving for them, and they weren't dead. They weren't dead.

"Kate," Arlene said, "have they found anything?"

"Nothing else," Kate said.

"Oh Kate, Kate," Arlene said, "I don't know why Billy picked on Danny. I'm sorry. I always liked Danny. Maybe it was my fault. I never told you this, but I used to . . ."

Arlene started to cry. George held her closely.

"Arlene," Kate said, "you don't have to say anything like . . ."

But Arlene waved her away.

"No, I want to. I don't want there to be any lies between us. I used to tell Billy he should be more like Danny, study harder. I used to tell him that it was kids like Danny who got ahead later in life. I think Billy really resented Danny for that. It was my fault. All of it was my fault."

She began to cry again and Kate found herself consoling Arlene.

"It's all right, Arlene. They're going to come back. I know they are."

The doors opened again and three dripping divers came in.

Brian hurried toward them and they talked in hushed tones. Then he came back toward the parents.

"Nothing," he said. "There's no sign of anything else."

"What does that mean?" George Conley said.

Brian looked at the families and chose his words carefully.

"It means we keep on looking. They could be held in the woods near here, too."

"God, won't you find them?" Arlene Conley said.

Kate looked at the well-manicured woman who was famous for her tough professionalism. In many ways, she seemed in worse shape than any of them.

"You want some coffee, Kate?" Brian said.

She nodded and they went over to a table where Flo Myers, the head of the P.T.A., was serving coffee and doughnuts.

"You should eat something," Brian said.

But Kate shook her head.

"You think they're drowned, don't you?" Kate said.

"I don't know, Kate. I'm not sure. Look at it this way. There's something too convenient about us finding those things here. It's almost like someone wanted us to. I'm not certain at all."

"He's alive, Brian," Kate said. "I feel it stronger than before. You've got to find him. Have you talked to everyone?"

"Everyone but one guy," Brian said. "Look, Kate, I don't know if he's alive or not, but I swear to you that no matter what, until we know for sure, I'll never give up, do you hear me? I'll never give up no matter what."

He looked into her eyes. Kate held onto him and hugged him. As she looked outside, two divers plunged into the deep river and disappeared.

Thursday, 7 p.m.

BRIAN DOLAN staggered to the office phone. His lack of sleep was beginning to catch up with him.

"Dolan," he said.

"Chief Dolan?"

"Yes. Father Lowery?"

"I have the information you asked for, Chief Dolan. Thomas Flannagan left St. John's in 1967. Under rather strange circumstances."

"What kind of circumstances?"

"Well, according to what I could get on such short notice, he started off as a good student. He did pretty well the first two years here, showed promise, especially in moral philosophy and theology, but by his third year he had tailed off badly. He failed some courses and he had personality problems."

"What kind of problems?"

"Hostility, bitterness. He began to attack people. Finally, and this must remain confidential, he left. Or rather, he was asked to leave."

"Do you know where he went?"

"We think he entered the diocesan Brotherhood at St. Jude's. A less demanding rule, you know."

Brian looked down at his watch. It was seven o'clock.

"Thanks, Father. I'll call there."

"That's a good idea," Father Lowery said. "Perhaps they can help you."

Brian put the phone down, called Boston information and got the number of the Brotherhood. Quickly he dialed it. As the phone rang, he suddenly had an image of three boys' bodies floating down the river toward the Atlantic, their faces white and bloated in death.

"Good day, St. Jude's."

"This is Chief of Police Brian Dolan, in William's Crossing. I need to talk to whoever's in charge. It's about a kidnapping case, an emergency."

"That may well be, sir," said a high-pitched voice that might have been male or female. "But this is Easter Week and the entire Brotherhood is in silence. No incoming calls have ever been placed in the history of the Brotherhood."

"Look," Brian said, "this isn't a request. It's an order."

"I'm sorry, sir."

There was a click, and Brian was yelling into a dead phone.

"Son of a bitch," he said.

Then he got out of his chair, grabbed his shoulder holster and started for the door. Outside, Judy Beth Traynor, the newswoman from News Team 7, smiled and moved toward him.

"Chief Dolan," she said. "Chief Dolan, please, can I have a word with you?"

Dolan pushed her aside and headed out toward the car.

"Get out of my way," he said, as two more newsmen came toward him.

O'Toole was coming up the path.

"I'm on my way to Boston," Brian said. "Stay by the radio. I have a hunch we're on to something."

"Right," O'Toole said. "But cool down, will you? You look like you're gonna blow."

"Don't worry about me, O'Toole," Brian snapped. "I'm calm, cool and collected."

"Yeah," O'Toole said, "and I'm Barry Fitzgerald."

Thursday, 7:30 p.m.

KATE WALKED to the car, supported by Maura. Or perhaps, Kate thought, it was she supporting Maura. The old woman had come over to offer support. Just now Kate couldn't bear to be alone. Thoughts of Danny's loafer, down by the Landing, an image of some man, some monster pushing her son's head under, bubbles coming to the surface as Danny fought back until exhausted. Oh God, Danny . . .

Now there was only one thing to do. Pray. And then after that get back over to see Father Joe. Sergeant Brown, a beefy young man, was manning the telephones for a while. The truth was Kate had about given up on the ransom call. There wasn't going to be any, she now knew. Only the calls from the crackpots and weirdos.

"I saw your son today out in front of my house with a tall, dark woman."

"I saw all three of the boys. They were ghosts and they came to me in a dream. They were carrying myrrh and frankincense. You see, they had become the three Wise Men."

"Your son is living in South America. There is

a Nazi there who steals children. Believe me,
this is true."

Now Kate helped her mother-in-law into the
car. Maura was trying hard to hold up, but the
thought of losing Paddy and now her only grand-
son was killing her, Kate thought. If Danny
doesn't come back she won't survive this. And,
thinking that, she realized how fragile they were,
all of them. They kept up a brave front, but
when something really horrible happened, they
fell apart. Walking around to the other side of
the car she found herself trying to imagine what
life would be like without Danny. Without his
laugh, and without his smile, and without his
great discoveries: "Mom, I found this great little
pond out in the woods with tadpoles"; "Mom,
have you ever seen *Attack of the Crab Monsters*?
I thought maybe you had, Mom, 'cause it was an
old picture, came out in the fifties, not that
you're old, Mom."

Kate gripped the door of the car and steadied
herself. She felt as though she were herself un-
derwater. Thousands of tons of pressure were
pushing down, down . . .

"Katie, are you all right?"

It was Maura inside the car. She had reached
over and pushed the door open.

"Yes, I'm fine, Maura. I'm fine. Let's go.
We'll be late for church."

On the way to St. Dominic's, Kate tried to think
of something else. Anything else. She thought
about the significance of Holy Thursday. After
Good Friday it was the most solemn day of the
Christian calendar. What had it been called be-

fore? Maundy Thursday. That was before the
Second Vatican Council. Oh Christ, she said silently. Oh Father, if I have been angry, if I have
sinned, then take me, but not Danny. He's an
innocent child.

She and Maura parked the car in the lot next
to the church. She looked up at the huge towers,
the stained glass windows. It was a magnificent
old church, the finest and oldest building in William's Crossing. Now, though, it looked somber
and foreboding. And the thought of the Mass
had, for Kate, a terrifying significance. Tonight
was the Mass of the Last Supper. Jesus' last
meal. As Kate sat down with Maura and the rest
of the congregation, she couldn't help but think
of Danny. If he was still alive, then what was he
eating? Was the person who had him worried
about his health, was he warm or was he cold
and wet?

Kate looked around the room. The Fishpaws
were looking at her. When she met their eyes,
though, they quickly turned away. It was as
though they had heard about the shoe and had
written Danny and the others off. She held
Maura's kind, rough old hands and tried to keep
herself in check. Concentrate on the ceremony.
Make it mean something.

She noticed that the Tabernacle was bare, as it
always was on this night, and prayed deeply as
the Gloria was recited and the church bells
pealed. Kate listened as Monsignor Merja read
from the Gospel of John.

"But if I washed your feet—I who am teacher
and Lord—then you must wash another's feet.
This is the gospel of the Lord."

She and Maura watched intently as Monsignor Merja washed the feet of some of the parish men, his obeisance to the holy tradition. As he got up to give the homily, his old hands grasping the lectern firmly, his voice booming, he said, "Tonight we celebrate the Holy Eucharist, the perfection of the Passover Meal. This meal was first celebrated on the night the Israelites went into Egypt. Subsequently, our Lord used the meal to illustrate our own journey through life. He promised us the Holy Eucharist would accompany us on that journey. And further, he told us in the Gospel of John, 'I am indeed going to prepare a place for you, and then I shall come back to take you with me, that where I am you also may be.' That is the word of our Lord. Christ is to take us on the journey through this life to the next one."

He bowed his head, signifying the homily was over, and then left the lectern. Kate repeated his words to herself. ". . . that where I am you also may be." Dear Danny, she prayed, I hope that is so.

Silently, she and Maura got in the line which formed down the center aisle for communion. As they advanced to the altar, Kate gripped Maura's hand and prayed for hope, for strength, for resolution.

And then she felt it again.

Danny's presence.

He wasn't dead. Somehow, he was still alive.

DANNY REACHED OUT on the cool cement floor. He felt weak, very weak. What had happened? He could barely remember it. Only that Billy had fallen against the coffins and then human skulls and skeletons had begun falling out of the coffins. Billy had screamed and fallen backwards. And then Danny had been scared. So scared that he didn't move for the longest time. The bones. The bones couldn't hurt him. It wasn't like in *The Twilight Zone* or *Night Gallery*. It really wasn't. Only he couldn't convince himself. To see Billy lying there for as long as he did, not moving, to see the skull gleaming in the darkness, staring at him. God, he could hardly move, and so he had stayed still for a long time. But finally, finally he had gotten up his nerve. He had to help Billy. Maybe the edge of the coffin knocked Billy out. Maybe Billy was going to die if he didn't help him.

And so he screwed up his courage and started to move forward.

But then he felt a hand on his arm, and he wanted to scream, but the gag was too tight.

It was the man. The man who had taken him. He tried to pull away, feeling an electric current of fear sweeping him. But then he felt something prick his skin and he fell back, deep asleep.

How long had he been out?

There was no way of knowing.

And when he awoke, nothing had changed. The smell, though, was just as bad as before.

Worse.

And Billy was still lying over by the pile of old bones.

Then a terrible thought entered Danny's mind.

What if Billy was dead?

He gave out with a little cry of fear, and then he noticed something. The gag around his mouth wasn't quite as tight. He could almost make a word.

"Bill . . ."

Billy Conley didn't move.

Danny began to crawl toward him. And toward the pile of bones. Funny, they weren't as terrifying now as before. No pile of bones would ever frighten him like the real, flesh hand that had grabbed him.

Oh God, don't let Billy be dead. Holy Father, please, please don't let Billy be dead. I know I've done bad things in the past, like the time I played hooky from school and went to the movies, and the time I got mad at Mom because she was beating me at Monopoly and I suddenly cursed out loud, and the time I got so mad at Daddy when he was dead. I was so mad at him and wanted to kill him, but he was already dead. I know that was really horrible of me, God, but I do love, and I did love Daddy. Mom said it was because I missed him so much that I got mad.

And I have been mad at Billy and wished him dead.

I know I have, God, but I want him alive now. I didn't really mean it. I didn't.

He winced as he crawled near the bones. Billy's feet were two inches in front of him and there was no way to get up near Billy's head without going over what looked like an old arm bone.

He was on top of Billy now. He put his head to Billy's chest and listened carefully. He listened and finally he heard it. Billy's heart was beating. But Billy was cold, very cold. Maybe he was almost dead. What did they call it?

In shock. Billy was in shock. He had to do something, he had to . . .

If he could just get the gag a little loose.

He hung his head above Billy's and rubbed Billy's nose with his own. He butted Billy with his head, and kicked at him.

I'm not trying to hurt him, God, I'm just trying to wake him up.

Billy groaned and moved.

Danny butted him again, using his chin, and kicked at him.

"Brrrrrrr."

It sounded like a growl, like he was a tiger. But he didn't feel like a tiger, he felt small and afraid, so very afraid.

"Ahhhhhhh," Billy said.

His eyes popped open and he look up at Danny with a look of pure, uncomprehending terror.

"Ahhhhh."

Danny looked down at the edge of the coffin

in front of him. It was sharp. If he could crawl over there and get the edge of the coffin on the gag, maybe he could stretch it and pull himself free. He had to talk to Billy.

He started forward.

"Oh Jesus, Jesus, I will always go to church, and I will always listen, and I will never, ever leave early and go to the drug store and drink sodas. I won't. I'll never have a bad thought. I won't. Just don't let me feel these bones."

Finally he got to the edge of the coffin and he got his mouth on the edge of the coffin and began to move his face up and down. He could feel the wood splinter off into his chin. It stung, and he knew that it was starting to bleed. But it was working, the gag was a little looser. He could almost talk.

"Bill . . ."

Too low.

He tried it again and again, and finally it was loose. He could, if he held his jaw tightly back, say words loudly.

"Billy. Billy, can you hear me?"

"Ahhhhhh."

"Don't try to talk. We're going to get out of here. I have to think. We could try yelling, but if the man is here, if he's around, outside, he'd come get us. We have to think."

Before Billy could answer, Danny heard the rumbling again. He'd forgotten about it, but now it came to him.

The rumbling noise. He had thought it was like a train or bus. But now he listened carefully. The noise wasn't like a machine at all. No, it was more like—like feet. Feet. That was it. Hundreds of people walking somewhere, heading up an aisle, like at Fenway Park, or at a theater. Or like . . . like . . . church.

Danny suddenly felt happy. In spite of everything, he felt happy.

He was in the church. He hadn't been taken anywhere at all.

The people were above him. Yes, and they were leaving Mass! It was Holy Week, but what day could it be?

Down below. The altar boys had all heard talk of the secret room below the church. But he had always thought it was just a story. Until he had asked Mom about it and she told him there were cool, dark places, caves sometimes, but sometimes secret burial rooms, built under churches so nobody could find them. With secret entrances. Made out of stone.

So this must be the coffin room and the loose bones were the ossuary, a common burial pit. Mom had said that in the eighteenth century parishioners had buried their dead under the church instead of in graveyards to protect them from their Protestant tormentors. Damn, these people must be old!

He was still at St. Dominic's.

"Billy," he said, so excited he could barely get the words out. "Billy, I know where we are."

Billy groggily sat up. He looked at Danny and suddenly his eyes got big. He tried to speak.

"Ahhhhh," he yelled.

Wildly he waved his head, as if to tell Danny something. Then Danny realized what it was. Behind him. He turned, and saw something in the shadows. The man. Oh God, if he had heard. He tried to scramble away, but the shape came closer.

"Who is it?" he said. "Who's there?"

"Skeeter," said a dry, raspy voice. "Is that you, Danny?"

"Skeeter Bannon?" Danny said, astonished. "Come here."

Skeeter moved forward on his knees. His gag had fallen off and was hanging around his neck like a cowboy neckerchief. He was pale and scared. Dirt and tears streaked his thin face.

"I just woke up," he said. "This thing wasn't tied very tight. He must have gotten scared when I fought back."

"Did you see who it was?" Danny said.

"No," Skeeter said. "He was waiting for me when I went across the Northwood Lot. He hid near the hedge there, and hit me from behind. Then he must have used some kind of drugs or something. Geez, is that Billy?"

"Yes," Danny said. "He might be hurt. Those coffins fell on him. We've got to help him. And we've got to get untied."

"Why don't we just yell for help?"

"Because he might be out there. The thing is, we have to get untied. I'll turn around backwards, and you see if you can work on my knots. All right?"

"Okay, Danny," Skeeter said. "Hey, you aren't scared are you?"

"Nah," Danny said, "we're gonna be out of here soon. Hurry, don't waste time. Try to get my knots. Here, turn around."

Danny turned around and looked at Billy Conley's crushed leg. Down around the knee it looked smashed. There was a thick clot of blood. He could see it clearly now. The coffin had crushed it. Billy tried to move it and winced in pain.

"Stay still, Billy," Danny said. "We're gonna get you out of here."

He could feel Skeeter Bannon's fingers fumbling with the knots. He had to act calm. Stay loose, as Daddy had always said.

But he knew for sure that the man would be back. They had to hurry, because Danny had a feeling that when the man found them untied and talking he wasn't going to like it at all.

Thursday, 9 p.m.

O'TOOLE HATED the Boston Underground Parking Garage. Why they had torn up the Boston Common to bury this monstrosity under it was beyond him. First, it never had any empty parking spaces so you circled and circled the long full lines waiting for a car to pull out and then you played chicken with some other driver to see if you could get the space. It was nerve-wracking business. And then you ended up in the fourth underground level and—you guessed it—no elevator running! Then you had to trudge your way to the street. It was worse than when they rebuilt the Arlington Street T-escalator when he was on the Boston police force and every day for six months he'd had to drag himself up the endless steps. No, these days he was quite happy working as lieutenant in William's Crossing. All these years he'd never regretted his moving from Boston to the small sleepy town on the Merrimack. That is, until this case. This was the worst thing he'd ever worked on. Three kids disappeared right into thin air. Who the hell would have the nerve to take them? And the whole town was hysterical. Only he and Brian Dolan were keeping their cool. You had to hand it to that Dolan. Nothing seemed to bother him. But he had something for Kate Riordan, O'Toole was sure of that. He saw the way he looked at her. She was an attractive woman. And they were both single. Besides, whose business was it anyway? None of his. That was for damn sure.

Brian had sent him to find the sister of Billy Riley, the driver of the car the night of that long-ago accident involving the missing boys' fathers. O'Toole had traced her to Dorchester and, after that, not much else. But then he got lucky. He put in a call to Roderick Blake, who was now with the Metropolitan District police. Rod had called all the local station houses for him. She had no convictions, but one of the cops remembered her. She'd been busted for soliciting. This cop had nailed her on Fresh Pond Parkway, but she beat the charge. Where had she gone? The cop wasn't sure, Roddy had said, but he had heard she was performing in the Combat Zone in Boston. Rod had gotten a good description of her—tall, red hair, and, most importantly, a limp. "My boy said she's working as a stripper at one of those joints. She moves around a lot. The guys who are into kink like to see her limp around and take her clothes off." Recalling that, O'Toole wished he was home with his wife Agnes watching the Thursday night pro wrestling on ESPN. Agnes was a lifelong Bruno Sammartino fan, and they had often gone to the Boston Arena to see Bruno wrestle in person. But now with that new cable stuff, you got good reception and a twenty-four hour sports channel as well.

After the wrestling tonight was Australian-rules football, and O'Toole knew he would miss that as well.

When he reached the corner of Boylston and Tremont he felt his stomach tighten; the neon almost blinded him. This was it. This was the depravity of Boston. One of the reasons he had moved to William's Crossing. Every marquee on the four-block strip advertised a different porno movie. There was Marilyn Chambers in *Insatiable*, Desirree Cousteau in *Captured*, Annette DeHaven in *Triple Vixens*. But it was the live clubs that bothered him the most. They all had their seedy, leering hawkers trying to steer traffic through their doors. "Hey buddy, come on in and see the best piece ever."

The thought struck him he was going to have to start to talk to these characters. After all, he had no idea where to look for Sherry Riley. He'd need their help. They'd be his partners in helping him find her.

After two hours he was nowhere. He had threatened, begged, even offered a bribe to one unsavory sort who hesitated but seemed like he might have known her. Either Sherry Riley had a lot of friends or no one particularly cared about her one way or the other.

He was tired and he was getting nowhere. He realized he was also getting hungry, so he walked along Boylston Street toward Chinatown for some good Chinese food. Now that was one thing you couldn't get in William's Crossing.

It was after eleven when he entered the small, nameless restaurant, but the owner offered to serve him at the bar. Too tired to argue,

.O'Toole accepted. A couple of Beefeater Specials would make him feel lots better anyway. A small blond-haired man sat next to him. He looked about forty or so. After the obligatory discussion of the Red Sox's chances, and what the Celts and Bruins would do in the playoffs, O'Toole asked about Sherry Riley.

"I know her. Yeah, that *used* to be her name. She dances now at the Samovar under the name of Princess Patricof."

Suddenly O'Toole wasn't hungry any more.

The Samovar was a dimly lit dive at the corner of Washington and Boylston. At one time it had been a Salvation Army station, and it did not bely its dreary origins. There were small rickety tables in front of a makeshift stage which served as a dancing platform. None of the dozen patrons stirred when O'Toole entered.

"Six dollar cover and two-drink minimum," said the waitress. She had on a dreary pink costume, a Playboy bunny retread, and looked sad. O'Toole paid without objection and inquired, "When is the show?"

The waitress shrugged.

"Princess can dance when she wants. Rule of the house. Anytime now she'll be going on."

O'Toole looked around the place. It hardly seemed like an expectant crowd. When the waitress came back with his JB and water, he asked directions to Sherry Riley's dressing room, which turned out to be a large converted closet next to the ladies' room.

She was a tall redhead who had seen better days. .

"Sherry," he said quietly, "my name is O'Toole from the William's Crossing police department."

The color drained from her worn-out face. She picked up a towel and placed it across her lap as if to cover her skimpy blue-sequined dancing costume.

Her voice was high and agitated.

"I haven't done anything. What are you hassling me for?"

"It's not you I'm after. I want to talk about your brother Billy."

She relaxed a bit and smiled.

"You can't pin anything on him either," she said with a chuckle. "He's dead."

"I know. Look, I know this is going to sound strange to you, but it has to do with the disappearance of those kids."

"Yeah, I saw that on Channel 5. That was awful. What kind of slime would do something like that?"

"Well," O'Toole said thoughtfully, "that's what we're trying to find out. Your brother knew the fathers of the boys involved. They were in the car with him the night he was killed."

She became defensive.

"So what are you saying? Billy came back from the dead to get their kids?"

O'Toole knew he had to win her over.

"Look, is there anyone who might want to get back at the boys' fathers? Anyone who blamed them for the accident?"

Sherry Riley was not a stupid woman. Unsteadily, she got to her feet and moved to her dressing table to get a cigarette. Lighting it, she turned to face the florid-faced O'Toole, who was now sweating profusely.

"Our parents are dead now. Bill's old girlfriends are long married to other guys. And there were no other kids in our family. If your hypothesis holds water, I'm a prime suspect, right?"

O'Toole was confused. He usually did the questioning, made the suppositions. He was uncomfortable in this role reversal.

"And there's something else you probably didn't know. Billy and I were twins. And we were very close. I guess after he died I got off the track and never really got back on it. That almost seems like another life now."

"You can account for your whereabouts this week, I take it?"

She looked at him sharply.

"An alibi? Sure, I always have lots of company, if you know what I mean. I sure don't lack for friends. But you can't know how painful this is. Every time I think I have Billy put away in a private place, someone comes along and dredges him up. Billy's death was when I first learned that you don't get everything you want out of life. I know how those parents must be feeling. How much it hurts to lose something that's a part of you. But I don't know anything about those kids, and I don't see how their disappearance can be connected to the accident."

"Did you ever meet any of the others in the accident?"

A small man with a crewcut opened the door to the room and said, "Five minutes, Princess."

She nodded and returned to O'Toole's question.

"I probably met them all at the funeral. It's a blur to me. I assure you I don't know what happened to any of them. I'm afraid I'm a dead end for you."

She stood again and, crossing to the cracked mirror, she took a feather headdress from the table and placed it on her head. In spite of the seedy atmosphere, there was something rather regal about her. He would have liked to stay for the show, but, after all, he was a professional and the interview was over. The Princess, he thought to himself, knew nothing about those kids. He would have bet any money on it.

Friday, 7 a.m.

BRIAN PULLED the Dodge up to the entrance gate of St. Jude's Brotherhood in Boston. The gate was wrought iron and had a large black cross hanging off it. Beyond the gate was a huge expanse of lawn, covered with fir trees and a beautifully tended garden of tulips.

He felt slightly sick. He was still running on pure adrenalin. He had to get inside the monastery. He had to find out where Flannagan was. And then it occurred to him that he might be wrong, that Mick was really the kidnapper, or even Merja. But the trail kept coming back to Flannagan.

Brian walked down to the fence and then decided that there was nothing else to do but go over. He found a toehold and began climbing. The wrought iron was slippery and he nearly fell. The fence had sharp spikes on the top, and he imagined what he would look like impaled up here. He could see the headline in the Boston *Herald* now—"POLICE CHIEF SPIKED IN KIDNAPPING INVESTIGATION."

But he managed to get over the top and then

he was falling down on the other side. The drop was further than he expected and, as he landed, he twisted his ankle. He felt a sharp surge of pain, but he hobbled to his feet and started running up toward the main stone house.

The pain still shot through his leg as he made his way past the shade of the fir trees up toward the garden.

He could see into the house now. Two brothers in brown robes walked by the window. They were carrying lighted candles, and then Brian saw four or five more. It looked like some sort of procession. Brian thought of when he had been young. The mysteries of the Church, the Latin and the stern faces of the priests had given a fearful order to his life. Now he knew that order was an illusion. Brian turned and started up the garden path. He was about fifty yards from the house when he heard a growling behind him. He turned and saw two Doberman pinschers coming toward him fast. They were maybe thirty yards away, and they were barking wildly and baring their teeth.

Brian didn't wait. He began to run directly through the flower beds, trampling the tulips as he ran. The dogs were gaining on him, but Brian saw the large oaken door of the Brotherhood house in front of him. He got to it and tried the door. No good. It was locked. Brian beat on the door with his fists, but no one answered.

He turned and saw one of the Dobermans come directly at him and begin to leap for his throat. Brian waited until the last instant, then turned and gave the dog a savage chop to the neck as the dog went by. The dog hit the door and fell over on his back crying. Then Brian turned. The other dog was ten feet away, growling. It was going to take its time, approach him carefully. The first dog got up now. It had only been stunned. It growled and started toward Brian. He backed off toward some bushes. Just beyond the bushes was a huge window which looked in on a great dining hall. Brian saw a wheelbarrow and a sack of fertilizer sitting by the side of the house. The dogs moved toward him, but he quickly picked up the sack and threw it at the first one. The dog jumped back and, as he did, Brian picked up the wheelbarrow and threw it through the dining room window. Glass shattered violently and then Brian retreated through the hedges, reached inside and grabbed the latch. The window frame opened and glass shattered on the tile inside.

Still no one came.

The dogs had backed off temporarily but finally started over the broken glass. They stood just outside the window, snarling and growling.

Brian stepped inside and looked around the hallway. There was a great long hallway to his left and he began to run down it.

This could cost me my job, he thought. Going on nothing more than a hunch. But he felt it. There was something here that had to be answered.

He stopped as he came to a big oaken door.

Then he heard the growling behind him again. The dogs were coming down the hallway after him. He pushed the door but it, too, was locked. The Dobermans were gaining on him. Brian went down the hallway. There was another door fifteen feet away.

He reached it just as the first dog reached him and began to rip and snarl at his pants leg. He could feel the teeth sink into his calf and he screamed out and gave the dog a brutal hit to the neck which sent it yapping away. The second dog moved in now and went for his hand. With his good right leg, Brian kicked it in the head, then pushed hard on the door. It opened and he fell inside.

The dogs stopped at the door, barking and looking at him. Apparently they were trained not to enter the room. Brian took a deep breath and turned around.

In front of him were over fifty Brothers, kneeling in front of an altar. They did not look at him. Indeed, they seemed not to have heard any of the commotion at all.

The service was in progress.

The Brothers clasped their hands together in prayer and looked straight ahead.

Brian ran among them screaming.

"Who's in charge here? Who?"

No one answered. It was as if he didn't exist. Brian stumbled over one Brother's robe and fell backwards. He righted himself by putting his hand out and using another Brother's head for balance. Then he went to the front of the room.

"Listen, I'm a police officer. This is a life or death situation. Some of you must have heard about the kidnapping of three little boys. You have to tell me who's in charge."

The Brothers continued to pray. The silence drove Brian mad.

"God damn you," he screamed. "God damn all of you."

He turned and looked at the large cross draped in purple on the altar, and he wanted to run over and pick it up and throw it at them.

Then he felt a powerful hand on his shoulder. He turned and saw a towering black man in a robe of bright red. The man looked down at him severely.

"Come with me," the man said.

"All right," Brian said breathlessly. "All right now."

Brother Andrew looked down at Brian and smashed his huge black hand on the desk of his study. Pencils and pens shook, and a paperweight with snow inside of it fell on the floor.

"What gives you the right, sir, to come crashing into this monastery in Holy Week, breaking our sacred vow of silence? What gives you the right to attack our dogs, break our windows, trample our flowers? Is this a police state?"

Brian looked at the man, and stood up to face him.

"My badge gives me the right, Brother Andrew, but beyond that, this case gives me the right. I called here. I explained the situation to the person on your switchboard and they still refused to put me through. Apparently the Church doesn't take the lives of its flock as seriously as it does its traditions."

"That is sacrilege, young man. Now, I would strongly suggest that, unless you have a search warrant . . ."

"No," Brian said, shaking his head, "I can see you still don't get it. There are three kids missing. They might be alive. They might have something to do with Thomas Flannagan, who studied here in the late sixties. He presumably got out of here and was made a Brother. Now what is his name?"

"I cannot give you that information. That is secret."

"I don't have time for your holy hocus pocus. You're going to give me the name, do you understand? Either that or I finish wrecking this place."

Brother Andrew looked at the wild-eyed man in front of him. His leg was bleeding, his shirt was torn, his hair stood out at strange angles, and he panted furiously, as thought he couldn't get enough air.

"I cannot get into the records. They're in a vault, locked away, and the only person with the combination is with the Master of Novices, Brother King, and he's away at the Vatican."

"Jesus," Brian said.

"Please," Brother Andrew said, "I do have some records though, photographic records, right out here in the hallway. Pictures of all the classes that graduated from here. Come with me."

He led Brian out into the hallway down which the dogs had just chased him. They remained there, growling menacingly.

"Here's 1967," Brother Andrew said, taking the picture off the wall. "Does anyone look familiar?"

Brian took the picture from Brother Andrew and looked at it closely.

"Everyone is so damn young and styles of hair have changed, I can't tell. Let me see 1968 and '69."

Brother Andrew took the two photos off the wall. Brian looked quickly at the '68 photograph, and then at the '69. He was about to give up in disgust when he picked up the '68 picture again.

"Wait," he said. "This guy on the end. He looks familiar. Let me see . . ."

He turned the picture over and began ripping the backing off it.

"What are you doing, Chief Dolan? Have you lost your mind?"

"No," Brian said, "I don't think so."

He pulled the picture out and then reached into his pocket and pulled out his pen.

"You're not going to deface the property of . . ."

"No, I'm just going to bring it up to date," Brian said.

Quickly he penned a beard in. Then he added longer hair, and he stood back and stared at the picture.

"Brother Michael," he said to himself. "Jesus God."

"Brother Michael? Wait," Brother Andrew said. "I remember people talking about him. He was a brilliant student who had to drop out of the seminary. It seemed he had this tragic brain dysfunction. Something that no one could help him with. Gradually he lost his powers. He couldn't concentrate. He couldn't really do the things asked of him."

"From the accident," Brian said.

"Accident?"

"Yeah," Brian said. "Let me use your phone now. I only hope to hell we're not too late."

Friday, 7:30 a.m.

MICK SHEA felt elated. He knew something was wrong with Brother Michael. It had been obvious for a long time and now it was becoming clearer than ever. He had first noticed it when Brother Michael used to ask him about the boys.

"Don't you think they're being spoiled?"

"Isn't it true, man to man, that things are too easy for them?"

"They don't understand what other people have gone through. They don't understand real suffering."

Mick had listened to all this with one ear. Vaguely, he supposed now as he waited by the rectory workshop, that he had been pleased by Brother Michael's flattery. Most people didn't understand, would never understand, how a kid's character needed to be formed by fire. No, nowadays there were child psychiatrists and special education teachers and P.T.A. groups, and a thousand other ways to make a kid into a soft little puddle of a person. That was what was wrong with the whole country—the weakening of the moral fiber. And it was the same with the

Church too. It had once been like, well, like
Mick himself. Staunch, upright, like a great stern
shepherd who took care of its flock, but was
quick to tell the wolves from the sheep. But
now, now it was simply like everything else. No
longer any Latin Masses. No, nowadays they had
Father Joe strumming his guitar. No mystery, no
dignity. Yes, he believed all these things, and he
was proud of it, but he should have seen, should
have known, nonetheless, that Brother Michael
didn't really know about these things. No, he
was just sucking up to him. The question was
why. Why did he show up at the football field to
talk to him? He had been around there for a few
years and he had never shown any interest in
sports before. And why had he asked about Billy
Conley's parents? Or Skeeter Bannon's after-
school job? It hadn't occurred to him really, but
it was suspicious, very suspicious. But now Mick
Shea felt elated because he was going to nail
Brother Michael himself.

He was going to watch him, and if he made
one false move then he was going to overpower
him and personally haul him into the police station. They said that his values were old hat.
Some of the parents said he had a John Wayne
complex. He knew they laughed at him, but he
was going to show them. He was going to show
them what one good man could do, if his hunch
was right. He was going to bring in Michael, he
was going to save the kids' lives, even though
they were little ingrates really, and he was going
to show up Chief Brian Dolan, that Burke fellow
from the FBI, and everyone else. He would be a
hero. He could already see the headlines:

"TEACHER CAPTURES KIDNAPPER." It would be like the old days when he got headlines for his touchdowns, but this would be even better. They'd all respect him again. Him and the things he stood for.

Now he waited by the rectory workshop. His friend Mrs. Mullen had told him there was something curious that had gone on the last few nights. Brother Michael had come in and was working on some kind of woodwork. Mick knew he had always been good with his hands. He was constantly on call to fix things around St. Dominic's, but there was something else as well. It was the hours Mrs. Mullen said Brother Michael put in. Last night he had worked for three hours, until two in the morning. Then he had left the workshop, headed back toward the rectory. Mrs. Mullen had been worn out staying up to watch him.

He huddled in the corner of the church. He'd been there since dawn. Finally at around seven he heard footsteps. Brother Michael was coming back to the shop. Mick pushed himself back in the shadows and crouched down by the hedges. Finally he saw Brother Michael go by him and walk into the workshop. The fluorescent light of the workshop went on and Mick heard the sound of nails being driven into wood. He looked up and tried to get a look at what Michael was working on, but he couldn't get that close to the window without running the risk of being seen. He crouched down, preparing himself for a long wait. It was going to be dull and boring, but if those penny-ante cops could do it, so could he.

To Mick's surprise, however, the wait was not

a long one. Suddenly the lights went out, and he heard Brother Michael walking toward the back door of the rectory. Mick waited, and then crept through the bushes. Suddenly he was struck by the possibility that he was all wrong. He hated to think of the embarrassment. He wouldn't actually accuse Brother Michael of anything—unless, of course, he caught him with the kids.

He crept to the edge of the hedge row and looked at the back door. Brother Michael had backed his Dodge van up to the door and was lugging something toward it. Mick could not make out exactly what the thing was. It seemed to be a number of long shafts. Stakes of some kind.

He waited until Michael had them loaded and then it occurred to him that he had again been stupid. Michael could simply get into the van and drive away. He'd never have time to run around and follow him in his own car.

But Brother Michael didn't get into the van. He started walking toward the church, the side entrance which led into the Robing Room. Mick crept along behind him, trying to avoid stepping on branches. He watched as Brother Michael opened the door slowly and walked inside. Mick hurried up behind him. He had been waiting for this, which is why he had conveniently forgotten to return Monsignor Merja's keys, borrowed the previous afternoon. This time, if Michael was in the church, he would find him.

But first he wanted to get a look in the van. Whatever had been put in there must be very interesting. Quietly he crept toward the van and tried the doors. Locked. He went to the back window, but there was a dark curtain pulled across it.

Mick was afraid to lose Brother Michael in the church. Quickly he ran across the parking lot and let himself in the Robing Room.

The room was dim at this early morning hour and he stumbled over a chair and could hear the sound reverberate through the place. If Michael heard that . . .

Mick moved forward slowly, trying to get his eyes accustomed to the dark. He made it to the other side of the room and then found the door to the sanctuary itself.

He opened it slowly, wincing as the hinges creaked. Then he looked out into the church proper. But there was no one there. No one at the altar, no one in the pews. There was still Monsignor Merja's office. He began to make his way across the pews when he heard a noise. It seemed to be coming from beyond the door to the cellar. Quickly he turned, went through an antechamber, and came to the cellar door. He saw a light coming from the other side of it, but then suddenly it went out.

Mick Shea began to sweat. There was a trickle which ran down his back, and another down his chest. He opened the door slowly and looked down into pitch blackness. There was something strange going on here. It occurred to him that he should call Dolan, but he rejected the idea. This was going to be his day.

He started down the dark steps, nearly tripping, and holding on to the old iron rail.

Slowly he descended into the cellar. And finally he was there at the bottom, but there was still no sign of Michael. What if all he had heard was a rat? And Michael had gotten away? What if he had invented all of this?

He moved down a corridor, past the old music room, past the storage bins, and then suddenly he heard something off to his right. He peered around the wall, and then he saw Brother Michael silhouetted by the flashlight in his hand. In front of Mick Shea was something he couldn't have dreamed of. The far wall of the basement was opening up, a sliding door leading into a secret room. Impossible. But then Mick remembered that the church had been built in Revolutionary War days. In those days, Mick recalled, a Catholic had a good chance of being called a witch and burned at the stake. So this was the old room.

He watched in mute fascination as Michael went inside the wall. He had to make his move now. The children had to be in there. There was no time to waste. If Michael got the door closed, he'd have to call the cops.

Taking a deep breath, Mick Shea started to run down the hallway. He could feel his heart beating, and his palms had gone cold. He made it to the doorway just as it was closing.

"All right, Michael," he yelled as he entered the dark room. "You may as well come out. I'm onto you now."

He barely saw the hand that came up behind him, striking him a tremendous blow over the left eye with a claw hammer. He could feel the hot blood drip on his neck, though, as he fell like a stunned animal to the floor.

Brother Michael stood over him, tapping the
hammer in his palm.

The idiot. Thinking he could outsmart him.
That was the trouble with all of them. They
thought they were smarter than he. They had
said so at the seminary. They told him it was un-
fortunate, but something had happened to him,
something which made him lose his memory,
something which had stopped him from being—
what was it? He could barely recall it now.
Something about the brilliant student he had
once been.

They all thought they were smart and he was
dumb. But he had proven it this time, hadn't he?
He had shown them all that he was still bright.
He deserved to be a priest more than anyone.
All the years he had suffered for it, had cleansed
himself of the sins of bodily desire, had given up
wanting women and money, and had dedicated
himself only to one thing—the Church. And
Jesus Christ Our Lord. That was all he cared
about, all he thought about, and what had happened? They had laughed at him. They had
made him feel small and insignificant.

"Brother Michael is very good with his hands."

"I hear he used to be a scholar, but that's hard
to believe. Not Brother Michael."

But it was true, he thought, as he dragged
Mick Shea's body up against the wall. It was
true, whether they believed it or not.

He had been a brilliant student until the accident. Until Paddy Riordan and his friends talked
him into breaking Retreat. They had laughed at
him and called him a creep. They had said that

he was afraid to do a little drinking. They made him feel like dirt, and so he had gone with them to show them he could drink as much as anyone else. And then they had had the accident. Bill Riley had died. Gus Coppazano had hurt his leg. But the others, the others had been in the back. Wasn't that the way it always was? The instigators got away clean while the innocent paid?

At first he had thought it was only a mild head injury. But then they had told him that something was wrong with his brain. It was a progressive case. They were sorry, really sorry, but there was nothing that could be done. The brain is such an extraordinarily complicated organ, Mr. Flannagan, and we really don't understand much about it yet. It seems that you will suffer from a deterioration of intellectual capacity, how much we can't say. By which they meant he would soon be so stupid that he wouldn't remember how bright he had been before.

Except he did remember it. He remembered it only too well. There were times, late at night, when he was sure it was coming back. He could remember whole chapters of St. Augustine, and he would feel a glow of happiness. He was going to be all right. He was going to be fine. They'd let him have another chance at the priesthood. They had to see how good he'd been.

He hadn't tried to get revenge on his enemies. He had been so good, so pure.

But finally they told him.

There was no hope.

He *was* going to get worse as he got older.

The deterioration was not going to be gradual any more.

And so he had decided to hurt them, the others, in a way that they could never forget. Take from them the things most precious to them. He would take their futures just as Paddy, George Conley, and John Bannon had taken his.

Their children. Their futures. Gone. In a way they would never forget.

He shut the door behind him and started toward the back of the old chamber. The boys would be tied up, like three little pigs. Oh, what a surprise he had for them. They'd see soon. They'd see how dumb he was.

He hadn't been dumb when he'd found the old church records and seen the buried area that dated to the eighteenth century. He hadn't been dumb when he'd found the old room and fixed the door so it worked well again. For a long time he had just come down here alone. By himself, and thought what to do. And then, finally, he had known. He had known and they would never, ever forget him now.

In a few hours it would be done. Yes, this would be a Good Friday they would recall the rest of their days.

He shone his flashlight into the corner where the boys were. Suddenly he felt a great panic. They weren't there. They had gotten away. He ran across the room and stared at the piles of bones. They had to be in here. There was nowhere for them to go. Then he heard something behind him.

They had waited behind the door. They had gotten out of their ropes and were trying to get away. He saw them struggling to open the old door. It was pathetic really. They couldn't get anywhere.

But they could rap on the walls and scream. Maybe someone would come. Maybe the janitor would hear them. No good at all. He had to stop them quickly.

"Come here, boys," he said, moving toward them.

There they were, up against the wall. Only two of them.

"Danny and Skeeter," he said, "where's Billy?"

Both boys held up boards to defend themselves.

Brother Michael smiled at them kindly.

"Danny," he said, "you're supposed to be the brightest. Do you think you have any chance against me?"

"You get away from me," Danny said.

"Look over there, Danny," Brother Michael said.

He pointed to Mick Shea, who lay bleeding up against the wall.

"The Mick," Skeeter Bannon said.

"Put down the boards, boys," Brother Michael said in a fatherly voice.

Skeeter Bannon started to lower his weapon, but Danny yelled at him.

"Don't do it, Skeeter. He's going to kill us like he killed the Mick."

Brother Michael moved toward them now. He watched as Danny raised the board and tried to swing it at him. With one hand he caught the board and ripped it out of Danny's hand. Then, with his other hand, he punched Danny in the face, knocking him up against the wall. Blood ran from the boy's mouth.

"Don't hurt me," Skeeter Bannon said.

He dropped the board at his feet.

"Now Skeeter, suppose you tell me where Billy is."

"He got away," Danny said. "He'll bring back the police."

Brother Michael smiled again, and slapped Danny up against the wall.

"He's under the coffins," Skeeter Bannon said, his voice a high-pitched whine. "We were just trying to trick you. I'm sorry, Brother Michael. I want to go home now. I want to see my Mom."

Skeeter Bannon fell to his knees and started to sob deeply. Brother Michael felt touched by the little boy's kneeling before him, a true supplicant. This boy knew the proper way to ask for mercy.

He patted Skeeter on the head.

"There, there," he said, taking his syringe out of his pocket.

"Now, now, Skeeter," he said. "No need for tears. Everything is going to be just fine."

Friday, 11 a.m.

KATE STOOD by Father Joe's bedside, Maura by her side.

"I don't know what good can come of you talking to a man in a coma," Maura said. "The last time you just got yourself in trouble."

"I know," Kate said, sitting in the chair next to the bed and taking Father Joe's limp, cold hand in her own. "But I know he said 'under.' I'm sure he knows where the boys are. He seemed to understand me. He really did."

Maura nodded and sat down in the chair opposite. She looked past Kate's head out the window at Mt. Olive.

"It's such a fine day," she said. "The trees must be looking beautiful on the mountain."

Kate felt something jerk in Father Joe's hand.

"Ma," he said.

Kate looked at Maura excitedly.

"What did you just say?" she said.

"I didn't say anything," Maura said.

"Yes. Yes you did," Kate said. "You said something about the trees."

"Oh that," Maura said. "That wasn't anything. I was just mentioning the fact that the trees look so nice up on the mountain this time of the year."

Father Joe's hand jerked again.

His mouth opened and he strained as though he had something important to say. But he sank back into his pillow without getting it out.

"Oh God help us," Kate said. "Did you see that, Maura? He knows. He knows something. What is it? The other day he said 'under.' Now you mentioned the mountain . . ."

"Under the mountain?" Maura said. "That doesn't make any sense."

"No, not under the mountain. There's something else. Father Joe, if you can hear me, please, please let me know where the boys are. Please try. You have to, Father Joe."

She pressed his hand tightly. But Father Joe didn't move. He stared serenely up at the ceiling, as though he had never made a sound at all.

Friday, 11:30 a.m.

BRIAN SLAMMED his hand onto the dashboard of the Dodge. In front of him was the yellow light which said CHECK ENGINE. Behind him drivers leaned on their horns. He was stuck all right, stuck near the damn Sumner Tunnel. His red emergency light flashed on top of his car uselessly. In front of him was sunlight and Route 93 back to William's Crossing. Christ, he had to get there quickly. He wanted to be in on the capture of Brother Michael. They had to get that maniac before he killed the kids, if he hadn't already.

He picked up his CB.

"Emergency, police officer stuck in traffic on Southeast Expressway. Need a ride out of here. Immediately. I've got a 10-4 in William's Crossing."

He turned and looked at the irate driver behind him.

"Hey pal, why don't you get that heap out of the way?"

Brian said nothing. He was too frustrated.

He got back in the car and turned the ignition

again. Nothing. The car had first overheated and then died. Now it wasn't going to start at all.

He heard a siren and saw a trouble truck coming through the traffic. Perhaps they'd give him a hotshot and get him moving again. Jesus.

He shut off the squawk of the CB and punched up the police station on his mobile phone. O'Toole answered the phone.

"O'Toole, this is Dolan. Did you pick up Brother Michael yet?"

"Not yet. There's an APB out on him. We've got every man out hunting for him. But so far there's not hide nor hair."

"Well, keep it up. He's got to be there."

"When are you getting here? You're very much in demand."

"I know," Brian said. "But the goddamn car just gave out on the expressway."

"I told the Mayor that we needed new auto appropriations," O'Toole said. "Now maybe he'll listen to us."

Brian hung up the phone. He was wired, wired, his nerves humming. But for now all he could do was sit still and wait anxiously for the trouble truck to bail him out.

"On Good Friday," Brian said. "And I need the CVS samaritan truck to help me out."

Friday, 11:45 a.m.

As THE congregation poured in for the noon
Good Friday Service, they barely noticed
O'Toole, his eyes roaming the inside of the big
church. Either his eyes were playing tricks on
him or he had lost his senses altogether. For he
had been sure he had seen Mick Shea's car not a
block away from the church. He had come up
rather quickly and saw someone—he wasn't sure
who it was—go into the church. Meanwhile
Brother Michael was nowhere to be seen. The
police had already checked the rectory, after
Brian's first call from St. Jude's, and asked Monsignor Merja and Brother Charles if they'd seen
Michael. No one had. If Michael had taken the
children, as Brian suggested, then he must be
holed up somewhere in town. But how did Mick
Shea fit into all this, and had he gone out of the
church through another entrance? O'Toole
doubted it. He had waited in the car from the
South Street entrance. He could see clearly
Mick's Landrover sitting in the parking lot. He
had to assume that Mick would come out the entrance closest to the car. But he hadn't. He

hadn't come out at all. Perhaps Mick had walked out of the other side of the church, left his car, but why would he do such a thing? Finally, he remembered the basement, and he had searched through the labyrinthine corridors only to come up again empty-handed. When he had reported this to Brian, the frustrated Chief told him to look again.

"Perhaps Mick is in with Michael. Find him."

And so, like the dutiful and persistent cop that he was, O'Toole had searched the entire church again. This time with two of William's Crossing's finest. And again they had come up empty-handed. It made no sense, no sense at all. He knew the Mick had come in here. He wasn't at home. He had to be still inside.

Now, standing in the back of the church, O'Toole half expected to see Mick Shea show up with the rest of the congregation to make the Stations of the Cross. But he was nowhere to be seen.

Monsignor Merja took his place in the pulpit and began the ceremony. O'Toole watched it all carefully. Ordinarily he would have been deeply moved by what he saw, but now he felt bothered again. Perhaps he hadn't really looked carefully enough in the basement. It was the only part of the church he was unfamiliar with. Slowly he walked to the back of the church and out to the hallway. He would look one more time. Quickly he headed to the door to the cellar and went down the steps. As he did so his heart sank a bit. He had been through this place twice already. There was definitely nobody here. But what if there was a clue he had overlooked? He had to try and find something that belonged to the Mick. But why would he come down here? It seemed senseless.

O'Toole went through the old storage rooms and found broken-backed chairs, some old pews that had been replaced, a long discarded marble Baptismal font. He wandered down the long, cool corridor and felt as though he were in an underground tomb. Was this how you felt when you were dead?

Meanwhile, above him Monsignor Merja led the congregation in the Stations of the Cross.

O'Toole came out of a room stacked with hymnals. Dust clung to his coat, and blew up his nostrils. He sneezed loudly and went down the hall to the next room. Inside was the huge, ancient boiler which heated the church. He looked at it, under it, and sneezed again. Goddamn this job. The man they wanted had disappeared, and now another one was gone.

He headed down the hallway. Above him he could hear the murmur of the congregation like a huge, monotonous hum. He walked on, his back aching, his head bent, feeling the cold, dark dustiness of the basement. It seemed to infect him and made his spirits drop. What good was all the prayer in the world if they couldn't get those children back?

And now he was there at the end of the corridor. There was no place else to go. He looked around carefully at the wall, got down on his hands and knees, though he felt the exercise was useless, and then he saw something, Something that he had missed before. He reached down to pick it up. It looked like an old piece of plaster covered with dust. But it wasn't. When he shook a little of the dirt off, it was bright red and it seemed to have bristles. Suddenly O'Toole realized what he had in his hand, and he felt ill. It was a piece of scalp. Those bristles were hairs, the red stuff blood. He felt a chill come up his mouth, and, not knowing what else to do, he began to yell.

"Mick? Mick! Are you around here? Mick Shea?"

There was no answer. He stared at the wall. Why was this here? And then he thought of Father Joe. Perhaps Mick Shea had gotten the same treatment that Joe had. Perhaps he had known about the altar boys and had a falling out with Michael. But where could he be?

O'Toole stared at the wall. Where did it go? It wasn't the outer wall of the church after all.

He began to pound on it with his fists.

"Mick? Are you in there?"

O'Toole felt like an idiot. Yet he, too, had heard tales of the secrets of St. Dominic's. What if there was some kind of room behind there?

O'Toole beat on the wall again. He listened for a hollow sound, but he couldn't tell for sure what he was hearing. These were heavy old stones. There was no way to tell what was beyond them.

Slowly he turned and headed away from the wall.

He had gone ten feet when he heard a beating back. It was weak at first, then stronger. A loud sound like a board being beaten against the wall.

O'Toole turned and began to yell Mick Shea's name through the wall.

At exactly 12:15, Monsignor Merja was leading the congregation through the Second Station of the Cross. Nearly all heads were bowed in prayer, and so only the Fishpaws and the Doughertys gasped when O'Toole dragged Mick Shea into the great church.

Mick collapsed on the altar at Monsignor Merja's feet. Slowly other people became aware of the disturbance and soon a collective gasp came from the faithful. There was a loud buzzing in the crowd, as people became aware of what had happened.

"What is the meaning of this?" Monsignor Merja said, his jaw set in outrage.

"I'm sorry, Monsignor," O'Toole said, looking out at the crowd. "We know who took the children. Brother Michael. He's had them just below here all the time. If any of you have seen him at all this morning, please come forward and tell me now."

There was a long silence, and then Jane Robinson, a nurse at Holy Redeemer Hospital, came up the aisle.

"Lieutenant O'Toole," she said, "I thought I saw Brother Michael just this morning. He was up on Canyon Street and he was driving the parish van."

"Thank you," O'Toole said. "The ambulance will be coming to pick Mick Shea up. Right now, though, he needs bandages. Can you help me, Mrs. Robinson?"

"Certainly, Lieutenant," she said. "I've got a first-aid kit in the car. I'll need some hot water from the rectory, Monsignor."

She stopped and looked up at Monsignor Merja, who looked pained, but slowly shook his head.

"Yes," he said. "Yes, I think we should all be of assistance here."

O'Toole looked at him and thought that perhaps miracles were possible after all.

Friday, 12:45 p.m.

BRIAN SWERVED out of the way of a Dodge van
as he headed down Main Street in the CVS
samaritan truck. He hit the accelerator and
turned down Spring Street. His leg was throb-
bing.

They had found the room. O'Toole had told
him. Under the church. So Father Joe hadn't
been talking about the river after all. Perhaps
the kids were still alive. The problem was they
had no idea where Michael was taking them. The
roads were blocked, and state troopers, FBI
agents, and the citizens of William's Crossing
were searching every available place. But what if
. . . what if he panicked and killed the kids?

Brian pulled into the side parking lot of the
police station. The media, with their cameras
and mikes and tape recorders, were all over the
front lawn. As Brian walked toward the front
door, he was besieged.

"Get the hell out of the way," he said. "There
are three kids' lives in danger. We don't have
time. No time. Let me through."

From the door he could see O'Toole. He

walked through the crowd and O'Toole dragged him inside.

"Any sign of him?"

"None yet, Chief," O'Toole said. "We checked the room. It was empty, and we found out where he got away. There was a tunnel. Apparently it was built during the Revolutionary War. It had been closed up, but he opened it. It came up on Cannon Street, almost a quarter of a mile away. He must have drugged the kids and taken them out that way."

"All right," Brian said, "now we've got to think. What the hell does he have in mind? Where the hell would he go?"

Friday, 1:15 p.m.

KATE SAT by Father Joe's bedside. He had
moved, she thought. Maura sat in a chair across
from her, her head on her chest. The poor old
dear is exhausted, Kate thought, but I know Father Joe knows. He's trying to wake up.

She sat and waited, holding his hand, and, for
what seemed like the thousandth time, she spoke
to him.

"Father Joe, you told me once. You said what
had happened to the kids. You said 'under.'
Remember, Father Joe? Now, please, please. I
know you must know something about it. I know
you can hear me. Oh God, Father Joe, tell me
something."

But Father Joe remained completely still.

Tell me, tell me, she wanted to scream. You
have no right to lie there silent.

"Lord forgive me for my anger," she said.

The ringing of the telephone made her jerk
back with fear. The phone had become the most
threatening instrument in her life. It could bring
news which would shatter her forever.

"Hello, Kate?"

"Brian? Have you heard anything?"

"Yes. The children were kept in an old room under St. Dominic's. It's been there for years and years, but no one knew about it. Brother Michael is the man we're looking for. He was Thomas Flannagan."

"Oh my God," Kate said. "But where is he? What of Danny?"

"We don't know, Kate. We've got roadblocks up, we've got everything going for us. He can't get away. I'm going out now to talk to the FBI. I just want you to tell Father Joe . . . tell him you know about Brother Michael. Maybe it'll shock him."

"Yes," Kate said. "I'll do it now."

"Wait, there's something else. Michael was found by Mick Shea. Shea followed him into the room and got hit over the head. O'Toole found Shea during Mass. But Shea doesn't know where he went. He did say something about his coming from the workshop with a bunch of boards before. I don't know what the hell he was doing with those. Shea is in pretty bad shape. Ask Father Joe. Keep at it."

"Yes, Brian. I will."

She hung the phone up and looked into Father Joe's eyes.

"They've found out it was Brother Michael. But you knew that, Father Joe. I know you can hear me. Please, if you know anything at all."

She squeezed his hand tightly, and suddenly Father Joe squeezed it back.

He opened his mouth and could barely speak. His eyes were bright with pain.

"The . . . cross," he said. "Cross . . ."

"Cross?" Kate said. "What do you mean?"

Father Joe tried to talk again, but his tongue was parched. The words would not come out. Kate quickly poured him some water, and held up his head.

"What's going on?" Maura said, waking up. But Kate hushed her with her eyes.

"The cross?" Kate said again.

"Mount . . . Olive," Father Joe said. "Black Rock."

Kate stopped and set the water down slowly. Her heart skipped a beat, and she suddenly felt as though she were going to faint.

She looked at Maura, who stared at her dimly.

"Call Brian at the police station," Kate said. "Tell him to bring all his men to Mt. Olive immediately, to the Black Rock. Tell him I'll meet him there. I can get there quicker than he can. It's just up the hill. Tell him the children and Brother Michael are there. And tell him to hurry."

She got up and moved quickly across the room.

"You can't go up there alone," Maura said.

"I have to," Kate said. "The police might not make it in time. I know what his plan is now."

"What?" Maura said.

"You don't want to know," Kate said. "This is Good Friday. From Black Rock you can see the whole town. He's going to take the boys there and put up crosses, just like the Crucifixion! They'll all be dead by three!"

Maura put her hand over her mouth in horror.

He hadn't really wanted it to end like this. There was no justice at all. None from the Church and none from the Lord either. That was what he had understood. Perhaps it was when he realized the Book of Job was a lie. Yes, that had been the day when it became clear. There was no justice at all. He had read Job and understood that there was never going to be any end to the tests that God had for him. And then it occurred to him that it wasn't God at all who was testing him. It was the Devil. He had already failed God. God had thrown him out. So now he had to please the Devil. He had to show them that they couldn't just shove him aside. He wasn't crazy. He wasn't just dirt beneath their feet.

Which was why he was using this old pine-covered back road up Mt. Olive. The three crucifixes waited for him and the three boys in their black sacks, tied and drugged. He was going to give them a Good Friday they would never forget. He was going to show them all. The pious phonies in the Church, the townspeople, and

God—God himself, now that his work was on the side of Satan. He was going to give them three sacrifices and, if God was really in Heaven, then he would bring them back from the dead.

He laughed bitterly to himself.

They wouldn't be brought back, just as his brain wasn't brought back. You could pray and pray and pray and nothing would change.

He gunned the van up the winding mountain road and headed for the very top. Yes, at the Black Rock. They would be so easily seen there. No one would be able to miss it. All the fake, pious people who had done him harm.

They would look up and they would see their precious children hanging there. And there would be nothing any of them could do.

He turned the corner and looked up the mountain. Only a short distance to go.

It was going to be easy. Easy. He had already put the crosses up this morning. Now it was going to be fun, a lot of fun for him and the kids. They would scream when he drilled the nails into their hands . . . .

Now they would see what they got for shoving him aside. They would see and they would all bow down to him. For the first time in his life he would show them all his power.

Friday, 1:45 p.m.

BRIAN MOVED for the car, O'Toole right behind him.

"The bastard can't be that crazy," O'Toole said. "He wouldn't . . . be thinking . . . of . . ."

"That's exactly what he's thinking," Brian said. "Those boards Mick saw. They weren't boards, they were poles. Let's go."

Brian hit the siren and turned on the engine.

Three newsmen jumped into a van in front of them. Brian roared past them, nearly sideswiping the truck. One of the newsmen screamed at Brian while the other flashed his camera.

"Kate's gone up there ahead of us," he said. "Christ, we've got to make good time."

Friday, 2 p.m.

KATE DROVE her Fairmont up the mountain. The road was steep and drenched in sunlight. Yellow daisies lined it, and giant sunflowers hung out over the car like antennae from some alien race. This couldn't be real. She couldn't be driving so fast up Mt. Olive that her car was nearly skidding off the road. This couldn't be the mountain where she went on church picnics as a girl, the mountain where she and Brian had climbed to neck as teenagers, the mountain where, later, she and Paddy and Danny had gone for picnics. It was impossible, too much to comprehend, that now she was driving past the old oak tree, and past Morgan's Creek and past Black's Farmhouse (where as a child she had looked for ghosts), past the place called Lookout Point, where tourists liked to get out of their cars and look down on the quiet little town that was nestled beneath them. It was impossible to comprehend it—that when she got to the top of the cliff, she might see her own child and two others in some terrible parody of the Crucifixion. She felt her stomach turn, felt her skin peeling off as

309

she drove. She could feel the nails piercing her own hands, could feel the heat of the sun—usually so reassuring, now a dreaded enemy. What kind of person could plan a revenge so horrible? And a man of the Church? It was beyond Kate Riordan's understanding of evil. She knew the world could be a violent place, that plans and dreams could be squashed like a bug on a windshield. She had learned that with Paddy's death. Life was indeed very, very frail. But this—there was nothing she could compare it with. She was taking the last turn to Black Rock. It would have to be here, for then everyone in town could see it. Here his deed would be public, his revenge perfect. She stopped the car in a grove of pines and got out. Then it occurred to her. In her haste to get up the mountain to save her son, she had forgotten any weapon. If she had thought of it, she would have stolen a scalpel from an operating room in the hospital, or she would have raced home—it was only two blocks away from the hospital—and gotten Paddy's old .45. Then she would have been in command. She had no doubt, none at all, that she could use it. The thought chilled her. All her life she hated violence, had spoken out for gun control, hated violent movies and TV shows. She wouldn't let Danny watch them. Yet now, if she had the gun, she would fire it into his face, over and over. Or would she? Perhaps she just felt that way because she didn't have it. Maybe she wouldn't be able to do it after all. But she had to do something.

She looked around and saw a limb of a tree. It might work as a weapon. If only to hit him with and keep him away from the children. She picked it up, feeling stupid, hopeless: She thought of the face of Brother Michael, the thick brows and his thick wrists and huge hands. He was always working in the tool shop. What effect was she likely to have on him? She started through the shaded path in the woods, climbed over a fallen oak tree, and pushed through the overhanging ferns and thistles which struck her in the face. Pine needles were strewn over the path, and once she had thought this a romantic place. But now she would never be able to come to this mountain again. The fear shot through her like an electric wire. She fought hard to keep from crying out. She turned the first corner, felt her feet sink in the mud as she walked over Morgan's Creek and then moved up the little rise toward the Black Rock clearing.

There was the Black Rock itself, a huge boulder which hung at a precarious angle over the edge of Mt. Olive. It was the town's one really sensational natural beauty. It must have been formed millions of years ago. She thought of the drop. It was a hundred feet, perhaps more. She moved through the thick underbrush now, holding the branch close to her. Then she came up over the last rise, just to the back of the opening.

When she dared to look up, she had to fight to keep from screaming. There in front of her was the unspeakable—three crosses, erected side by side, and on them were three children. She felt the blood rush to her head. Oh God, there in the middle was Danny. He lay against one post with his head on his left shoulder. Stripped to the waist with only his shorts on. To his right was Billy Duncan, to his left, Skeeter Bannon.

Down below them walked Brother Michael. At his feet was the portable ladder, and in his hands . . . in his hands Kate saw the hammer and nails. She looked back again at the boys. They were merely tied to the stakes now. Then she wasn't too late. She had to act, act fast. But Michael had picked up the ladder now and was turning it toward the boys.

He set it down and then he called up to them.

"Danny," he said in a small, almost childlike voice. "Billy . . . Skeeter . . . time to wake up. Time to come out of your sleep. It wouldn't be any fun if you slept through it. You understand. It would ruin the whole thing if you were asleep."

Kate started forward, then stopped. The way to catch him was on the ladder. Yes, if he was up there and she could get across to him in time, then, for that brief moment, he would be at her mercy. Maybe she could knock him off the ladder so hard he would be knocked out. No, he was tough. The most she could hope for was that he wouldn't be able to move for a second and she could come over and hit him with the club. But could she raise the club and strike someone lying on the ground? She looked back at her son, tied with rope to the cross. Yes, she could, and she would. Brother Michael wasn't human any more. Whatever had happened to him in the past, there could be no excuse for what she was seeing. She would hit him all right. He was at the foot of the ladder now.

"I'm coming to see you now, Danny," he said. "I'm coming to see you now. And I want you to know who I am. Wake up, Danny. Wake up. I'm

going to give you a surprise, Danny. You like
surprises, don't you Danny?"

Kate felt the bile coming up in the back of her
throat.

Why didn't he go up the ladder? Why didn't
he make his move? She didn't want Danny to
wake up and see what had happened to him. She
wanted to stop this madman before he opened
his eyes.

"Danny . . . Danny, you're the brightest of
the boys. You'll understand. I know you will,"
Brother Michael said. He smiled broadly, reveal-
ing yellow jagged teeth.

On the cross, Danny opened his eyes and
looked down. He tried to move his arms and
realized they were tied. The sun was so hot. At
first it seemed like a blessing. He was at last out
of the dark, cold place. Then he felt the pain in
his arms. They were being pulled out from him.
They were stretched so tightly that he could
barely stand it. And the pain in his feet. His
ankle bones were bound together, and were rubbing each other, and when he tried to move
them at all, they simply rubbed more, causing a
terrible pain which traveled up his leg.

"Danny," a voice said beneath him. "Danny,
you see where you are?"

Danny Riordan looked down at Brother
Michael and suddenly, without the crazy, smiling
man saying a word, he knew what had happened
to him. How many millions of times had he seen
the picture which terrified him? The picture of
Jesus on the Cross in his loincloth, his long hair
hanging down his back? How many times had he
seen the picture in his mother's bedroom? With

storm clouds in the background, and the two
thieves on either side of him. Danny turned his
head to the right and saw Billy Conley, his eyes
still shut. Then he heard a cry to his left, and
looked that way. Skeeter Bannon was staring
into his eyes. Skeeter's own eyes were gigantic
with fear.

"Danny," he said. "Danny, we're nailed up.
We're nailed up here."

"No," Danny said, holding back the fear that
was closing in on him like a hand over his face.
"No, we're not. We're only tied here. It's a joke.
Isn't that right, Brother Michael?"

Down below him Brother Michael got a confused look on his face.

"What did you say?" Brother Michael said.

"I said," Danny said thickly, his mouth so dry
he could barely speak at all, "I said that you're
playing a joke on us. You're kidding around with
us."

"No," Brother Michael said, holding on to the
ladder. "No, I'm not. It's no joke."

Brother Michael held out the nails and the
hammer.

"Do you see these?" Brother Michael said.
"Do you?"

Skeeter Bannon began to cry loudly.

"You aren't gonna stick us with those?" he
said.

"Yes, I am," Brother Michael said. "But don't
worry, Skeeter, you won't be the first. No, the
first one will be the one who gave me all the
trouble. Danny Riordan."

From the bushes Kate started forward. Then
she realized she must wait. She had no chance at

all, even with the tree limb, if he was on the ground. She clenched her teeth and watched her son.

"I know it's a joke," Danny said.

"Why do you think it's a joke, my smart little friend?" Brother Michael said, putting his foot on the first step.

"I know it is," Danny said, "because you know the Bible. The Bible said that when Christ was crucified, He had a choice. He could either be nailed up or He could be tied to the cross. Christ chose the nails. You must know that. If you were really going to leave us here, you'd give us a choice."

"What are you talking about?" Brother Michael said. "Are you telling me I don't know the Bible? Do you think I've forgotten it? Is that it? Do you think I'm so dumb I've forgotten it?"

"No," Danny said, looking over at Billy Conley, who was awake now and staring down at Brother Michael with a fear so great that he could barely breathe.

"I know you're smart, Brother Michael. That's why I know you're just kidding around with us. You love the Bible and the Church, and you know it better than anybody. That's why you wouldn't make a mistake like this."

Brother Michael stopped as though he were perplexed.

"It's not a mistake," he said, looking up at Danny. Brother Michael's voice was a whine. He seemed like a small child who had been badly annoyed.

"I know exactly what I'm doing," he said. "They never gave Jesus any choice and they never gave me any choice. And I'm not giving you any. This is what you were *born* for, boy."

He started up the ladder, deliberately, one step at a time.

"You don't want to do this," Danny said. "They'll hunt you down. You'll be put in prison."

His voice cracked now and the two other boys began to cry in fear. Brother Michael moved faster as he neared the top of the steps.

"You tried to trick me," he said. "You think I'm stupid, like all the others, don't you? But I'm not, do you understand? I remember everything anybody ever did to me. You see that?"

He stopped near the top of the ladder. His face was only six inches from Danny's. Danny looked at him and saw the wildness in his eyes, felt his hot, stinking breath.

"Now you're going to know what it feels like to be me," Brother Michael said, raising the hammer and the nails.

Kate Riordan was up from her crouch behind the hill. She slipped as she moved forward, but pushed herself off the ground and started running toward the ladder.

On the cross, Brother Michael put the nail directly into Danny's palm. Danny could feel the hot point of it. Panic engulfed him. He nearly fainted from the nail's touch. Then suddenly he cleared his throat and spit directly into Brother Michael's face. The Brother was shocked, so shocked he dropped the nail out of his hand.

"You little bastard," he said, striking Danny with his open hand so hard that it made the boy's nose bleed. "You'll pay for that. You will pay for that dearly."

He looked down at the bottom of the ladder and saw Kate Riordan three feet away. Without saying a word, he jumped from the ladder and landed in her path, the hammer in his hand.

"Well, well," he said. "Mommy has come to save the babies. How touching."

"You let them go, Brother Michael," she said, raising the branch of the tree above her head. "You let them go now, do you hear me?"

"Yes," he said, "I hear you. Very amusing. Very, very amusing. You think I went to all this trouble to be stopped by a woman? What a joke you are."

He moved toward her. Kate swung the branch and clipped him on the right shoulder.

Michael went down to one knee, and Kate hit him again, this time on the top of the head. He bowed from the blow. She raised the branch again, but before she could hit him he had dived under her and grabbed her leg with his right hand. She could feel herself slipping, and then she was down on her back and he was on her. She felt his rough hands on her throat, felt the pressure and the pain. He was ripping her throat apart. Quickly she brought her knee up in between his legs. Michael gasped and fell limp. His head was curled backwards, but he smashed her in the face with his left hand. Kate saw white lights from the blow and tasted blood in her mouth. She tried to knee him in the groin again, but he had clasped her legs down with his own. Now she was totally helpless.

"You bitch," he gasped. "You worthless bitch."

She opened her eyes and tried to scrape his

face, but he struck her again. She didn't feel the blow as solidly this time. She was numb. But the blood started in her mouth again. Then, from some distant place. a voice out of a tunnel, she heard the sound of a man's voice.

"All right, Michael, hold it there. You're completely surrounded."

Kate felt rough hands pulling at her. She tried to resist but he had his huge hand around her mouth and nose, cutting off air.

Suddenly she felt something else, something cold on her throat.

"Go ahead and try it," Michael said, dragging Kate to her feet. "You make one move toward me and I finish off Mrs. Riordan here. Now let me tell you what I want."

As he talked, Brother Michael moved toward the Black Rock. Kate felt herself pulled along like a doll. Deep within her an anger, a new anger, was born. This madman . . . just because he was bigger and stronger than she, thought that he could carry her off, use her as a hostage. She reached up toward the knife, but felt the point cut into her neck.

"I wouldn't try it, Mrs. Riordan," Brother Michael said. "I wouldn't try it. I can cut your throat in a second. Right in front of your son. That would be a nice memory for him, hey?"

Kate felt her feet hit a hard substance and knew without being able to look down that she was on the Black Rock.

He dragged her across it and held her tightly.

"I've got Mrs. Riordan here," Brother Michael said. "If you make a move, I throw her off the Rock. I want you to get back. I am going

to get out of here and take Mrs. Riordan with
me. Do you understand?"

Kate waited, barely able to breathe. She
looked up at the cross and saw her son hanging
there. He looked at her with terror in his eyes.

She had to survive this, though part of her was
already giving up. She could feel it. Go ahead,
kill me, I've saved my son. She had to fight that
impulse with as much ferocity as she had fought
to save Danny.

"How do you like it, Mrs. Riordan?" Brother
Michael said. "I want you to look down. You
hear me? Look down."

Kate Riordan felt the pressure on her mouth
lessen slightly. She looked over the edge of the
Rock and felt dizzy, and terror swept her again.
The drop looked endless. Far below her was a
stand of pine trees.

Suddenly from in front of her, Kate heard
Brian's voice.

"You make one false move and I kill you. I
promise I can do it."

Brother Michael turned to the right and
looked at Brian Dolan. He stood not more than
five feet away. While the other police had
bunched together where Kate had made her
hideout in the trees, Brian had gone around to
the north. Now he was in a good position for a
shot at the Brother.

"I see you, Dolan," Michael said. "Very
clever. But you don't quite get the picture. I still
have Mrs. Riordan. You make one move and I
pull her over with me. You shoot me and we
both die."

"But what's the point?" Brian said. "She's

innocent. I know all about the accident. I sympathize with you. But it's not Mrs. Riordan's fault. She couldn't help it. It's a terrible thing that happened to you. Nobody really knows what you've been through. Why don't you talk with me about it?"

Kate felt Michael's hand slacken slightly.

"That's right," he said. "Nobody knows how . . . I never wanted to go out and get drunk. I never wanted to leave Retreat. It was Riordan, Bannon, and Conley who made me feel guilty for not going. They said I was a fanatic. They made me feel as though I wasn't a . . . a man if I didn't get drunk with them. Then they went out and had the accident. All of the so-called real men went out and got drunk and smashed us up. Do you know what they did to me, Chief Dolan? Do you know how they ruined me?"

"Yes. Yes, I do," Brian said. "I know what happened. But listen, it's not too late. You haven't been to the best doctors. You could get help. Quit now before you really get in trouble."

There was a brief pause. Kate could feel Michael's hand loosen again.

"I devoted my whole life to the Church," he said. "There is nothing else for me. So I might as well take someone with me."

Kate felt the hand tighten on her throat. Michael was turning toward the ravine. It was now or never. Quickly she put her foot behind his and pushed back with her body. He fell backwards and she landed on top of him. His hands still grasped her tightly. Kate slammed her elbow into Michael's ribs and then she rolled to the right, laterally with the great rock. Her feet hung over the edge.

Quickly she tried to scramble forward but he was on top of her, pulling her back. She heard Brian move forward, but Michael once again started to put the knife to her throat. She tucked her head so he couldn't reach her neck and then bit down hard on Michael's wrist. He gasped and pulled back. Kate put her knees on the Rock and stood part way up. Michael tried to pin her back down, but she managed to stumble forward. He lunged at her, but Kate stepped back. She nearly eluded his grasp completely, but he grabbed her foot. Kate kicked at his head. Michael got up and pulled her with him. She heard Danny scream "Mom" and then she saw the knife descending toward her.

At that precise moment she heard the crack of gunfire. Michael screamed as the bullet passed into his shoulder. Then he lunged at her again. Kate saw the bloody patch.

She turned to run, but he grabbed her. With all her might Kate pushed his head away and brought her hand across to his neck. Michael stabbed at her arm, and the knife came down in her right shoulder. As she fell she heard him cry and then, suddenly, he was gone. Reflexively, Kate threw out her hand to him, but he was screaming and sailing through space. He hit the top branches of the trees and fell to a shady spot below.

Kate felt the blood run down her arm. She tried to stand, but she was dizzy, so dizzy. She staggered halfway to her feet and heard Brian's voice.

"Kate, stay down, darling. You're hurt. Stay down."

She wanted to fall back on the comforting mass of the Rock. But she didn't know where it was any more. She staggered and fell forward into Brian's arms.

Friday, 8 p.m.

"MOM," CAME the voice behind her. "Mom, it's me. Do you hear me, Mommy?"

Kate looked up at her son, Danny. He was clean-faced and his hair was combed and he wore a dark blue shirt.

"Mom, it's me. Danny."

"Danny," she said.

She opened her arms and Danny came to her then. She hugged him and felt the warmth of his body, the fresh smell of his skin, the soft spot by his ear.

She cried good tears, full of relief and a happiness that seemed frightening in its intensity.

"My baby," she said. "My baby."

And Danny was kissing her and hugging her back. This time he didn't mind her calling him a baby. He was there in his mother's arms at last, and there was no better place in the world.

She held him for a long time, and then he pulled away a little and looked down on her.

"You're okay," he said to her. "You fainted when Brother Michael fell off the mountain and they brought you down here. It's funny, Mom, I was the one who got kidnapped and you end up in the hospital."

"Yes, my darling," she said. "That's funny. Oh God, are you all right?"

"Sure, Mom. I was brave. I helped get Skeeter and Billy loose. We almost got away too. But he knocked me down. But it didn't hurt."

"Are you sure?" Kate said, holding him to her again.

"Sure. Hey, that was something when Brian shot him. Wow, that was something."

"Yes, dear," Kate said.

She saw someone coming into the room. It was Brian and Jerry Manning, and she smiled at both of them.

"Hey, you're a hero," Brian said.

He held up the Boston paper to her.

"MOM SAVES KIDS" was the headline.

"They are really going to be after you for the talk shows now," Brian said.

He sat down on the side of the bed, and Kate quickly clasped his hand.

"I won't go on any of them," she said, "unless you come with me."

"Yeah," Danny said, turning toward the Chief.

"I see," Brian said.

"You will see soon," Kate said, squeezing his hand. "And how is Father Joe?"

"He's okay," Brian said. "He's somewhere around. It seems that he was suspicious of Brother Michael when he caught him working in the carpentry shop on the crosses late every night. He followed him to the mountain and watched him. Only he got careless and was caught. Brother Michael knocked him over the head and panicked, leaving him for dead. Then he must have phoned Monsignor Merja and pretended he was Father Joe and was staying out of town for a few more days."

"I see," Kate said. "Then Ed Devlin happened by and brought him down. God, what luck for us. It was Father Joe who gave it all away."

"Thank God he lived," interjected Jerry Manning.

"Yes," Brian said, "but it was Kate who stopped him."

"That's right, Mom," Danny said, holding his mother's hand. "It was you. You were a real hero."

"Heroine," Kate smiled. "But I couldn't have done it alone. Thank God you got there when you did, Brian."

"Yeah," Brian said. "It looks like we make a pretty good team."

He reached down and with his other hand squeezed Kate's hand tightly.

"Brian," she said softly.

"Oh Mom," Danny said, embarrassed. But he looked at Brian and smiled widely.

"Well, look what we have here," said Jerry Manning.

He took off his hat, scratched his great woolly head and stared down at the three of them with a great, beaming smile.

Holy Mother, pierce me through
In my heart each wound renew
Of my Savior crucified.

—*From the last page of*
  Brother Michael's book